NEEDING A HERO

BAYTOWN HEROES

MARYANN JORDAN

Needing a Hero (Baytown Heroes) Copyright 2023

All rights reserved. No part of this book may be reproduced or transmitted in any form or by any means, electronic or mechanical, including photocopying, recording, or by any information storage and retrieval system without the author's written permission, except where permitted by law.

If you read this book and did not purchase it, you are reading an illegal pirated copy. If you are concerned about working for no pay, please respect the author's work! Ensure you are only reading a copy that the author has officially released.

This book is a work of fiction. Names, characters, places, and incidents are products of the author's imagination or used fictitiously. Any resemblance to actual persons, living or dead, events, or locales is entirely coincidental.

Cover: Graphics by Stacy

ISBN ebook: 978-1-956588-25-5

ISBN print: 978-1-956588-26-2

❦ Created with Vellum

Author's Note

Please remember that this is a work of fiction. I have lived in numerous states as well as overseas, but for the last thirty years have called Virginia my home. I often choose to use fictional city names with some geographical accuracies.

These fictionally named cities allow me to use my creativity and not feel constricted by attempting to accurately portray the areas.

It is my hope that my readers will allow me this creative license and understand my fictional world.

I also do quite a bit of research on my books and try to write on subjects with accuracy. There will always be points where creative license will be used in order to create scenes or plots.

1

"Have you got everything you need, sweetheart?"

Ivy smiled as she drove, knowing her mother would fuss and worry even though Ivy was almost thirty years old and had lived independently since college. "Yes, Mom, you and Dad left everything in perfect order. I've filled up the refrigerator and pantry. I couldn't believe that Mrs. Tomlinson was still working there! I swear, she looked just like she did when I was little. I accused her of finding an ever-timeless potion. Plus, I moved in only my needed possessions, and the movers took everything else to the storage facility outside Baytown."

"I just hate that we won't be there."

"It's fine, Mom. Honestly, Grandma needs you, and that's where you and Dad should be right now. I'm just grateful that I don't have to look for an apartment. Moving back into your house until I find something more permanent is perfect."

"Well, I'd tell you that you can stay with us forever." Her mom laughed. "But I know you'll be looking for your own place soon. I'm just so glad you're taking the job in Baytown. You can't imagine how excited your father and I are to have you close again."

"Me too. Listen, you and Dad take care of each other and Grandma. I'm getting ready to get on the Bay bridge-tunnel, so I'll lose my connection in the tunnel. I'll talk to you in a couple of days."

"Love you, Ivy."

"Love you, too. Give my love to Grandma."

Disconnecting the call, Ivy moved through the toll gate on the Virginia Beach side of the Chesapeake Bay Bridge Tunnel. There was a little traffic, and as she drove over the water, her grin spread across her face. Home. Home on the Eastern Shore.

Her phone rang again. Pressing connect, she heard Sybil's voice. "Are you almost there?"

Laughing, she replied, "Just got on the CBBT."

"Okay, then I'll get off. But I can't wait for us to live close to each other again. I hate that I'm not there to welcome you. Of all the times for us to have planned a winter trip to Disney World!" Sybil had married her college boyfriend, moved back to the Eastern Shore, and now had a five-year-old son and a four-year-old daughter. "I told Ricky and Jessica to find something for their Auntie Ivy from Mickey Mouse."

"I look forward to seeing you all. I'll call once you get home next week. See you soon."

Disconnecting again, she still had her smile firmly in place. It was time… time to return to her roots. She'd left the Shore, gone to college, earned her degree in systems engineering, and worked in Richmond for an engineering firm focused on construction. When the Chesapeake Bay Bridge Tunnel advertised for a systems engineer, she decided to apply. And when the job offer came through, she packed up her belongings from her small apartment and moved back to Baytown.

CBBT had two administrative locations—one on the Virginia Beach side and one on the Eastern Shore side. With her office at the entrance on the Shore side, she was now living only about fifteen minutes away from her new office.

She'd started her new job a few weeks ago, commuting the distance. But today, she'd enjoyed a trip over the Bay for a goodbye luncheon with her former coworkers in Richmond. Now heading home, she approached the first tunnel, glad for only a few vehicles on the road. Driving through a tunnel that went underwater never bothered her, but she hated to get behind someone traveling slowly. She looked to the side at the new construction. A second tunnel was being built to handle the summer traffic.

Her new job had her right in the middle of the new work, and she loved it. With the complexities of systems needed to maintain the current bridge and tunnels and the new construction, she had a hand in addressing multiple factors throughout the design.

Coming out of the tunnel and onto the last section of the bridge, she looked over the water and watched as gulls flew alongside the bridge. "Oh, Mr. Thomas, I can still hear you." Thinking of her high school history teacher, she continued in a singsong voice, "Over seventeen miles of bridges and two tunnels. For three hundred and fifty years after the first settlers set up the colony of Virginia, the crossing was completed by boats, ships, and ferries. And what a wonder of modern technology it is."

Keeping to the speed limit, she was anxious to get home while enjoying the view. A vehicle only had room to pull off in case of an emergency in a few places on the bridge, but she'd never seen anyone there other than an occasional CBBT police officer. But looking ahead, a blue minivan was parked, and a man stood next to the edge of the bridge with a child in his arms.

The unexpected and unusual scene triggered her to slow as she approached. Gasping, she watched as the man paced close to the edge, dangling the child as he yelled.

"Oh God, oh God, oh God!" she chanted as she slammed on the brakes, causing her car to squeal to a stop as she jerked behind his.

Hitting the emergency call button on her phone, she barely gave the dispatcher a chance to answer before she cried, "I'm on the CBBT, near the east end approaching Fisherman's Island. There's a man at the pull-off with a child, and he's screaming, and it looks like he's threatening to drop the child over the edge!"

She threw open her door and raced out of the vehicle, ignoring the 911 dispatcher telling her to stay in her car.

With her heart pounding a rhythm that threatened to beat out of her chest, she lifted her hands in front of her. When the man whirled around, he was younger than she thought, barely more than a teenager. The child was crying. Its little face scrunched up with fat tears rolling down his cheeks.

"Please, please, don't do this. Whatever's happening, don't do this. Hand me the baby, and it'll be all right."

"Back up!" he yelled, only making the baby cry more.

He wore an oversized black jacket, but it was unzipped, and the sides flapped in the breeze. It was enough to remind her that she'd left her coat in the car, and the chilly breeze blowing across the water made her shiver.

"No. I can't do that. Listen, you don't want to hurt the baby. Let me help. This is not what you want to do. That poor baby doesn't deserve this." The child was in a onesie with a sweater buttoned but no hat. Its face quivered, and her fingers itched to pluck the child from his arms.

The sound of approaching vehicles and sirens grew louder. *Oh, thank God, someone is coming!* She tried to steady her voice without taking her eyes off the baby. "Let me hold your baby. He's crying, and your arms are probably getting tired. Just let me hold the baby, please."

Though she was terrified to move closer, her fingers itched to reach the child in his arms. She watched the wild expression on the young man's face, seeing indecision as well as desperation. She inched forward but stopped when he swung back toward the edge of the bridge once more. Her gasp turned to a choking sob as the air stuck in her lungs, terror flooding her veins. She spared a quick glance toward the water. The breeze was blowing, and the water below undulated gently. They were near the end of the bridge, close to the shore.

While the bridge height was not high over the water where they were, the baby would never survive the fall. Her knees shook, and she locked them to keep them from dropping to the concrete surface. "Please," she begged again, her body quivering. "Tell me your name."

"Larry," he whispered, his eyes wide. He stared at her as though surprised to find himself on a bridge with a baby.

"Hi, Larry," she whispered in return. "I'm Ivy." She shuffled a step closer. "What's the baby's name?"

He mumbled as he looked down, his gaze registering surprise as though he'd just realized what was in his arms. His expression morphed into fear and then anger. "How the hell should I know?" he barked.

She blinked, jerking slightly. "Uh…"

Sweat dripped down his face, and he jerked his gaze behind her at the sound of boot steps approaching. Afraid to turn away, she lifted her hands slightly to the side so no one would think she was threatening the child.

The police approached, announcing their presence, and for the first time since she'd arrived, she let out a sigh of relief. They would take over, and she could step back to let the professionals handle Larry and save the baby. As she moved a foot away, Larry shouted, "No. You stay! Everyone else, get back! Get back, or I swear I'll jump!"

Her heart jolted once again, but staring at the desperation in Larry's eyes, she stayed in place. "Larry, please. Please let me take the baby." Her arms ached as her entire body quaked with shivers. She gazed to the side, seeing the police encircling them but not coming too close. "You don't want to hurt your baby."

"It's not mine!" he screamed, spittle flying from his mouth as his eyes darted behind her.

Oh shit! Oh shit! "Come on, Larry, then let me help. Whatever this is, let me help."

The child wailed louder, and her attention snapped to the bridge's edge. She moved closer to him once again.

2

Andy Bergstrom raced onto the pier where the Virginia Marine Police had their boats docked. The sky was clear, but with the holidays just a few weeks away, the cold had settled in, and he could see his breath in front of his face. But with the emergency callout, his thoughts were firmly on the situation they were heading into.

He jumped onto the boat he and his fellow officers had recently taken out on patrol. They'd just come back for lunch when the call came in. Callan Ward and Joseph Newman joined him, and on the other vessel were Officers Jose Martinez and Jared Dobson and Chief Ryan Coates. They pulled out of the Baytown Harbor, heading south at top speed toward the Chesapeake Bay Bridge Tunnel.

The CBBT had its own police officers, but it wasn't unusual for the VMP and Coast Guard to assist in emergencies. With Joseph behind the wheel, he listened as their dispatcher relayed information.

"Ten forty-four," Bobbie Jean called out. "CBBT and

state police are at the scene. Close to Fisherman's Island."

"Jumper?"

He looked toward Callan and shook his head. "Not sure, but thank God they're not far from the shore. If they go over, they've got a better chance of survival."

Even as the words left his mouth, he knew survival was not guaranteed. While the main bridge was only about forty feet above the water, the distance would seriously hurt someone who went over the side. Being closer to the shore decreased the distance between the bridge and the water, making a fall or jump much less devastating, but that didn't include landing near one of the concrete pilings or the currents taking the body away.

Bobbie Jean radioed, "It's a child. A man is threatening a child."

Andy's head whipped around to look at Callan, his eyes wide. "Fuck!"

Callan and his wife, Sophie, had given birth a couple of months ago to a little boy, and Callan had just commented yesterday that he was "living the dream."

He felt the vessel's speed increase as Joseph pushed the boat to get them to the scene as fast as possible.

Bobbie Jean continued, "There is a female bystander who is with him. CBBT says she's at the edge of the bridge, too."

He stepped out of the wheelhouse and was hit with a blast of cold, briny air. His trimmed beard kept his face warm, but blinking in the wind, he was grateful for the heavy coat. Sucking the air in deeply, he filled his lungs before letting it out slowly. He focused his attention on the bridge as it neared, then glanced behind to see the other VMP vessel nearby. With their chief, Ryan, on board, he would take charge, and as the senior officer, Callan would also be directing.

Andy looked at Callan, whose binoculars focused on the scene. Flashing emergency lights filled the area on the bridge, which had been cleared of other vehicles.

"Vessel four, go under to the south side. Vessel two will follow," Ryan radioed.

Once under the bridge, Andy twisted his head upward to see the events unfolding. Both Ryan's vessel and theirs were also tied into the radio system used by the state police and CBBT police.

"Status?" Ryan radioed.

The CBBT communications officer replied, "Man. Twenty-one. He stole a van at a gas station in Virginia Beach. Got on CBBT and discovered a baby in the back. Panicked. Knows this ups his charges. He stopped and was pacing the side when a female bystander saw him and called it in. She's trying to get him to let the child go. When officers arrived and asked her to step back, the man threatened to toss the baby over the edge if she left."

"Shit," Andy cursed under his breath.

"Fuckin' hell," Callan's curse joined in.

Andy grimaced, knowing Callan was thinking of his own son.

"Whoever the woman is, she's gotten his trust," Joseph surmised.

Andy looked over as Joseph managed to keep their

boat close, battling the current and waves that knocked against the bridge pylons. "Or he just knows that she gives him one more hostage."

The police radio on the bridge picked up the woman's voice. "Please, please, give the baby to me. It's so cold, Larry. The baby needs to be warm. If you need someone, then just keep me. You don't need the baby now."

Andy's gaze shot back to the woman, who was visible as she stood several feet from the man who walked back toward the edge with the small child in his arms. She was much smaller than the man, both in height and weight, barely coming to the man's shoulder. The scene sent chills throughout his body that had nothing to do with the weather. Her arms were stretched out and had been since they arrived. She wasn't wearing a coat or jacket. *She must have jumped out of her car to rush to the scene without putting her coat on.* With binoculars, he could see her arms and hands shook and knew both fear and cold were the cause.

Her auburn hair was pulled back in a ponytail, but tendrils had come loose and whipped about her face from the increasing wind. The original call came in over twenty-five minutes ago, so she'd been out on the bridge for that long and must be exhausted as well as cold.

"She called him Larry, so maybe he does trust her," he radioed softly. "If she can get her hands on the child, then the police can get the man."

"Be prepared," Ryan radioed his warning. "He could jump... either with the baby or after giving the baby up."

"Fuck," Andy cursed under his breath again. He and Callan moved in sync as they readied the flotation devices while Joseph kept the vessel close. The VMP boats had moved back slightly so if someone went into the water, they could get to them quickly while not being in danger of the person hitting the boat. Andy looked at the shore, seeing the distance to Fisherman's Island. Here, the bridge was only about twenty feet above the water. *But no way the child can survive that drop.*

The shouts from above drew Andy's attention, and his gaze stayed riveted on the scene. Through the binoculars, he could see the pale complexion of the woman as she braved her fear to try to save a child she didn't know. Something moved inside his chest, and he winced at the fleeting but sharp pain. He knew a woman who would never try to save a child... or even stick around to see them grow up. The bitterness he thought was long gone slid back into his consciousness. *Funny how emotions can sneak up when least expected.*

"Larry... please," the woman on the bridge begged.

The crackling sound of an officer's voice came through the radio. "Sir... Larry, you know how this will go. You can make this easier on yourself. Just kneel and place the child safely on the bridge. Then—"

"Shut up! I can't think!" he screamed, making the baby cry louder.

"Larry, please, I'm begging you. I know you can do this. I know you have it in you to do the right thing here. Please."

The last plea from her lips seemed to have reached something in the young man's mind. He cast a gaze down to where Andy and the other VMP and Coast Guard vessels looked up at him.

The fight seemed to leave him, and he turned back toward the woman. Slowly, he moved closer to her and said, "I'm setting the baby down. Don't shoot."

"We're not going to shoot, Larry," the state trooper called out. "We just want everyone to leave here safely."

"I don't trust them," Larry said, gazing at the woman. "Get over here. I want you close."

The breath caught in Andy's throat as he watched the woman inch toward Larry, her arms still out. Seeing them together, he realized how petite she was compared to the much taller young man.

"Not gonna give the baby to you. Gonna lay it on the bridge. I want you close so I don't get shot," Larry said.

The woman slowly lowered her arms as though they were stiff and unused to moving. "Okay, Larry. Just lay the baby down."

Andy kept his eye on the woman as Larry's head lowered, and then he stood quickly, grabbing the woman and holding her in front of him as he returned to the edge of the bridge. Heart pounding, sure that hers was synchronized with his, Andy held his breath as Larry appeared more agitated now that the baby was no longer in his arms. The back of Larry's hips pressed against the bridge railing.

"Larry, please, let's go over there so they can take care of us," the woman begged.

"You know there's no way out of this for me. I can't go to prison. Not for this." Larry gave the woman a small push, then turned to leap over the bridge.

Andy watched in horror as the woman screamed and whirled, reaching out to grab Larry's back to keep him from plummeting over the bridge. But the movement didn't halt the larger man's progress, and her body flipped over with his. They plummeted into the water where the Chesapeake Bay swallowed them.

3

"Fuck!" Andy shouted as he raced to the front of the vessel, his gaze trained on the water where the two went under the surface. While Callan called out instructions for Joseph to move the boat forward, Andy whipped off his coat, ready to jump in.

A splash sounded ten feet to his left, and Larry's head came to the surface. Jose had Jared move their vessel closer, and he reached out to grab the back of Larry's jacket. As Ryan and Jose pulled Larry aboard, another splash sounded closer, and Andy watched as the woman's head barely broke the surface before going back under, then resurfaced again. Not waiting, he leaped off the end of the boat with a flotation device in his hand.

With only a few strokes, he came to her and wrapped his arms around her. "Ma'am, I've got you."

Spluttering was all she managed to get out. Uncertain what injuries she might have, he worked the device under her head and neck, then turned to see that Callan was already close enough to assist as Joseph expertly maneuvered the boat.

"Careful," he warned Callan even though the words were unnecessary. He hauled his body over the side as they gently lifted her onto the boat.

Callan had laid her gently onto the stretcher, and as soon as Andy's feet hit the deck, they each picked up an end and carried her into the wheelhouse.

"Report?" Ryan called out.

"She's in and out of consciousness," Andy reported. "We're heading to the hospital." She'd spent the past hour of her life terrified, cold, and trying to save a child she didn't know. And for some strange reason, he wanted to be the one to care for her. He knew they could get her there much quicker than if they tried to get her to shore and taken by ambulance.

Without hesitation, Ryan agreed. "Roger that. We'll follow with Larry."

Receiving acknowledgments from the state police and the North Heron sheriff's department, they pulled away from the bridge and left it behind as their vessels powered through the water.

Callan closed the wheelhouse door so they could keep the heat contained. Wrapping her in several warming blankets, Andy knelt next to the stretcher, waiting until Callan took her blood pressure and temperature. "Temp low but not dangerous. Blood pressure elevated."

Hating to lose hold of her, he stood to the side and quickly stripped off his shirt, then ran a towel over his torso and hair. Reaching into a pack they kept on board, he pulled on a fresh shirt, shivering in the process. He shifted to his ass and reached out to wipe a few wet tendrils from her face. Pale with a bluish tint, her skin was cold, and the side of her face had slight swelling. Her eyes blinked open, showing light brown eyes filled with pain and confusion.

"Ma'am, we're with the Virginia Marine Police. My name is Andy, and this is Callan. We're taking you to the North Heron Hospital."

She blinked, and he wasn't sure she understood what he said. "Can you tell me your name?"

"I… ee," she croaked. Swallowing water had affected her voice, and he nodded, not wanting her to try to speak again.

"Okay, ma'am. Don't try to talk. I'm going to hold your hand." He slid his hand under the blankets, but when his fingers reached her, she cried out. "Shit," he muttered, then lifted the blankets to see her wrist already swelling and turning blue. "Possible broken arm," he said as Callan radioed to the hospital.

Looking at her other hand, he noted her cold, delicate fingers appeared uninjured. Taking hold, he leaned closer again. "Can you squeeze my fingers?" He waited, then instructed again, "Can you squeeze?" Feeling a slight pressure, he nodded toward Callan.

"Good, good. Now, I want you to squeeze once if you're in a little bit of pain and twice if your pain level is high." Waiting, he grimaced at the feel of her tightening her grip two times.

Looking at Callan again, he said, "High pain."

Without taking his eyes off her, he called out, "Joseph, ETA?"

"Ten minutes," Joseph replied.

Callan was in the process of communicating with the hospital ER, then said, "They'll be ready for her. They said to pull into the Parkside Harbor, and they'd have an ambulance to take her straight to the ER."

The Parkside Harbor was only a two-minute drive to the ER. "Ma'am, we're less than fifteen minutes away from getting you to the hospital."

She squeezed his fingers, and he smiled. "You're very brave, and they'll take very good care of you." She squeezed his fingers again, and he breathed a sigh of relief that whatever injuries she might have, her cognitive function seemed to be intact.

Hating that her wet hair kept her chilled, he grabbed a clean towel and gently patted her hair. "Let me know if I hurt you."

He couldn't do anything about her wet clothing underneath the warming blankets, but with Callan monitoring her temperature for hypothermia, he was doing all he could until they could get her to the hospital.

Looking up, he caught Callan staring at him with a questioning expression. He mouthed, "What?"

Callan only smiled and shook his head, then looked back down at the woman, taking her blood pressure again.

"Almost there," Joseph called out, slowing the vessel.

Twisting around, Andy spied the dock with two

ambulances parked nearby, their engines running, and the EMTs waiting outside the vehicles with stretchers. Two North Heron sheriff vehicles were also in sight, and next to one was Sheriff Colt Hudson. They stopped with barely a bump against the dock, and Callan moved outside to toss the rope to a waiting harbor employee who tied them off before running to the other vessel and doing the same.

The next few minutes were a flurry of activity as Andy and Callan carried her stretcher off the boat. Andy grumbled every time they jostled her, but Callan's concentration stayed intact with only the hint of a grin at Andy's under-his-breath cursing. They lifted her onto the gurney, and he walked alongside as she was transported into the back of the ambulance.

Forced to step back, Andy stood to the side, his hands clenched into fists, the desire to climb in with her almost overwhelming. He was barely aware of the other activity taking place around him. Just before the ambulance doors closed, she lifted her head, and her pain-filled eyes captured his gaze. His breath snagged as their gazes remained locked until the doors broke the connection. When the ambulance pulled away, his attention jerked back to what was happening around him.

Larry was also strapped onto a gurney, but his wrist was handcuffed to the side. Listening to Larry crying and complaining, Andy was filled with rage and stepped forward, his hands curled into fists.

"Back down," Callan said in a soft voice that no one else could hear, but he grabbed Andy's shoulder. "I know something is going on with you and the pretty woman, but man, don't fuck up your career over this."

With his lips tightly pressed together, he offered a curt nod and stepped back as Larry was placed in the next ambulance, and a deputy climbed in with him. Once they pulled away, Callan maneuvered him down the dock to where Ryan and the other VMP officers stood with Sheriff Colt Hudson.

"According to the State Police, he stole the vehicle from a gas station on Shore Drive in Virginia Beach. The owner of the vehicle, who was at the pump, immediately began screaming since her child was inside. The police were called. He got on the Bay bridge, and it was there that the child in a carrier in the back seat began to cry. From what the police on the bridge said, he immediately realized his charges went from just theft to include kidnapping. He freaked the fuck out and went crazy, even considering getting rid of the child."

The angry murmurings from the others resounded. Colt continued, "But thank God, he didn't have it in him. By that time, though, the bystander saw him and stopped. She called it in before she exited her vehicle."

"What will happen to her car?" Andy asked, realizing it was almost an hour's drive south of the hospital.

"I've got a deputy bringing it to Baytown. Once we know when she'll get discharged, we'll arrange to get it to her," Colt replied.

"Do you know her name?" Andy asked, hoping his interest was kept hidden from the others. No one seemed to pay attention to his question except Callan, whose lips twitched.

"Not her first. Watkins is what I got from the state police officer." Colt's phone rang, and he answered, saying little as he listened. Disconnecting, he said, "Looks like we won't interview her today. They've taken her in for surgery."

"Surgery?" Andy barked out, his brows lowered in concern. He knew she probably had a broken arm, but the idea that she might have other, more serious injuries sliced through him.

"I don't know anything else," Colt said as he reached out his hand. "Ryan, I'll see you at the next law enforcement leaders meeting. And when I get more information from Ms. Watkins, I'll send it your way for your reports." With a wave toward the others, he called out, "Good work today."

Andy and the other VMP officers circled as Ryan scrubbed his hand over his face and sighed. "Just as Colt said, good work, men. While this rescue wasn't ordinary, the baby stayed safe, and we got to the two who entered the water. Joseph, Jared... excellent vessel handling. Jose, we got Larry in with no trouble and managed to care for him while ensuring he was secured. Andy, you had to go into the water. Good decision... you probably saved her life. She appeared too exhausted to stay afloat in the cold water for very long. Callan... your care made sure the ER knew what to expect. All in all, I'd say this was successful. Let's get back to the station, debrief, and get reports written."

As the others moved back to the boats tied at the dock, Andy stared in the direction of the road where the ambulance had disappeared from sight. Sighing heavily, he turned and followed Callan.

Once on the water, he and Callan stayed in the wheelhouse with Joseph, tidying the area and noting what they'd need to restock when they returned to the station. He stripped out of his wet pants and slid on an extra pair kept for emergencies.

"You okay?" Callan asked. "You just seemed really… I don't know… invested in her."

"She needed saving," he answered, keeping his face averted. When silence met him, he looked up to see Callan and Joseph both grinning. "What?" he grumbled.

"I don't know. Why don't you tell us?"

"Nothing to tell," he argued. "She just seemed like a nice lady. Stopped when she didn't have to. Got involved when she didn't have to. Stayed with him and tried to talk him down when she didn't have to. And then, when he decided to go over, she tried to stop him." Shrugging, he said, "I'd say that makes her worthy of someone being invested."

Callan nodded his agreement. "You've got that right."

Andy stayed busy for the rest of the trip, trying unsuccessfully to keep his mind off the woman in surgery. Glad when they arrived at the Baytown Harbor, he threw himself into restocking the vessel for the next callout or patrol. He headed inside to take a hot shower in the locker room. Dressed in clean, dry clothes, he walked into the larger office with unassigned desks available for whoever needed to do desk work. Adding his comments to the report Callan had already started didn't take long. After he sent it to Ryan, he stood and met the others outside, ready to leave for the day.

"You heading to the pub?" Jose asked.

At first, he shook his head, then changed his mind. "Yeah. I've got time for a drink before heading home."

Soon, the group was ensconced at the pub, his mood lifting as they laughed with the owners, Brogan and Aiden MacFarlane.

"The dumb fuck stole a minivan at a gas station and didn't even look in the back?" Aiden asked, incredulity mixed with anger.

"If someone took my kid, that's the last thing they'd ever take," Brogan growled next to him.

"Damn straight. No one would ever find their body," Aiden agreed with a rare frown on his face, slapping the cloth in his hand onto the bar.

Andy remembered the MacFarlane brothers in high school even though he was only in middle school at the time. They were part of the original Baytown Boys, named after the close friends who played baseball together. Now, as adults, they were still with the same friends, but having begun a chapter of the American Legion in Baytown, they extended the special friendship to all the locals who had served in the military. Whereas the teenage Andy would have scoffed at being part of the *in*-crowd, he now appreciated the adult camaraderie.

Knowing their penchant for protection, especially since many of them were now fathers, he understood their anger toward a foolish young man who'd made a decision today with far-reaching ramifications. Even though the woman wasn't *his*, she'd touched the protectiveness inside.

Ryan walked over to their table with Mitch Evans, Baytown's police chief, and Lance Greene, Grant Wilder, and Ginny MacFarlane, all Baytown police officers.

The conversation moved from the day's rescue to the latest fundraising project for the American Legion. After a few minutes, Andy scooted his chair back and stood. "Hate to drink and run, but I really need to get home. I'm supposed to have dinner with Dad and Aaron tonight."

With a wave to the others, he was glad he had a ready excuse to leave, considering his mind was not on the AL's projects. Instead, as he climbed into his SUV and headed down the road, his mind was firmly on the pretty woman who gave so much for a child and a man who were strangers to her.

4

Ivy blinked her eyes open, then squinted at the light in the room. It wasn't a bright light, but enough that she wondered why she fell asleep with the lamp next to her bed turned on. She swallowed, then winced at the sting. Her tongue felt too large for her cotton mouth, and her lips were desert dry. Blinking several more times, she fought to wake fully, not understanding why she was sleeping on her back. Ivy had always been a side sleeper, curling up as she cuddled her pillow.

She tried to sit, but before she was able, a woman walked into the room. Gasping in surprise, she blinked several more times as the woman approached. *Nursing scrubs?*

"Oh, Ms. Watkins, you're awake. Good. I'm Kelly, your nurse. I was just coming to check on you. I'll let the doctor know you're awake as soon as I check your stats."

"Wha—" she croaked.

"Here you go." The nurse held a cup with a straw down to Ivy's lips, and she drank thirstily.

"I don't… where am I?"

"You're at the North Heron Hospital. You had surgery earlier today on your arm after the accident."

"Accident?"

Kelly continued to check the monitors, but Ivy's mind struggled to make sense of the little information Kelly had given. Suddenly, her body jolted with the shock of memories. *The bridge. The baby. The man. The begging. The fear. The desperation.* A weight pressed down on her chest as more memories forced their way through the fog of her mind.

He went over the edge. I tried to grab him. Lost my balance. His coat slipping from my grasp. Weightless. Falling. Screaming. Hitting. Plunging. The cold. Then nothing.

"Okay, okay," Kelly said as the beeping from the machine next to her bed increased. "Take deep breaths with me. You're fine. You're going to be fine." Another nurse stuck her head in the room and Kelly called out, "Get the doctor."

Ivy kept her gaze on Kelly as she slowed her breathing. As her thoughts slowed, allowing her to process, she gasped again, jerking upward. "The baby! What happened to the baby?"

Kelly leaned close, patting her arm. "He's fine. I heard one of the other nurses say that he was taken to a hospital in Virginia Beach and reunited with his parents."

"Oh, thank God." Falling backward onto the stiff mattress, she winced.

"The doctor will be right here," Kelly said, still monitoring the attached machines.

The baby is fine. The baby is fine. She closed her eyes, and another memory slid into the forefront of her thoughts. *There was another man. Arms that encircled me through the pain. Arms that dragged me to a boat and lifted me. Then he'd held my hand.* Everything was fuzzy, but she remembered feeling safe as long as she could feel his hand holding hers.

Ivy shifted, now more alert, and looked around. Typical hospital room. Ugly blue gown. And an even uglier left wrist. A scar with puckered reddened skin and black crisscrossed stitches lining it met her gaze.

"Good evening, Ms. Watkins!"

Her brow furrowed as she looked up to see a smiling man walk in, wearing a white coat with the requisite stethoscope around his neck.

"I'm Dr. Neilson, an orthopedic surgeon here at the hospital."

"Hello," she greeted, anxious for him to tell her what had happened.

He stood at the end of her bed, his smile beaming toward her before he moved closer. "Do you remember why you're here?" he asked.

"Yes. I fell into the water. Or was pulled… never mind. I… fell." While the details were now crystal clear, she was certain he didn't care about them.

"You had quite the day. Even made the evening news, although your name wasn't mentioned."

She blinked, unsure what to say to that announcement. Glancing down at her arm, she said, "So… um… my arm?"

"Yes, yes." He nodded, his smile still as bright. His blond hair was swept to the side, neatly styled. He was handsome in a classic pretty-boy way, but she had an inkling that he was used to more adoration than she was willing to give at the moment.

Holding his gaze without offering a smile seemed to bring him back to the matter at hand. "The ER evaluated you when you came in earlier. They completed an MRI and full-body radiographs. You're quite lucky. Their reports found that you have no swelling of the brain, although you have minimal swelling on the left side of your face. No internal injuries, and no other broken bones other than a distal radius fracture of your left wrist. A very common fracture for someone who has fallen. You probably placed your hands in front of you to protect your face– a very natural, instinctive reaction. And since the break was only with your left wrist, your body probably hit the water on that side, therefore having your wrist take the brunt of the force."

"Oh," she muttered, her chest deflating as the air rushed out.

"It was easily set with a few screws and plates. You'll have a cast set tomorrow before you're discharged. You'll wear that for two weeks and then be given a removable splint to wear for about four more weeks. I'll give you a referral for physical therapy and, of course, a script for pain relievers for a couple of days. After that, you can transition to over-the-counter pain meds. Kelly will have all the details for you. You'll make an appointment to return to see me at my office in two weeks, and we'll see how things are going then. Sound good?"

Her brain struggled to catch up to his rapid-fire analysis and instructions. "Um… yes, thank you."

"I'm sure you're concerned about the scarring," he continued.

A scoff slipped out, but she covered it with a quick shake of her head. "No, actually, that's irrelevant. What I am concerned about is my job. Driving. Going into work."

"Oh," he said, brows raised as he smiled. "Well, you can't drive until you're off the prescription pain medication, but that should only be for the next few days. Then driving might be awkward with the cast, but it's certainly doable."

"I'm an engineer at the CBBT. Any restrictions there?"

His brows lifted. "Oh, an engineer. Well, I would imagine that computer keyboard use will be limited for a while. You're right-handed?"

"Yes."

"Until you come back for your two-week appointment, I don't want you to carry anything with your left hand that puts any strain on you. Certainly, you can balance a book or small item with your cast, but there's no reason to take a chance on re-injuring yourself with anything heavy."

She sighed but nodded while thanking him again. As he walked out, she tried to wrap her mind around everything that had happened. *How did I go from driving across the bridge toward home to here?* She stared down at her left arm as it lay propped on a pillow. The swelling of her hand, fingers, wrist, and lower arm, as well as the angry surgery site caused her to groan. She shook her head slowly. *And now this.*

She thought of her new job and grimaced. "Shit," she muttered. Fatigue weighed down on her shoulders, and she closed her eyes, but her rest only lasted a moment.

"Hi again," Kelly said brightly, walking back into the room.

Plastering a smile on her face, she opened her eyes. Before she had a chance to speak, Kelly looked over her shoulder as she washed her hands.

"I think you made quite an impression on Dr. Nielsen. It seems like most patients are worried about scars, and your questions seemed well thought out for someone who just woke up."

Looking down, she shrugged before lifting her gaze. "There's nothing I can do about a scar. I'm more worried about making sure I can work. I just moved back into town and am new to my job."

"Then I'd suggest you at least take several days to give your body a chance to get over the shock. You know, as the surgeon, he's really just concerned with your wrist. But what you went through today… well, from what I heard, it was traumatic."

She nodded, not wanting to spend much time rehashing her morning. Too many practical decisions needed to be made, starting with how she would get to her car, which had been left on the bridge.

Exhaustion continued to pull at her, and she was desperate for more pain medicine. A knock on her door sent her attention to the two men in uniform who entered her room. One was slightly older with dark-brown hair cut in a military style, and he wore a kind but no-nonsense expression on his face. The other was younger, his light-brown hair neatly trimmed, and when his gaze landed on her, a wide smile crossed his face. He was good looking, but she couldn't imagine why he was smiling, considering she no doubt looked as ragged as she felt.

"Ma'am, I brought your purse to you," the younger one said.

"Oh!" She looked to see his name on his uniform. "Thank you, Officer Jenkins."

"It's deputy, ma'am," he replied affably.

"Deputy Jenkins," she amended, clutching her purse with her good hand, grateful to have it with her.

He stepped closer, leaned his hips against her bed, and dropped his hand to rest on her blanket-covered foot. For a second, she wondered if he wasn't paying attention to what he was doing when the other deputy growled in a low voice, "Hands to yourself, rookie."

The younger deputy jerked his hand back but winked at her. She blinked, her brain foggy, and could only imagine the pain medicine had her reactions slowed.

Clearing his throat, the other man turned his attention back to her. "I'm Detective Shackley, Ms. Watkins. We've come to ask you a few questions about this morning if you're up to it."

All she wanted to do was forget about the morning, but she knew she had no choice but to relive it again.

After assuring them she was able to give her statement, she answered their questions as fully but succinctly as she could. *No, I didn't know the man. I stopped because I saw him pacing in what looked like agitation with a baby in his arms near the edge of the bridge. I just got him to talk to me. I tried to calm him. I didn't know what he'd done or what he'd planned.*

By the time they'd finished and thanked her, she quickly asked, "My car? Where is it?"

"It was driven to the Baytown Harbor, Ms. Watkins," Detective Shackley answered. "Our sheriff had us leave it at the Virginia Marine Police station so it would be safe until you could retrieve it."

Deputy Jenkins grinned and winked again as he dipped his chin. "Your keys are in your purse. I'd be happy to assist you in retrieving it when you're discharged."

The hopeful specter in his eyes was almost endearing, but Ivy was exhausted, in pain, and felt as gross as she knew she looked. "Thank you, Deputy, but I'll manage. I appreciate you bringing my purse, though."

He reached into his pocket and pulled out a card. After scribbling on the back, he handed it to her while Detective Shackley rolled his eyes. "Here you go. It's my *personal* number, so if you decide you need assistance, just give me a call."

Her lips were pressed into a thin line, but she attempted to force them into a slight smile. Uncertain if she had achieved the modicum of politeness, she thanked him again. After they walked out, she breathed a sigh of relief.

Gratitude spilled forth when Kelly returned with a pain reliever and assisted her to the bathroom.

Finally, she closed her eyes, willing the day to end. But her dreams were filled with remembrances... a crying baby, a terrified young man, and falling into an abyss. The dark below extended, and she fell and fell and fell. Jolting awake just before she hit the water in her dream, the image of a dark-haired, bearded man with deep chocolate eyes came to her mind. He held her hand and whispered words to her as he wrapped her in warmth. Blinking in the light peeking through the hospital window blinds, she vowed to find the hero who'd come just when she needed him. And for the first time since she'd stopped her car on the bridge that morning, she smiled.

5

"Andy, glad you made it!"

He grinned as he walked through the door leading into his dad's kitchen. Arthur Bergstrom stirred a pot while standing at the stove, and Andy's brother, Aaron, was grabbing beer bottles from the refrigerator. The scene was familiar—he and his brother tried to have dinner with their dad once a week unless their schedules didn't agree.

Raised on the Eastern Shore, he'd spent his fair share of time on the water, considering his dad worked for one of the larger fishing businesses on the shore. But Andy had always known that fishing wasn't for him. Not that he had anything against the job. Hell, it had provided his family with their livelihood, but he'd been anxious to get away from the area and see more of the world at eighteen. Joining the Navy had allowed him to do just that, although his dad always laughed at his military job description.

"Boy, you left the shore to become a marine engine

mechanic with the Navy. Hell, you could have just stayed here and learned from me!"

Still grinning at the memory, he shook his head. While his dad joked, he understood Andy's need to find his own way in life. But life often took twists and turns, and the job he'd originally wanted to do fell away when a new opportunity presented itself. Becoming friends with a fellow sailor at the base who was an MP, he became interested in law enforcement. After a tour as a mechanic, he'd applied and received permission to change his MOS and enrolled in military police school. After that, two more tours were all he'd managed before the Eastern Shore called once again.

His younger brother had followed in his footsteps, although when he'd joined the Navy, he was accepted immediately into MP school. Aaron had only completed one tour before he was ready to return to his roots and was now a deputy for North Heron.

Accepting the cold bottle from Aaron with one hand, he fist-bumped him with the other. He and Aaron shared the same dark hair and dark eyes, but at five years younger, Andy could swear his brother didn't have the crow's feet extend from his eyes that he did. Plus, his brother had kept his face clean shaven, also making him appear a lot younger.

The kitchen had changed little in the years since Andy and Aaron grew up in it. The tile on the floor and the countertops were old but scrubbed clean. The cabinets had been painted several years ago, and the appliances had been updated as the older ones needed replacing. The table in the eat-in kitchen was the same wooden one from his childhood, but his dad had replaced the chairs several years ago. It was still the hub of the house, a place where the three gathered.

Moving closer, he clapped his dad on the shoulder as he leaned over to see what was in the pot. "Damn, Pop, you know the way to bring us home," he moaned appreciatively as he spied the homemade Bay chowder. It was his dad's recipe, and he changed it with whatever fresh fish from the Bay he could get. Sometimes it was chunks of rockfish, Bay scallops, and clams. Other times, it included oysters and blue crab. But whatever he added to the creamy broth with onions and potatoes, he also would throw in some cooked, crumbled bacon.

As soon as the trio sat down at the table with full, steaming bowls in front of them and a platter of rolls with butter, they dug in.

"Heard you had some excitement this morning," Aaron said. "I wasn't on duty, but everyone talked about what happened on the bridge. I heard it was on the local Virginia Beach news stations."

His dad looked up, brows raised. "What happened, Son?"

Swallowing his spoonful, he took a swig of beer, then related the morning's events from when they got the call to watching the man pull the woman over the edge. He finished by telling them about going into the water after her and talking to her as they headed to the hospital by water.

"Holy hell," Aaron said, shaking his head. "What a dumbass! To steal a vehicle right in front of the owner and not even think there might be a passenger in the back. Shit!"

"But thank God, the baby was fine," his dad said, a crease forming along his forehead. "What about the woman? That was a mighty brave thing for her to do."

Andy nodded, his mind filled with thoughts of her. "Yeah, she was amazing." He could see her so clearly as though he still had her centered in his binocular view. Auburn hair whipped in the breeze. Her pale complexion. The way she kept her arms outstretched while pleading for the baby. And how easy it would have been for her to turn away from the man who'd held them all captive.

"Kind of reckless, though." Aaron shrugged while spreading an excess of butter all over his warm roll.

"Reckless?" Andy barked, shooting a glare toward his brother. "There was nothing reckless about her. She was standing in the cold without a coat for over half an hour, begging the man to give the baby to her. Then she could have just let him jump, but she tried to help." His nostrils flared with irritation as his words poured out. Chest heaving, he focused on the two pairs of eyes staring at him.

Aaron licked the butter from his fingers while his brow lifted to his hairline, the beginnings of a smile curving his lips. "Damn, bro. Looks like I touched a nerve, but gotta ask, are you sure she's just a rescue? Kinda sounds like a bit of interest there."

His chin jerked back, and he shook his head. "Sure… admiration. But… I mean, I don't know her… it's not…"

Aaron laughed, his eyes twinkling. "I think it sounds like quite the crush."

"Shut up, asshole," Andy grumbled but couldn't get the image of her lying on the stretcher in the wheelhouse out of his mind or how cold her pale, almost bluish complexion was under his fingers when he brushed her wet hair back from her face. And the squeeze of her fingers on his.

"Sounds like there's a good reason for your brother's admiration," his dad said, admonishing Aaron. Turning toward Andy, he continued, "You ought to check on her."

He hated to admit that he'd already had that thought, but looking at his father and brother, who knew him better than anyone, he shrugged. "I don't even know if she's local. She may have just been passing through."

Aaron shook his head. "Nope, I heard Josh Jenkins say she was new to the area and working in Baytown." Shaking his head, he scoffed. "That idiot thinks he's got a chance with her."

At that, he jerked, causing the soup on his spoon to drop back into the bowl. "What are you talking about?"

"He was one of the deputies who went to the hospital today to get her statement. They took her purse to her and had looked at her driver's license. He said that even though she looked like hell in the hospital, he knew she'd clean up good. Then he gave her his card with his cell number and wanted to take her to her vehicle parked at the Baytown Harbor tomorrow. Figures he can get a date out of her once he comes to her rescue." Shaking his head, he added, "I thought Sam

Shackley was going to take Josh's head off, but that guy has thought his shit didn't stink ever since high school."

Lips pinched together as his fist gripped the now-empty spoon, Andy was filled with unexpected anger. "What the hell? She'd clean up good? Jesus, with everything she went through today, she shouldn't have to even breathe his air, much less worry about him sniffing around!"

Aaron and his dad shared a look before Aaron said, "Anyway, don't you have tomorrow off?"

"Yeah. What does that have to do with anything?"

"Go see her. Check on her. Tell her you were the one from the VMP who rescued her."

"I wasn't the only one, you know—"

Aaron waved his hand dismissively. "Stop deflecting. You know what I mean."

They continued eating their dinner, finding other subjects to talk about, but the seed had already been planted. The idea of stopping by to check on her and then volunteering to take her to her car sounded like a good plan. *At least I'd get to see her again.*

Aaron said goodbye soon after since he had to get home for an early shift the next day. Andy and his dad grabbed a second beer and wandered into the living room, where his dad took up his usual place in the easy chair facing the television. Leaning back on the old, worn but comfortable sofa, Andy plopped his feet on the coffee table. Like the kitchen, the living room had only changed over the years as furniture needed to be replaced. But it still exuded warmth with framed photographs of the three of them on the mantel.

"I'm real proud of you, Son. Proud of both of you." His attention swung over to his dad, and he was struck with the knowledge that his dad had never shied away from telling him and his brother that he cared about them and was proud of them.

"Even when I was a fuckup of a teenager?"

His dad chuckled and shook his head. "You were never a fuckup, Andy. Hell, you never snuck alcohol other than a few times when your friends did. You never used drugs. You always worked hard. God knows I needed the help, and if you resented it, you never let me know."

"I didn't resent it, Pop."

Aaron was five years younger than Andy and born prematurely. In and out of hospitals for the first couple of years of his life, Aaron then lagged in development for a few more years. As they grew up, Andy always watched out for his younger brother.

He sighed. *God knows Mom didn't try.* Not interested in caring for a child with so many needs, by the time Aaron was two, their mom had packed her bags and left. Andy never had any contact with her after that. First, because for years she didn't want any. By the time he was a teenager, she'd reached out to their dad. Pop would have put all of his feelings of anger and abandonment aside if that was what his sons wanted. But as far as Andy was concerned, he didn't have a mom, so he'd refused any contact. Aaron was approaching middle school but took his cues from his idolized older brother and refused as well. After a while, their mom stopped trying. Once again, she didn't have it in her to stick out anything difficult.

While he'd like to think he was a well-adjusted adult, he knew his lack of a family with a loving mom at the center had skewed his thoughts of women in general when he was younger. So much so that he was often sullen to some of the female teachers and sure as hell surly to some of the female students who seemed to have everything he didn't. It wasn't until he was in the military and had the error of his ways forced into his sight, that he finally realized how piss-poor his attitude had been.

"Son, it's no lie that when your mama left, she left a big hole in you and Aaron. I tried to fill it, but—"

"Don't even go there, Pop. Believe me, you filled it. I took out my anger about her on a lot of people who didn't deserve it. Looking back, some of my biggest regrets were in high school. I wish I'd been a better man."

"Hell, boy, I'd say you've redeemed yourself over and over with the man you are today."

Andy snorted. "Maybe…" He took another swig of beer, then fiddled with the label.

They sat in silence for a few minutes, then his dad finally said, "There was nothin' any of us could do to keep her here, you know. I thought she was a good woman when I married her, but she wasn't very maternal. She had a selfish streak that I didn't realize until too late. I think back, and it was as though she didn't really take to motherhood. And that had nothing to do with you or your brother. It was all on her. It wasn't too bad with you, but when Aaron was so ill when he was little... well, she just didn't know how to cope and gave up."

His gut clenched like it always did when he thought of his mother. He'd finally come to terms with her abandonment, but thinking about her turning her back on Aaron when he was so young could still bring anger to the surface.

As though his dad could see the flinch Andy thought he'd hidden, his dad leaned forward to make his point. "I get it, Son. I was able to let go of my feelings about my wife leaving a lot easier than I was able to let go of the feelings about the mother of my children leaving them. But I had to jump in and do the best that I could for you and Aaron."

His gaze whipped to his dad, seeing the deeper lines creasing his face. "Pop, you did a fuckin' amazin' job."

"Hmph." His dad snorted. "I know I'm proud of the way you two turned out. Figure the good Lord and some good people helping had a lot to do with that."

A knock on the back door sounded, and Andy looked over in surprise when his dad jumped up to answer it, his eyes twinkling and an expectant smile on his face.

"Sally, come on in," he called out as he threw the door open wide.

Andy watched as their neighbor walked into the house, her hands full of a cake plate and a soft smile gracing her face. She was in jeans, but he noticed her pink blouse brought out the slight blush on her cheeks. Her silver-blond hair had been in a just-above-the-shoulders cut for as long as he could remember, but tonight, the sides were pulled back with shiny clips. And he could swear she had a dash of lipstick and mascara on.

Sally and her husband, Toby, had been his dad's neighbors for as long as he could remember, and he knew they were two of the good people his dad had just referred to. They'd never had children but pitched in whenever they could. Toby helped with the exercises Aaron needed to strengthen his muscles when he was little and later taught Andy how to drive. Sally would chauffeur him and his brother around when his dad was working and babysat whenever needed. And her prize-winning cakes always found a way onto their table. Toby had died just before Andy had left the Navy, but Sally had stayed in their little house next door.

Now, looking at the blush on her face as she stared up at his dad, an easy smile slid into place. *Looks like Dad has a girlfriend.*

He quickly stood and walked over to greet her. She wrapped her arms around him tightly as she always did. "Ms. Sally, good to see you."

"Me or my cake?" She laughed, the familiar sparkle in her eye.

He lifted the aluminum foil cover and spied her apple spice cake. "Oh, that's a toss-up."

She laughed again and swatted his arm before turning back to his dad. "Arthur, I realize I missed Aaron, but you make sure to save him a piece." Walking into the kitchen, she set the plate down on the counter and then turned, her gaze darting around as though suddenly uncertain.

He'd never known her to be nervous but covered his knowing smile with a slight cough. "Well, Pop, I've got to get going."

"Oh, please don't leave on my account…" Sally began.

"No, no. I need to get home to… um… well, I've got things I need to do." He bent to kiss her cheek and then turned to clasp his dad's hand.

"Well, let me cut you a piece." She quickly sliced a large section and placed it into a plastic container, snapping on the lid. Handing it to him, she smiled. "A treat for a sweet boy."

She'd always said those words to him when he was younger, and somehow, they soothed the ragged edges his mother had left. Bending, he kissed her soft cheek and murmured his goodbyes.

"I'll see you out, Son. Sally, hang tight, and we can share a piece of cake."

Still grinning, Andy walked out into the evening chill with his dad, and they stood on the back patio. Inclining his head toward the house, he lifted his brows. "You and Ms. Sally?"

"Now, boy, don't be impudent."

Clapping his dad's shoulder, he shook his head. "Dad, you've been alone for a long fuckin' time. Ms. Sally is one of the best women I've ever known and deserves another good man. If the two of you have more than friendship happening, go for it."

His dad looked down as he rubbed the whiskers on

his chin for a moment before raising his gaze back to Andy. "You don't mind?"

Staring at the man who'd not only given him life but had given him nothing but the best, he shook his head again. "Hell no, and Aaron will tell you the same. No one deserves happiness more than you."

At that, his father straightened and squared his shoulders, giving a curt nod. "Well, alright. You take care, and I'm going back inside to have a piece of cake."

Jogging over to his SUV, he climbed inside and cranked up the heat. As he backed out of the drive, he looked through the window to see his dad and Ms. Sally standing in the kitchen, smiling at each other. Something warm moved through his chest.

That feeling remained all the way home as he now considered visiting the beautiful, brave stranger the next day.

6

Andy walked down the hall of the hospital, hating the smell. It reminded him of the many times they'd had to come when Aaron was young. Eventually, Aaron grew stronger and healthier, but Andy was always amazed at how the scent of a place could bring back such evocative memories. Even though he'd only been a kid himself, he'd sit in the corner of the room, angry when his dad would have to say that he was a single parent to whoever asked if the mother was coming.

Pushing those thoughts to the side, he approached the room he was visiting. The door was partially opened, and he hesitated, hearing voices from inside.

"Kelly, I need to call for a taxi. I don't have a way to get to my car."

"A taxi will cost a lot from here to Baytown. Are you sure?"

"I have no choice. I'm new to the area... well, new for now. I grew up here but haven't lived here in years.

My parents are away, so it's just me at their house for now."

"Okay, let me go to the nurses' station and find the number for a taxi."

As the nurse stepped out of the room, he softly called out, "Nurse?"

She turned and smiled, tilting her head to the side. "Yes? May I help you?"

"I was one of the officers at the scene who helped bring Ms. Watkins in yesterday and just came by to see how she was doing. I didn't mean to eavesdrop, but I can take her if she needs a ride to get home."

He felt like a bug under a microscope as she stared, then slowly nodded.

"Well, I'll have to ask her, and the doctor is completing her discharge papers now. But if you wait out here, I'll let you know."

He nodded his agreement, and the nurse went back into the room. He stepped back, refusing to listen at the door, but excited that she was well enough to discharge and that he might be able to spend more time with her. A moment later, she came back with a smile on her face. "She said she would appreciate a ride. If you want to get your vehicle, you can pull it up to the side entrance just beyond the ER. She'll be wheeled down shortly."

Dipping his chin, he thanked her, and with a grin crossing his face, he headed back to the elevator. He was surprised she'd agreed so easily but wasn't about to look a gift horse in the mouth. Once he got to his SUV, he drove to the patient discharge pickup lane and parked. Climbing down, he walked to the passenger side and leaned against the door, his gaze trained on the hospital door, anxious to see her again.

"You don't seem very excited to have a handsome man come pick you up," Kelly remarked, helping Ivy pull on a pair of scrubs. Her clothes from the previous day had dried and been stuffed into a plastic bag. The scrubs were hardly flattering, but considering she hadn't had a shower, she was glad Kelly offered them to her. And the top certainly made it easy to get on over her casted wrist. Her slightly swollen cheek made speaking difficult without feeling the tightness.

Ivy thought of the flirtatious twinkle in Deputy Jenkins's eye yesterday, and while grateful she didn't have to spend money on a long taxi ride, she wasn't in the mood to talk to a stranger for an hour while trapped inside a vehicle. *Maybe I can pretend to sleep.* Seeing Kelly's expectant expression, she muttered, "I'm just a little tired, that's all."

"Well, that's normal. Remember what I said... take care of your mind and body."

Settling in the wheelchair with her purse, meds, and discharge papers in her lap, she waved to Kelly as the aide rolled her down the hall.

Once on the first floor and heading to the discharge door, the aide said, "You don't have a coat, and it's cold outside. Let me know when you see your ride, and I'll wheel you out."

At the wide glass door, Ivy looked at the vehicles

parked in a line but didn't see one from the sheriff's department. *Maybe he brought his personal vehicle.* But she didn't see Deputy Jenkins anywhere. "I don't know. I don't see him."

Just then, her gaze landed on a dark-haired, dark-bearded man leaning against an SUV, his eyes staring straight at her. She gasped, recognizing the man who'd pulled her from the water and held her hand while being transported to the hospital. "Him?"

"Oh Lordy." The aide laughed. "What a gorgeous man to come to whisk you away. Makes me almost wish I was in your shoes!"

Ivy stared as the man walked toward her, pulling off his thick black jacket as the aide rolled her outside. "Hello," he greeted. With a soft smile, he whipped his coat around her shoulders to keep the chill off before walking beside her as they approached his SUV. She was immediately engulfed in the warmth of the material and the scent of him surrounding her. Without thinking, she leaned her face to the side, burying her nose in the lining and inhaling deeply.

Looking up, she realized he was watching, his smile still in place and the crinkles emitting from his eyes deepening. He opened the passenger door and reached over to lift the plastic bag and her purse from her tight grip. "I've got the heat on for you." He turned to set her purse and bag on the floorboard, then returned to take her by the arm as the aide helped her stand from the wheelchair.

She hesitated as she looked at her casted left wrist and wondered how she would climb into his vehicle. It didn't help that at only a little over five feet tall, she'd need her left hand to pull herself up.

"May I assist?"

She turned and looked up. Even with her standing, he towered over her. She was used to being shorter than everyone, but he had to be well over six feet tall. And built. She held his gaze, seeing the sincere expression on his face, and liked that he asked first. Nodding, she replied, "With this cast, I can't figure out how to do it myself. Plus, I'm a little short."

His brows lifted. "A little? No… you can't be serious."

A small bark of laughter erupted at his joking tone. Her heart felt lighter than it had since she'd stopped on the bridge. He moved closer, and with one arm under her knees and the other around her back, he lifted her into the seat, making sure to buckle her in. Once he climbed behind the wheel, she blurted, "You're not the deputy who took my statement yesterday."

He blinked and cocked his head to the side. "Oh, I'm sorry. Were you expecting someone else?"

She swore she saw the disappointment in his eyes as well as heard it in his tone. "No," she rushed. "I… the nurse just said that the officer from yesterday came to take me to my car. So, um… he'd offered, but I didn't take him up on it. I just assumed it was him. But this is fine. I mean, more than fine. I had no desire to ride with him. Not that there was anything wrong with him." She blew out her breath. "Jesus, I'm sorry. I'm not usually a blabbermouth, but the pain meds must have loosened my brain and tongue." She leaned her head back against the headrest and closed her eyes, embarrassment racing through her.

He chuckled, and the sound released the tension that had coiled in her body. She rolled her head to the side and stared at his profile as he pulled out of the line of cars picking up patients. His nose had a tiny bump at the top, and she wondered if he had broken it at some time. It didn't matter because it did nothing to detract from his attractiveness. Dark brown hair trimmed neatly at the sides and a little longer on top. Angular cheekbones and jaw, the latter covered by a trimmed beard.

Not in uniform, he wore jeans that molded to his thighs, boots that had stood firm as he helped her into his SUV, and a hunter-green crewneck shirt. And, of course, his warm black jacket that was wrapped around her and smelled deliciously of salt air and pine.

Pulling out of the hospital parking lot, he said, "I'm Andy."

She assumed he knew her name. "And you work with the police?"

"The Virginia Marine Police. I was one of several who answered the emergency call and was in a boat underneath the bridge."

"Does it sound terrible to say I barely remember seeing boats below?"

He looked to the side and shook his head. "Not at all. I watched you. I could hear a lot of what you said. Your focus was on getting that baby to safety."

Nodding, she blew out a long breath. "I was terrified to take my eyes off what was happening."

"I need to ask if you've taken any pain medication today."

"Yes, they gave me some this morning before they took my IV out." Wondering why he asked, she suddenly jerked. "Oh, my God. I'm not supposed to drive, am I? Shit! Now, what am I going to do?"

"I can take you to your home and make arrangements to bring your car to your house tomorrow."

"Oh, I can't ask you to do that."

"You're not asking me to do anything. I'm volunteering. If you give me directions to your house, I'll ensure you get there safely."

Her fuzzy mind reminded her of her college years when she'd drink and get a buzz. She'd always been a lightweight with alcohol, and it didn't take much for her to become tipsy. The pain meds Kelly had given her this morning had the same effect. It crossed her mind that she was having a stranger take her to her house, but she realized that was no different than if she'd taken a taxi or driver service. *At least I know he's a police officer.*

She rattled off her address, but as they approached Baytown, she pointed him down several streets toward her parents' house outside of town.

"Are you new to the area?" he asked.

"No, I grew up here. But I've been gone for a long time. In fact, we're heading to my parents' house. They're in North Carolina taking care of my grandma right now, so I'm staying at their place until I find something for myself. I admit, it feels a little weird to move back into the house I grew up in, but there was no reason to start paying rent now. Plus, while they're gone, I can keep an eye on their place for them."

"I know what you mean. When I first moved to the area, I lived with my dad until I found the house I bought. It's small, but it's mine."

"Sounds perfect," she agreed. "That's what I'm hoping to find too." She looked out the window and lifted her right hand. "You can turn here. It's the white house on the right."

He slowed to almost a stop before turning into the drive. She looked toward him, but he was staring at the house with his mouth open. She shifted her gaze out the windshield to see if something strange had caught his eye, but everything appeared the same. Looking back at him, she blinked as she found him staring at her, his mouth still open and his eyes pinned on her, his gaze roving over her face.

He jerked his attention back to the vehicle as he parked next to the house. "Uh... so, um... Ms. Watkins... um... let me help you in, and then I've got to... well... um..."

He threw open the driver's door and climbed down, and she watched as he walked around the front. She couldn't account for the change in his demeanor, but disappointment spread through her. He opened her door and assisted her, careful not to bump her cast. Once they reached the front porch, he waited until she unlocked the door and stepped inside. She turned to see if he would like to come in, but he'd jammed his hands into his front jeans pockets while looking down at his boots.

Having enough presence of mind to realize she still wore his coat, she slipped it from her shoulders and handed it to him. "I want to thank you, Andy, for… well, for many things. For coming today and offering to drive me home. For offering to bring my car back to me tomorrow. For the use of your coat. But most of all, for being the type of hero who would jump into the water to help a stranger."

During her speech, his head lifted, and he held her gaze as a slight tinge of blush hit his cheeks above his beard.

"Ivy, you don't have to thank me. It was an honor to be able to help. If anyone was a hero, it was you. That baby sure as hell needed one, and I suppose the man did too."

He stepped back from the doorway. "Take care of yourself. I'll get a coworker to accompany me tomorrow when I drop your car off."

"Oh, you'll need the key fob." She fumbled awkwardly as she reached into her purse but finally handed the fob to him. As their fingers touched, she felt a tingle. It was so light she almost wasn't sure it was real until she saw his eyes widen. Knowing he felt it, too, she curved her lips up into a smile.

"Goodbye, Ivy," he said, then turned and jogged back to his SUV.

She waved, unable to shake the finality of his goodbye as she closed the door and locked it behind her. Tired to her bones, she dropped her purse on the dining room table as she walked past the living room and into the kitchen. The pain medicine that had made her so loopy earlier was wearing off, but she didn't want to take anything stronger than ibuprofen. Finding some in her parents' kitchen cabinet, she popped several and filled a glass of water from the tap, drinking to wash the pills and quench her thirst. Figuring she should get something in her stomach, she fiddled with the twist tie on the bread and pulled out a slice with difficulty.

Not feeling up to battling the jar of peanut butter, she ate the bread plain and then headed upstairs. She walked through her bedroom and into the Jack and Jill bathroom shared with the other guest room. Now, under the bright lights, she looked at her reflection in the mirror.

She snorted, now understanding why Andy had not wanted to stick around. She was pale with dark circles under her eyes from exhaustion and smeared mascara, and her hair gave proof that she'd jumped into the Bay, and then it dried while she slept. At least the swelling on her face had gone down.

She brought up her discharge paperwork and read through it, not surprised to see she wasn't supposed to get her cast wet. *Well, this will be fun.*

Forgoing a shower, she decided a bath was just what she needed. Running the water, she stripped with difficulty, then stepped into the tub, sinking into the warm water and leaving her casted left arm resting over the side. After relaxing, she scrubbed off with only one hand, then used the handheld attachment to wet her hair. Again, she worked the shampoo through with one hand, then rinsed. It wasn't perfect, but she figured she'd soon become proficient.

Once she got out and dried off, she struggled into sweatpants, fuzzy socks, and a zip-up hoodie. She went downstairs to pile up in the living room, too tired to do anything else. Flipping through channels, she found nothing interesting to take her mind off the past day's events.

Was it only yesterday that I was on the bridge coming home? Only yesterday that I became involved in trying to save a baby and a man? Only yesterday that I fell off the bridge and into the water?

She shook her head, stunned when she thought of everything that had happened. Then Officer Andy filled her mind, and she sighed. *Was it only yesterday that he'd held my hand, making me feel that everything would be okay?*

She couldn't stem the disappointment at the thought of his quick dismissal. She should be grateful, and she was. *He helped me at a time when I needed it. And that's all.* When she finally succumbed to fatigue and fell asleep on the sofa wrapped in a soft blanket, she dreamed of a dark-haired man holding her, the scent of the sea and pine surrounding her.

A few hours later, waking from her nap, she remembered that he called her Ivy, and something in his voice sounded like regret.

7

Driving down the road, Andy was in shock as disbelief hit him in the gut, making it hard to breathe. Ivy Watkins. *What the fuck... Ivy Watkins?*

He hadn't recognized her, but then he hadn't expected to know the woman from the bridge. As soon as she'd pointed out the house that belonged to her parents, he was transported back in time. Back to the days of high school. He remembered parking outside when he'd been forced to pair with her for a project.

No, that's not true. I wasn't forced. He had been assigned to work with her, but it wasn't a hardship. She was smart, and being with her was the reason he got a high grade. But being at her house was a stark contrast to his own. Her mother baked cookies even after she'd spent the day teaching at the middle school. She also ensured they had the necessary resources, including their computer. *God knows, my mom couldn't be bothered to care for the basic needs of Aaron and me, much less stick around for anything else we might need as we grew up after she walked out.*

As an adult, he could easily admit the stupidness of his former attitude, but back then... *Poison Ivy.* It was an asshole nickname he'd used, and he grimaced again at the memory of what a prick he'd been that went way beyond just a bad attitude.

Scrubbing his hand over his face, he tried to shake the heavy mantle of the past. He'd planned on heading straight to the VMP station to make arrangements for her car, but it seemed his inner thoughts had a different destination. Before he knew where he was going, he turned into his dad's driveway. Parking, he didn't alight from his vehicle. Instead, he just sat and sighed as memories flooded back.

Adolescence had sucked. The best thing he had going for him was his size and looks. Being bigger, he didn't have to worry about being bullied, and he made damn sure his brother wasn't either. He was athletic and played sports when he could squeeze in the time between helping with Aaron and his dad. It was enough to keep him popular, and in high school, that was all that really mattered.

But when did I become such an asshole to her? He closed his eyes and sighed. He remembered having Mrs. Watkins as his eighth-grade English teacher in middle school. Her husband had been the principal at the elementary school, not that he'd spent any time in the principal's office. While he wasn't a stellar student, he'd stayed out of trouble. But that day, he was in Mrs.

Watkins's room after school while waiting on the bus. He was pissed, but it wasn't until Ivy skipped into her mom's classroom that his anger shot upward. Mrs. Watkins and Ivy shared a hug as she asked about Ivy's day. And even as a thirteen-year-old boy, he could see that she really gave a shit about everything that came out of Ivy's mouth. *Something I'd never had in my whole life from my mom.*

Ivy. For some reason known only to that jealous adolescent boy, she became the object of his surliness. Just enough to be a thorn in her side when he'd call her Poison Ivy.

A sharp pain struck his chest, and he wondered for a moment if he was having a heart attack. Rubbing over his sternum, he knew it was more like a bolt of conscience.

"You gonna sit out there all day?"

He jerked, then looked through the window at his dad standing on the front porch. Climbing down, he jogged over. "Pop, you should be inside where it's warm."

His dad lowered his brows. "Boy, I worked on fishing boats on the Bay during all kinds of weather. Think I can handle some chilly wind while on my porch."

Andy knew his dad was right, but since having been forced to settle into an administrative job with the fishing company after his arthritis kept him from being on the boats, Andy couldn't help but worry. They walked into the house, and after a few minutes of working side by side, they fixed large sandwiches packed with roast beef and cheese. Sitting down, they ate in companionable silence.

The back door opened, and Sally walked in. Her smile lit her face as her gaze landed on the two men. "Oh, Andy, I didn't realize you'd come for lunch. I'll just—"

"No, Ms. Sally," Andy hurried to say as both men stood from the table. "Please, join us. There's nothing we can't talk about with you here."

"Well, if you're sure." She sat down, placing the plate of brownies on the table.

After they'd finished the dessert, his dad pushed his plate away and leaned back in his chair. Pinning Andy with a brow-lifted stare, he said, "You gonna talk? Don't mind a visit on a day when we both have off work, but I got a feeling something was going on when you were sittin' in my driveway looking like a lost puppy."

Andy scrubbed his hand over his face and squeezed his eyes close for a few seconds. "I went to the hospital this morning to see the woman from the bridge."

His dad leaned back in his chair and settled his arms around his middle with his fingers clasped. He looked at Sally and said, "Andy was the one who dove in to get her."

Sally nodded, her attention riveted on Andy as his dad dipped his chin, indicating he was ready to listen.

"Outside the room, I overheard her tell the nurse she didn't have a way to get to her car, so I offered to drive when the nurse came out. The nurse checked and said that was fine, so I went back outside to get the SUV.

When the aide wheeled her out, I could tell she was surprised but seemed glad to see me."

At his dad's lifted brows, he explained, "She remembered me from the day before. As soon as we started down the road, I realized that taking her to her car didn't make any sense because she was on pain medication and couldn't drive. So I offered to take her home and get her car to her tomorrow."

"Okay," his dad said, nodding. "So far, sounds like a nice story. But from the hound-dog look on your face, it all goes to hell. What happened?"

Sally leaned forward, her forearms resting on the table as she offered him an encouraging smile.

"When she gave directions and pointed out where she was staying, she mentioned it was her parents' house. She grew up here, left the area, and has come back. Since her parents are out of town, she's staying at their place until she gets a place of her own. It just so happens that I recognized the house. And then I recognized her."

His dad's eyes widened. "Hell, Son, I know you weren't a choir boy in high school, but I also know you weren't a big player. But please tell me she wasn't just somebody you had fun with under the bleachers!"

"Arthur!" Sally admonished.

Andy barked out a laugh, recognizing his dad's attempt to lessen the tension. "No, she wasn't. She was a nice girl. Pretty. Sweet. Came from a good family. Her dad was the elementary school principal, and her mom was my English teacher in middle school. And I wasn't very nice to her."

Sally huffed and shook her head as though she couldn't believe his words. His dad's chin jerked back when he couldn't hide his surprise. "What the hell are you talking about? I know you were angry, Son, and walked around with a chip on your shoulder, but I never knew you to be cruel."

"Most of the time, I wasn't. I did a good job of being surly, and only as an adult did I realize that a lot of my attitude came out toward some of the female teachers. But it was Ivy who I teased. I was sitting in your driveway thinking about the first time I noticed her and her mom one day after school. They were happy, and her mom was so totally into her."

"And you were envious," Sally said softly.

He nodded at the statement. "Yep. And like a stupid teenager, I gave her the nickname Poison Ivy. She hated it but either ignored me or gave attitude right back. I think that just made me angrier. In high school, it didn't help that she was super smart. Somehow, I projected that her life was perfect and mine was shit."

He didn't miss the wince that crossed his father's face. And he rushed to amend, "Pop, my life wasn't shit. My life with you and Aaron was good. But as a fuckin' teenager, Jesus Christ, I had attitude."

Sally pinched her lips. "You're being too hard on yourself, Andy."

Chuckling, his dad nodded. "I think the definition of a teenager is the attitude."

"Yeah, you're probably right." He sighed, his chest deflating. "I recognized her house because she and I got assigned to work on a couple of projects together in high school. I got another front-row view of her mom as she helped us out. I gotta admit, though, Ivy stood strong. She gave back as good as she got. Anyway, after high school, she went off to college, and I joined the military. To be honest, I never thought about her again. Hell, I tried not to think about high school at all after I left."

Sally leaned back in her chair but glanced at his dad. Pop was quiet... so much so that Andy began to wonder what was going through his mind. But that was his dad's way... carefully considering what he would say. Andy eventually picked up that trait from his dad as an adult, and now, he really wished he'd had that discipline when he was younger. If so, he wouldn't have given a stupid name to a girl who didn't deserve it just because he was pissed at his own mom. And, if so, he'd be at Ivy's house right now, making sure she was okay instead of sitting at his dad's house like a wimp, spilling his guts.

"What are you going to do?"

Leave it to his dad to cut through the crap and get to the crux of the situation. "Well, I promised to get her car to her. I can leave it and hope she doesn't recognize me."

His dad barked out a laugh. "Yeah, you could. But...?"

"But I'm not a teenager anymore, so hiding behind anger or embarrassment isn't really an option."

"I think you owe forgiveness to yourself," Sally said. "And you owe it to her to be able to give her forgiveness, too. I also think you owe it to yourself to realize what a good man you are regardless of the teenager you were."

He thought about seeing Ivy standing on the bridge, doing everything possible to save a child and a man she didn't even know. And he thought about how she hadn't left his mind since that moment. He'd wondered if his mom had left him with a legacy of never being good enough for her... or any woman. But now... Christ, all he wanted was a chance to be with someone who gave everything of themselves.

"Son, I told you that you had to learn to let go. Sally and Toby used to tell me that I had to forgive myself every time something happened. I always wondered if I'd only done more, your mom might've stayed." Pop reached over and placed his hand over Sally's. "I also had to learn that I deserved good things, too. I've got my boys. I had good friends. And when Toby died, and we learned to deal with our sorrow, I had the opportunity to have a new chance at love beyond friendship. I want that for you, too."

As he held his dad's gaze, his resolve slid into place like the final piece of a puzzle. "First of all, I will get her car to her. Then I'm going to tell her who I am. I'm going to apologize and hope like fuck she forgives the teenage asshole that I was. I hope she'll give me a chance to show her who I am now."

Sally giggled softly, and his dad's lips quirked upward but didn't stop until a wide smile crossed his face. "Well, all right, Son. Sounds like this woman means something to you besides just a high school memory that you'd rather forget."

Nodding, he stood and walked to the door. With a kiss on Sally's cheek and a hearty, back-slapping hug from his dad, he waved goodbye and walked briskly through the cold to his SUV. Nerves speared through him, but there was no way he would back out now.

"Heading to Youngers Creek."

Andy jolted at Joseph's callout. They were out on the water, but his mind was on the woman he planned to see after work.

Joseph slowed the vessel as they approached several fishing boats, and Andy moved to the side, calling out, "Harry! How's it going?"

"Not bad. Got a good load. Better than last month so far. I'll take what the good Lord gives. How's your dad?"

"He's good," Andy replied. "He'll be glad for warmer weather, though. The arthritis is worse when it's cold."

"Yeah, my grandpa had the same problem. You tell him I expect to see him at the pub sometime."

With a chin lift, he signaled Joseph to move on to the next boat. Callan called out to check the licenses and registrations since they didn't recognize the fishermen. They'd spent the entire morning the same way—a bit boring, but that was what Andy liked about patrols. He got out on the water, and no two days were the same. Considering some days were hectic as hell, the easy ones just gave him time to get to know the men and women who made their living on the Bay.

"Ready to head back for lunch?" Joseph asked.

He and Callan nodded, both moving into the wheelhouse. He looked at Callan. "How's the baby?"

Callan's smile widened. "Phillip's great. Finally sleeping through the night, so Sophie is getting more rest."

Callan and Sophie grew up in Baytown as neighbors, dated in high school, and then went their separate ways when Callan joined the Coast Guard. Reunited years later when he'd been assigned the Baytown Coast Guard station, they were now married with a little boy.

Andy couldn't deny that his friend was truly happy. Turning to look over his shoulder at Joseph, he said, "And you? Are you living the dream?"

"Hell, yeah. Shiloh said yes, and we're getting married in a few months."

Andy would be jealous if he wasn't so happy for his friends. They were good men who deserved and found good women.

He had a history with both Callan and Joseph before they started working with the VMP. Callan had been part of the Baytown Boys, so while he was several years ahead, Andy remembered him. And once he'd gotten out of the Navy, Andy worked with Joseph's brother, Wyatt, as a police officer for a small town north of Baytown.

After they docked, they headed to the Seafood Shack with Jose, Jared, Bryce, and Ryan. Once they'd ordered, he turned to the others and asked, "Any chance I can get two of you to help me get the car to the woman from the bridge? I told her that I'd get it to her today."

"Sure," Jose agreed readily. "But why do you need two of us?"

The conversation around them halted as all the

attention from those at their table came to rest on him. He reached behind him and squeezed the back of his neck. "I need someone to drive my car while I drive hers and then someone to drive to take the other back." Realizing that statement was more convoluted than he'd intended, he started over. "I want to stay and talk to her, so not only am I dropping off her car, but I'll need mine there too."

"No problem. I can go, too," Jared said. "Billie is off today, so I don't have to get home to let the dog out." Jared and his girlfriend, Billie, had a rocky start but now lived together. Andy anticipated more engagement announcements soon.

"Thanks." He nodded toward them. "Appreciate it." Taking a sip of the water that had been delivered, the silence at the table had him looking around, seeing the gazes still pinned on him. Sighing, he knew they were curious. "Look, I went by to see her yesterday at the hospital to check on her. And since she didn't have anyone else to help, I gave her a lift home. Once there, I realized I knew her."

"Knew her?" Jose asked, his brows raised.

"You didn't realize it when you first saw her?" Callan asked.

Bryce's chin jerked inward. "How'd you know her?"

"Whoa," he called out with his hands raised in front of him. "Not so fast." The server arrived with their food, and he was grateful for the interruption. But when she left, it seemed his friends' attention was still on him. "Look, I realized I knew her from high school."

"I thought someone said she was just passing through," Joseph said, digging into his burger.

"She was born and raised out here. I knew her when we were in school together. Then she went to college, and I guess she's been working elsewhere. She's just come back into the area, and her parents are visiting a relative, she said. Unfortunately, she had no one else to call on to take her home from the hospital. I happened to be at the right place at the right time."

"She must've been surprised to see you, too," Callan said, passing the ketchup around.

Snorting, he shook his head. "It's hardly a story like you and Sophie's. We didn't date in high school. In fact, we weren't even friends."

"Well, it looks like you've got a second chance, anyway, if you're interested. And if you visited her at the hospital and told her you'd get her car to her, it sounds like you're interested," Jared added.

"I don't know about a second chance. Not only were we not friends but, well, the truth is, I was a real asshole in high school. For reasons I won't even begin to explain, it seems like I was mostly an asshole to her."

Joseph scoffed. "Teenagers can be assholes." Joseph had a teenage stepdaughter, and while she was well-behaved, Andy knew she'd had trouble with other bully teenagers several months ago.

"The least I can do is apologize for my behavior," Andy admitted.

"Adolescent angst is real," Ryan said, shaking his head. "Not saying it's worse for girls than guys, but my Cindy feels things real deep. Trevor is much more likely to let things roll off his back." Ryan had two teenage children, so Andy figured his boss knew what he was talking about.

"Yeah, but it's been years," Bryce argued. "Surely she won't hold a grudge this long."

As they ate, the conversation flowed all around, but Andy's mind was still firmly on his visit to Ivy. And the sick feeling in his gut that she'd slam the door in his face as soon as she found out who he was.

8

Ivy had had a miserable day. Between the constant ache in her wrist and the stabbing pain she'd felt every time she'd rolled over in bed, she'd slept poorly.

It was hard to dress with one hand. She'd struggled to make a sandwich for lunch with one hand. She'd even peed on herself when she couldn't get her stretchy sweatpants down quickly enough.

And that didn't even take into account that she could not seem to get the events from the bridge out of her mind. She'd been so groggy in the hospital and then just concerned with getting home, it had been easier to push it away. But now, with the silence of her parents' house, she lived inside her head. And currently, that wasn't a very friendly place to exist.

The events played on a continuous loop that she couldn't seem to break. The sight of the man pacing with the baby dangling in his arms perilously close to the bridge's railing. The desperate 911 call she made. Racing toward him with no plan other than to get to the child. She couldn't have imagined that thirty minutes later, she would still be standing close to him with the police kept at a distance while she begged him to give the baby to her.

And as though it was happening at the moment, she could feel the chill as it settled in her body without her coat, making her even more scared for the child who wasn't sufficiently bundled, either.

She remembered looking at the water beyond the bridge's railing, thinking how beautiful it was. She also remembered being so preoccupied with what was happening directly in front of her that she hadn't realized police vessels were nearby.

And as she turned the events over in her mind, she continually questioned if she'd said or done the right things. And when he gently laid the baby down, and she finally thought the nightmare was over, she remembered feeling as though she could breathe again.

At least until she looked into his eyes and saw that his manic desperation had given way to a stalwart decision. At the memory of him lurching toward the railing, watching his body vault into the air, she gave no thought to what she was doing other than to try to stop him.

There was something strange about falling. It was so quick that she barely knew what was happening, yet she could remember her body lifting into the air, the feel of the railing at her hip, and then the weightless feeling of nothing between her and the depths below other than air. But the acute fear and the instinct to save herself filled her consciousness just before she hit the water.

She remembered the pain exploding, and the instant she wondered if she would die. She should be grateful she was not injured more severely, but the replay of fear kept gratitude at a distance right now. But then, if they'd been farther along on the bridge at a higher point above the water, she could have been killed.

Stop it! She tried to force a break in the brain loop, thinking of anything she could besides the events on the bridge, but Kelly's words came back to her about trauma. While everything had turned out okay with the baby and the young man not dying, she wasn't sure how long it would take before she could sleep.

Blowing out a breath, she looked out into the driveway, hating she didn't have her car, even if she had nowhere to drive. *The officer... Andy said he would bring it to me today.* She glanced at the clock on the television and knew it was almost time for the sun to set, and soon it would be dark. *I guess he's not bringing it after all.* She had to admit that the idea of not seeing him stung as much as not having her vehicle.

When he'd called her Ivy the day before, she assumed her name was on whatever report they'd had to file. Yet his tone was something far away and almost sad.

The sound of more than one vehicle approaching caught her attention, and she twisted to look out the living room window. Seeing her car being driven in the front, she let out a sigh of relief. Then seeing two other vehicles follow closely, she wondered who else was coming.

Andy climbed from her vehicle and turned to the

other two. Another officer in uniform got out of the second vehicle and tossed a set of keys to Andy while calling out, "Good luck," before walking to the third vehicle. Andy waved as they pulled away. Realizing that he wasn't just dropping off her vehicle, but it seemed as though he might stay, she wished she'd attempted a better job at brushing her hair.

Hurrying to the front door, she opened it as he approached. "Thank you for bringing my car back!" she gushed, her gaze drinking him in. Seeing him in his uniform reminded her of when he'd leaned over her and held her hand after pulling her from the water. Only then, his hair had been wet, and she'd been fascinated watching a few drops roll down the side of his face. Now she longed to reach up and run her fingers through his dark hair.

He handed her the keys but didn't attempt to come in. She wasn't sure he wanted to but wasn't about to squander a chance to talk to him more. "Can you come in? I can't promise you a great meal, but there's beer in the refrigerator."

He chuckled, the sound coming from deep in his chest before it wrapped around her. "I'd love to. I brought you some dinner, but I left it out there in case you were sleeping or not hungry."

"I'm definitely hungry," she replied, her mouth already watering for whatever he would bring that she didn't have to fix.

"Great. Close the door so you stay warm, and I'll be right back." He turned and jogged back to her car, and she watched in curiosity, ignoring his order to stay warm. He leaned into the passenger side and grabbed two plastic bags, then jogged back onto the porch and through the front door she held open for him.

Immediately, she was hit with a delightful scent of Mexican spices. "Oh my God, that smells divine! Did you bring Mexican, or am I dreaming?"

"You're not dreaming." He laughed. "Mama June makes the best Mexican takeout around here, so when you eat it, you'll think you're in heaven."

Laughing, she let him into the kitchen. "Good answer!"

She lifted her right hand to get plates, but he stopped her. "Let me." He reached up and grabbed two.

His height easily reached over her, and she tried not to sniff him in a way that he'd notice. Sea air and pine. It had become her favorite scent.

He nudged her. "You sit down and rest."

"I feel like all I've done today is rest. Well, rest and think and remember."

He jerked slightly as he set the plates on the table. His gaze shot to her. "Remember?"

Nodding, she pulled out the plastic forks from the bag. "Yes. I keep replaying the bridge scene in my mind."

He let out a deep breath that almost sounded like relief. She looked at him, but his head was down as he pulled out the food containers. Giving her head a little shake, she continued, "I find myself wondering if I said the right things, or did the right things, or made things worse, or could have—"

"Hey." He interrupted, placing his hand on her arm

and giving a little squeeze. "Stop torturing yourself. You saved that baby's life. And probably his, as well."

She looked into his deep brown eyes and stared. His hand on her arm was warm and comforting. He was so handsome it was almost hard to hold the stare, but she didn't want to look away. His eyes held warmth and understanding. And strangely, she felt as though they held…

"You ready to eat?"

His words snapped her out of her staring stupor. Blushing, she rushed, "Yes. Sure. I'll get a beer—"

"Nope. You sit. I'll get us something to drink."

His hand left her arm as he walked to the refrigerator, and she immediately felt the loss of his touch. She looked down, wondering if there would be a branding print of his fingers. Giving her head a little shake, she decided she needed to back away from the pain medicine if hallucinations were one of the side effects.

He walked back to the table with two water bottles in his hands. Grinning, he said, "I know you can't drink with the meds you've been on, and I don't need to either."

Soon, the only sounds heard were the occasional groans from her as she devoured the delicious food. Finally, coming up for air, she wiped her mouth and smiled. "That was amazing. Where did you say it came from?"

"Mama June. It's a food truck not too far from here. The food is delicious and authentic. She can make it as spicy as you want, but I asked her to go mild."

"You made the right assumption." She smiled. "Most people seem to like hot food, but I'm boring."

"I'd hardly call you boring," he protested forcefully.

She wondered if she'd said something wrong. Tilting her head to the side, she asked, "Is everything okay?" She waited for the hasty confirmation, but it didn't come. Instead, he swallowed deeply, his gaze focusing on his hands resting on the table. *Oh shit. I've totally read this wrong.* It hadn't been hard to think that maybe he was interested since he'd come to visit and taken her home, then brought her car and food. But something clearly had him uncomfortable, and since she hadn't said anything out of the ordinary, it must be her.

"Why did you do it?" he asked softly, staring down at his empty plate.

Chewing on the corner of her bottom lip, she shook her head. "Do what?"

His head lifted, and she was captured by his gaze.

"Stop on the bridge. Stay. Keep talking to Larry when you were cold and afraid. Why did you try to grab him once the baby was safe?"

Not expecting those questions, she opened her mouth to offer a pat response, but the intensity of his gaze shut down her superfluous reply, and she snapped her lips together. The memory of the cold water and becoming disoriented as she tried to claw her way to the surface hit her.

Slowly, she shook her head. "I don't know."

It was obvious her reply surprised him when his chin jerked back.

"I mean... I stopped because I've been across the

bridge-tunnel a million times but had never seen anyone pulled to the side. And when I saw him near the edge holding a baby, I just... I knew something was wrong. I thought maybe his baby was choking. Or had pooped, and he didn't know how to change the diaper. Or... I don't know. But I needed to find out."

"But you called 911."

She nodded. "By the time I stopped, he was holding the baby too close to the edge. Something was wrong. Horribly wrong. I called 911 because I was scared for them."

"And you ran over to them."

"The police would take a while to get there. Even the CBBT police would take a few minutes. I couldn't take a chance. I just wanted to help. I had to help."

He remained quiet, his gaze still holding hers. She cocked her head to the side. "Why are you asking?"

"Just trying to figure you out, that's all."

Wanting to squirm under the scrutiny of his stare, she stood quickly and grabbed the plates. "I'll stick these in the dishwasher and pack the leftovers for you." Turning before he could stop her, she tried to carry both, but a sharp pain in her left wrist caused one plate to clatter onto the floor, breaking into several pieces. "Oh damn!" She battled tears, both at the pain and because she felt a strange discomfort from him.

"Ivy, no, let me," he said, hustling to the pantry to grab the broom and dustpan. Bending, he swept the pieces up and efficiently deposited them into the garbage under the sink.

Ivy watched as he moved about the kitchen as

though he'd been there before. There had been no hesitation as he gathered the items he needed. No looking around or asking. He'd moved with swift surety.

He turned, and when he looked at her, his eyes widened slightly before an uncomfortable specter moved through them. "Ivy…"

"Do you know my parents? Have you been here before?"

Their gazes held for what was only a few seconds yet felt like an eternity. The admission that he'd met her parents and had been in the house before should be easy. But the tightness of his body and the clenching of his jaw showed that nothing he felt was easy.

"Yes." He sighed heavily. "Yes, I've met your parents. And yes, I've been in this house before. But it was many years ago. And it was with you."

Her body jerked in a physical startle as her gaze roved over his face. Dark eyes that could pin her with a stare. His jaw had a thick, neatly trimmed beard. Dark, thick hair cut short on the sides would have waved if it were longer. *Andy. Andy.* Then like a slap in the face or a nasty nickname called out, she jerked again. "Andy? Bergstrom?"

He nodded slowly as she stood in silent shock, trying to reconcile the angry teenager that hurled insults her way with the caring policeman who'd saved her life standing in front of her. She opened her mouth to speak, but no words came forth. She was blank—completely, totally, one-hundred-percent blank.

Memories rushed forward, most having been locked away in the mental box labeled hurtful-adolescent, not-worth-worrying-about, and things-to-forget. But the box lid sprung open, and only two words spilled forth in a barely breathed whisper as she stared at the man standing in her kitchen while seeing the boy with the smirk in the same place. "Poison Ivy."

9

Tenth Grade - Baytown High School

Ivy pressed her face against the school bus window, smiling as they passed black tail gulls flying next to the bridge. She recognized a V of black pelicans gliding over the water and peregrine falcons sitting regally on the light posts above. The surface of the Bay was calm, and the sun was shining. Even though the boys in the back of the bus were noisy, she sat near the front to hear her history teacher as he lectured. The field trip to the Virginia Marine Museum in Virginia Beach had been exciting, but she loved the trip back to the Eastern Shore.

"The Chesapeake Bay Bridge Tunnel is one of fourteen bridge-tunnel systems in the world," Mr. Thomson said, standing at the front of the bus full of teenagers. "Before the 1950s, travelers crossing the Bay had to travel by ferry. This ferry system grew from the original boats that the original settlers in the 1600s used. In the

1960s, the building of this modern wonder began. Who can tell me how long the CBBT is?"

Ivy's hand shot up, her smile widening as Mr. Thomson dipped his chin in acknowledgment. "Seventeen and a half miles long, with two tunnels that go almost one hundred feet under the water for the large ships to travel over."

"Excellent! That's exactly right—"

"Hey, Poison Ivy! Got any other stupid facts stored in that big brain of yours?"

Her smile dropped as her lips pressed together tightly. Turning, she glared at the boys in the back. "I'd rather have a big brain than a tiny one like yours," she retorted.

"Nothing *tiny* back here, *little* girl!"

"Boys!" Mr. Thomson warned, and the noise settled down.

She whirled around to face the front again, her face hot with embarrassment and anger. Tears prickled as they gathered, and she blinked furiously to keep them from falling.

"Don't pay any attention to them," Sybil said, rubbing Ivy's arm. "They're just stupid boys and are jealous because you're so smart!"

She nodded, both grateful for Sybil's support and even more glad she was sitting near the front so the stupid comments and laughter from the back were less likely to reach her. A late bloomer, she was only five feet two inches and barely weighed over a hundred pounds. In fact, she'd never really paid attention until last summer when a group met at the Baytown beach. For the first time, it was glaringly apparent with the girls in their bikinis, whose adolescent bodies had matured faster than hers. *Almost everyone!*

Crossing her arms over her chest, she felt anger slam into her again at the memory of a few of the boys' demeaning comments thrown her way. "Jerks," she mumbled, turning her face toward the window again, not wanting them to ruin her trip.

She loved traveling over the Chesapeake Bay Bridge Tunnel. When she was with her parents, her father would point out the different bird species, and her mother would comment on the many ships that passed into the Bay. Naval ships, pleasure boats, cruise ships, fishing vessels, and massive cargo ships filled with containers going to or coming from Norfolk and Baltimore floated over the vehicles that crossed underneath in the tunnels. She and her parents made a game of trying to guess what the ships were carrying and where they had traveled from.

The quest for knowledge came naturally with her parents in education. Her dad was the principal at the Baytown Elementary School, and her mom was a middle school English teacher. "There are no useless facts," her father always said before he'd spout something interesting.

With her forehead resting against the cool glass window, her lips curved slightly as she spied a cargo ship, containers stacked with precision. *How do they keep from tumbling into the ocean when waves come? What countries has that ship been to? What port will it dock to unload? Where do the workers on board sleep?*

Raucous laughter came from the back of the bus again, and she battled to tamp down her irritation. Refusing to look over her shoulder, she already knew the ringleader. A boy in her class had taken it upon himself to be the biggest jerk of all.

"Have you decided what to do for your science report?" Sybil asked, then laughed. "I don't even know why I ask. You've probably had it figured out since last year."

Ivy nodded, her shoulders relaxing. A giggle escaped because it was true. She'd had everything planned out since they were told there would be a science report at the beginning of the year. When she'd told her parents, they'd loved her idea—a study of the materials used for CBBT tunnel building. Leaning back in the uncomfortable school bus seat, she relaxed. Chorus and running cross-country were great for the camaraderie with others, but working on a science project alone gave her the freedom to follow her quest for knowledge her own way. *This is going to be so much fun!*

"I hate him!" Ivy cried, plopping down at the kitchen table. She slung her backpack to the floor, and it landed with a crash against the table leg. Her auburn hair had escaped her ponytail, and as she huffed, tendrils floated away from her face.

Her mother had just gotten home from work and was fixing both of them a snack. Looking over her shoulder, concern in her eyes, she asked, "What's going on?"

"Mrs. Blackstone, my science teacher, has paired us up to work on our reports. We couldn't even pick our partners! In fact, it seems like she picked the smartest kids in the class to work with the—"

"Careful, sweetie." Her mother lifted her brow, and Ivy sighed.

Huffing, she continued, "I wasn't going to say the dumbest, Mom." With both parents in education, she knew that all students had potential and some learned faster in certain subjects than others. "I was going to say they paired us up with the *less motivated*."

Her mother nodded approvingly. "I can see why she did that. It gives students who might not have thought of particular subjects a chance to work on things that perhaps they wouldn't have been exposed to."

"Yes, but I got stuck with the biggest jerk in the class. He said my idea was dumb."

"Well, maybe he thinks it's dumb because it's something he hasn't learned yet."

"He's in most of my classes, and I hate that he's going to share my project, as well! He calls me Poison Ivy because he thinks it's funny. And he laughs at me because I'm short and smart. He said my big brain kept the rest of me from growing."

Her mom walked over with her plate of brownies and set them on the table, along with a glass of milk. Sliding into a seat, she sat across from Ivy and held her gaze.

"Ivy, you're a beautiful fifteen-year-old."

"Maybe," she pouted. "But I want to look like a beautiful eighteen-year-old!"

Her mother laughed. "Oh, well, I'm afraid only time and patience will take care of that. But you normally have such confidence, honey."

She took a bite of brownie, the chocolate gooeyness melting in her mouth, and moaned. Her mom's brownies could almost make all the ills of the world fall away... almost. Chewing, she swallowed and then sipped her milk. Finally nodding, she confessed, "Being a fifteen-year-old is hard."

"You're right about that, sweetheart."

Finishing her snack, she wiped her mouth on a napkin. "Well, I don't care what he says. I'm sticking to my report, and if he wants to do something else, he can. Although I know he won't. I overheard him tell one of the other boys that he got stuck with the smartest girl and would let me do all the work, and he'd get a good grade." She snorted. "I ought to give him the worst parts of the research to do."

Her mom smiled gently and reached across the table to squeeze her hand. "You know you won't."

"Yeah, because I'm a pushover, you mean," Ivy grumbled.

"No, because you're much too nice." With that, her mom stood and returned to the kitchen to fix dinner.

As Ivy pondered her fate, she frowned. Made fun of for being smart and short... and stuck with a jerk for a partner. *Life sucks.*

Eleventh Grade - Baytown High School

Standing at her locker, Ivy smiled at the boy next to her. Now a junior, she and the president of the debate club had been flirting for a while, and he'd hinted that he'd like to ask her out. They shared a few classes, but with his locker beside hers, it was easy to see him often during the day.

She smoothed her hand over her dark auburn hair, having brushed it to a gleam before coming to school. Her modest, pale-mauve shirt draped over her late-blooming figure that had finally matured, but she couldn't quite get used to showing too much skin. Still, she could see his appreciative glance as his gaze swept down her. *Come on... ask me out!*

"Ivy, I was wondering if you'd like to... well, maybe if you're not busy... we could—"

"Hey, Bobby. I see your locker is next to Poison Ivy's. You'd better watch out. Touching her will make your balls itch!"

Ivy battled a grimace, refusing to listen to the taunts coming from the same jerks she'd dealt with for the past years. Keeping her gaze focused on the cute boy in front of her, her heart nosedived as Bobby's eyes turned from her, a blush filling his face. "Just ignore them, Bobby. I always do—"

"Sorry, Ivy, I've got to get to class. I'll talk to you later."

Her breath caught in her throat as she watched him scurry past the group of boys standing on the other side of the hall.

Lifting her chin, she held her head high as she sailed

past them, trying to disregard their laughter. Ignoring them had become second nature to her, but it didn't seem to matter. They had been paired together for their project last year, and her parents had welcomed him into their home as they worked together. Or rather, she worked, and he just copied what she was doing. She'd wondered if he would be nicer to her, but that had been a foolish notion.

The bell rang, and everyone scattered to get to class. Stopping, she looked over her shoulder and saw him standing by himself. He leaned against the wall as though he had all the time in the world.

"Better luck next time, Poison Ivy," he said. "Maybe one day you'll find a date who won't run away."

Suddenly, seeing red, she stomped over and tilted her head back to meet his glare with one of her own. "Andy Bergstrom, you're disgusting, you know that?" With her teeth clenched tightly, she shoved him as hard as she could and gasped when he toppled to the side, bumping into a stack of boxes and knocking them over. Horrified that she'd placed her hands on someone else in anger, her face crumpled as tears pricked the backs of her eyes.

"What's going on out here?"

Her heart skipped a beat at the sound of their science teacher's strident voice. Eyes wide, she gasped, turning toward the stern face staring at Andy. "I'm sorry—"

"I just fell," Andy said quickly.

Her gaze snapped to him, and her brows lowered in confusion.

"Well, pick those boxes up and get to class," the teacher ordered, then walked into her classroom.

Still staring at him, Ivy opened her mouth to apologize again, but he cut her off. "Don't get any ideas. I didn't rat you out because I don't want the hassle. Got it?"

Lifting her chin, she hissed, "Got it! Loud and clear!"

Just then, the teacher popped her head out of her classroom and looked at them again. "You know, your science teacher told me last year that she paired you two up for the project. She said it was an excellent presentation. I won't mess with a good team, so you two will be assigned the junior science project this year in my class. Don't disappoint me." With that, she turned and disappeared back into her classroom.

Ivy's eyes widened as she looked up at Andy, seeing a smirk on his face. He leaned closer and whispered, "Looks like I get another good grade this year."

"You're... you're... impossible!" Turning, she rushed down the hall to lunch. Finding Sybil in the cafeteria, they joined their friends, and she regaled them with her tales of woe.

"Maybe this is like a movie... you know where the mean guy falls for the sweet girl," Jane said, her nose scrunched.

"God forbid." Ivy shuddered at the idea of how many girls he'd been with under the Baytown High School stadium bleachers.

Sybil shook her head. "You know, he's kind of right about Bobby, though. You deserve a guy who won't run off at the first sign of trouble."

Barking out a snort, she said, "Even if the trouble is just a jerk?"

"Well, yeah," Sybil said. "After all, Andy showed you what kind of guy Bobby is. I don't care if he's the debate team and math league president. If Bobby doesn't stick up for you, then screw him! Just keep waiting until the right one comes along."

The girls continued their lunch, but Ivy tuned out the small talk, suddenly tired of high school and ready for adulthood.

When the school day had ended, she walked toward her small used car in the student parking lot. Hearing an angry voice, she turned to see her devout critic with his back to her, talking on his phone.

"Pop, I'll pick him up after practice. Yeah, I'll get him, take him home, and make sure he eats. No... no! I told you that I don't care if Mom wants to see us. She can deal with the fact I don't want to see her. It's okay, Pop. I'll get him. You've got to work. I'll make sure he's okay. Yeah, bye, Pop. See you tonight."

Ivy slowed her steps, uncomfortable at overhearing someone's private conversation. Uncertain if she could make it to her car without being seen, her hopes were dashed when he turned around.

Immediately, he jerked slightly, narrowed his eyes, and then sneered. "Damn, Poison Ivy. You gotta be everywhere?"

"Just going to my car," she muttered, rolling her eyes as she passed him.

"Well, you can forget anything you heard. None of your business, anyway."

Whirling around, she speared him with a glare. "I assure you that nothing you had to say was of any interest to me at all!" Leaning closer, she added, "And you'll be happy to know that I've already talked to Mrs. Greenway, the senior science teacher, and asked her not to pair us together for our senior project next year. Two years of working together is quite enough for both of us. You can earn your passing grade the hard way... on your own!"

She could've sworn something flashed through his eyes, but as another smirk filled his face, she knew she'd only imagined it.

"Fine by me. At least next year, I won't get stuck with the brain of the class trying to outdo everyone else with those dumbass project ideas."

She rolled her eyes. "Brain? Is that the best you can do?"

He stepped closer and looked down at her, a sneer on his face. "Yeah... all brain and no body."

Blinking at the insult, she slung her purse around as rage rose inside, causing it to slam against his chest. He grunted in surprise, and she forced her lips into a tight line when all she wanted to do was scream. His hand lifted to rub his sternum, and guilt speared through her. Again. She'd never resorted to violence, and having given in to the urge twice in one day now made her feel worse. "I'm sorry," she grumbled, her shoulders slumping even though he deserved what she had to dish out.

His eyes widened slightly at her apology, then his expression morphed into indifference. "You couldn't hurt me on your best day."

Sucking a deep breath through her nose, she turned and stomped to her car. Settling into the driver seat, she slammed the door, stunned that she'd lost control… again. *He's the only person who makes me want to scream.* After starting the car, she pulled out of the lot, unable to keep her gaze from looking in the rearview mirror to see him staring after her. And for some reason, her righteous indignation sat like a stone in her gut.

Twelfth Grade - Baytown High School

Ivy stared out over the crowd in the football stadium filled with fellow high school seniors and family members, smiling from the podium at the crowd. As valedictorian, she had the honor to turn the tassels of the graduates after they accepted their diplomas from the principal. She'd already given her speech, and now, as the other seniors crossed the stage, she relaxed and laughed with them as her hand reached up to flip the tassel from one side of their caps to the other.

Some she'd known since kindergarten. There were friends, athletes, cheerleaders, and club members. Some had joined every activity, and others had watched from the sides. And then her gaze landed on the one who'd frustrated her at each turn.

"Congratulations," she murmured as she turned his tassel.

"Gee, thanks, Poison Ivy." He smirked, walking past her and down the steps.

Rolling her eyes, she smiled at the next student until the whole class had received their diplomas.

Moving through the crowd as she looked for her family, she caught sight of him at the edge of the gathering, standing with a lone man and a younger boy. Suddenly, she recalled the conversation she'd overheard about his mother, and a sense of sadness moved through her.

But her attention was quickly diverted once she'd found her family and was surrounded by her parents, grandparents, an aunt and uncle, and two cousins who'd made the trip to see her graduate. Grinning, she fell into their embraces, preening for the camera. Finally, she was ready to leave Baytown, high school, and adolescence.

10

Present Day

Fuck. Andy stared as Ivy's gaze sharpened on him, and realization dawned on her face. And then she whispered the words that he'd once said with the intent to irritate but now hated. He hated the words. He hated the way the light dimmed in her eyes. And he hated that lashing out at her hadn't made him feel any better back in high school, and he sure as hell regretted it now.

Lifting his hands, palms up, he sighed heavily. "Ivy, I'm so sorry."

Her chest deflated, a scoff leaving her lips. Her brow lowered as she glanced back to the leftovers on the counter. She huffed and shook her head. "So... all this... was just... a joke? A chance to get one over on little ole me?" She lifted her gaze, showing a spark of fire in her eyes. "Thank you for bringing my car and for dinner. Pardon me for not offering dessert." She turned and walked toward the front door.

He followed, then hesitated, not wanting to leave. He

was desperate for a chance to explain. "Please, Ivy, let me apologize."

His gaze followed every movement she made, and he caught the slight hesitation in her step. She stopped at the front door but turned before reaching for the handle. Grabbing every opportunity, he rushed, "I was going to tell you tonight. After we ate. After I had a chance to make sure you were okay. After—"

"After I became indebted to you for the rescue, your generous offer to bring my car to me, and the added bonus of dinner? Then you'd laugh and reveal who you were? Well, the joke's on me, isn't it?"

"No!" How could she think that? But then the answer was standing right in front of him. "Jesus, Ivy, that was a long time ago. A lifetime ago. The man I am now isn't the teenager you knew. And I'm here to fully admit I was an asshole. And I'm more sorry than you'll ever know."

She stood ramrod straight. Her hands reached toward each other as though to clasp fingers, then winced at the movement. Her right hand shifted to hold the cast on her left wrist instead.

The dark shadows underneath her eyes stood out in stark relief to her pale skin. The specter of pain in her eyes hit him squarely in the chest. He wanted nothing more than to talk. To explain. To purge the teenage memories that plagued him and, from all appearances, plagued her too. He wanted to plead for forgiveness and ask for a chance to let her discover who he was as an adult.

But seeing her shoulders sag and her back loose

some of its stiffness as though the effort to remain standing was taking all her energy, he sucked in a deep breath and let it out slowly as resignation filled him. Now was not the time. And that gutted him.

He started toward the door, bringing him closer to her. She stiffened again as he stopped directly in front of her. Reaching out, he placed his hand over hers, his thumb gently rubbing over the fingers holding her cast. "You need to rest, Ivy. As much as I want to talk to you and tell you again how sorry I am, I know you need your rest."

She lifted her chin and held his gaze, numerous emotions swimming in the depths of her eyes. She was so petite, his chin touched his chest to keep his eyes on her. He leaned forward slowly, giving her every opportunity to tell him to stop or to step back. She remained ramrod stiff, but when she didn't back away, he placed a chaste kiss on her cool cheek, straightened, squeezed her arm, and walked out the front door, inwardly cursing every step.

Once he walked through his front door and kicked it closed behind him, he immediately headed into his kitchen. He opened the cabinet where he stowed his alcohol. Not a big drinker of hard liquor, he kept whiskey on hand for when a few of the guys would come over. He poured a few fingers of the amber liquid into a glass and walked back into the living room. Taking a large swallow, he relished first the burn and then the flavor of the whiskey as his taste buds caught up to the peaty scent.

He closed his eyes, but the vision of Ivy standing in

front of him, disbelief morphing into disgust as the realization of how they used to know each other slowly dawned.

Hating that vision, he opened his eyes and stared across the room, a framed photograph catching his attention. Like so many pictures people have in their homes excitedly hung on walls or prominently placed on tables and shelves, they're often ignored and become part of the background. He didn't have many photographs up, but the ones he did were special. And now, he focused on the family photo Aaron gave him for Christmas several years ago.

It was a picture taken by one of his dad's friends when they were fishing one day. Andy was in high school, and Aaron was in middle school. Aaron had his head thrown back in laughter, their dad wore a massive smile with his arms around his sons, and even Andy had a carefree expression. *The three of us.*

He'd always liked that picture and was pleased when Aaron had a copy of it made to give to him. But now, looking at it, his mind rolled back to their mom. She wasn't in the photograph, long gone by that time, but her image came to the forefront of his mind anyway.

She was almost as tall as their dad, and he topped at six feet. Her hair was dark and long, and with her blue eyes, she looked like one of the queens in the fairy-tale book he had as a child. She cooked dinner most nights, but he remembered her grumbling about all the work she had to do to clean the house and take care of him.

It wasn't until he was in kindergarten that he noticed the difference as other mothers hugged their kids hello and goodbye. His mother barely looked him in the eye at any time. But when she'd let Aaron cry in his crib and just sit in the living room watching TV, he really began to see that she just wasn't like the other mothers. The arguments he'd heard his parents have when he was younger grew more frequent and louder.

And then, one day, when Andy was seven, she was just gone. He'd woken on a Saturday morning, headed into Aaron's room to help him get dressed, then held his brother's hand as they came downstairs for breakfast. His dad was sitting all alone at the table with a cold cup of coffee in front of him and a sad expression.

The news didn't come immediately, but as soon as Aaron went to play in the living room, his dad told him that his mother had left.

"On a trip?" he'd asked.

"I think she's gone away," his dad replied.

"Is she coming back?"

His dad shook his head, his eyes filling with tears. "I don't know, Son. But I don't think so."

Sally came over a few hours later, bringing dinner and ensuring the boys were bathed and ready for bed. She organized a small group of friends to help with meals and figure out transportation for him and Aaron while their dad was at work.

Andy couldn't understand at the time what was happening but overheard some of them murmuring about the shameful way his mother had abandoned her babies and husband.

"How can any mother do that?" one woman had clucked to the others.

"I don't know, but she doesn't deserve to be called a mother," another replied.

"Those poor boys will never be the same after this. It's cruel... just cruel."

"How on earth will Arthur raise these boys on his own?"

He'd raced to his room, buried his face in his pillow, and cried. His heart broke at the thought of his mother leaving. *Didn't she love us? Did we do something to make her leave? Did I? Maybe I didn't help her enough. If I promise to do better, maybe she'll come back.*

After a while when his tears had turned to sniffles, he heard Aaron crying in his room and rushed across the hall. Aaron had fallen, and Andy helped him stand, holding his brother's hands until his weak-muscled legs could bear weight again.

Even at the age of seven, he knew his dad needed him. His brother needed him. He'd cried daily for the first few months, but she never returned. On his eighth birthday, after the party that his dad, Sally, and Toby had thrown for him, he'd sat on the front porch and waited, thinking that surely his mom would not forget something so important as his birthday. And his tears fell as the sun lowered in the sky. Finally, his dad and Aaron came out to sit on the porch with him. No one spoke for several long moments. Not even three-year-old Aaron.

Looking over at his brother sitting in Pop's lap, he leaned against his dad's shoulder. After another moment, he swiped at his tears and took a shuddering breath. "It was a good birthday, Pop."

He heard the choked voice return, "Only the best for my boys. Happy birthday, Andy."

And that was the last day Andy cried over his mother.

Ten years later, his dad told him their mom had been in contact and wanted to see the boys. He'd been stunned. And pissed. But then, pissed had been the emotion he most felt since he'd hit puberty. Pissed at females in general. Pissed at happy families where both parents loved their children. And pissed at others who hadn't gone through his pain.

He'd told his dad he didn't want to see his mom and never regretted that decision. He knew his dad had had a few conversations with her, but he'd never asked nor cared what they'd talked about.

He took another large swig of whiskey and waited until the burn passed down his throat before sighing heavily. Scrubbing his hand over his face, he grimaced as Ivy's image filtered through his mind again. Thinking of when she'd put her hands on him and shoved him into a stack of boxes, he snorted. He'd known back then that she had a spine of steel and tough resolve. Strong character wrapped around a good heart.

Tossing back the last of his drink, he grimaced once more because those thoughts haunted him most of all.

11

"Hey, Mom," Ivy said, trying to gather enthusiasm. She was resting on the pillows piled against her headboard, having gone to bed soon after Andy left, unable to focus on the television or the book she'd started. She was tired and frustrated, and her mind refused to slow down the tumultuous thoughts racing at her.

Andy Bergstrom. The cute boy who never seemed to like her. It had always bothered her that she could never figure out why. She'd had many friends in high school, and while she never considered herself popular, most people liked her. Except for him. His taunts making fun of her name or her good grades, or her petite stature had irritated her. She had self-confidence and mostly ignored him, yet he always seemed to know what to say to get a little dig in.

But now, sitting in bed sifting through her high school memories hadn't reconciled the boy she knew with the man she met.

"I told your father I was going to call you in just a

little bit to see how you were doing," her mom said. "We were talking about leaving him here and letting me run home for a few days to check on you."

"Mom, that's not necessary at all. In fact, after tomorrow, I'm going to work."

"Is that wise? I can't believe the surgeon cleared you to go to work after only a few days!"

She crinkled her nose, now wishing she hadn't said anything to her mom about her plans. "Well, technically, I'm not going to *work*. I'm just going into the office to check on things. I want to make sure everything runs smoothly."

"Just don't overdo it. I know how you are. When you make up your mind about something, you're dogmatic until the task is accomplished."

She laughed and shook her head. "I wonder where I got that trait from?"

Her mom's sweet laughter sounded. "It must be from your dad. But seriously, honey, how are you doing? Have you been eating?"

Heat moved through her at the thought of the handsome man who delivered her dinner. "Yes, I did, and there's a story there that I wanted to tell you about."

"I'm all ears!"

"Well, the officer who jumped in to save me and then held my hand on the boat to assure me that I would be okay came by the hospital yesterday and volunteered to drive me home since I didn't have my car."

"That sounds like a lovely thing for somebody to do."

"Well, Mom, the story continues. This evening, he brought my car along with dinner."

"Oh my. The story gets better and better. Do I dare ask if he was handsome, as well as nice and heroic?"

Settling back deeper against the cushions, she couldn't keep the smile from her lips. "Yes, I would have to say that he was gorgeous. And I had no idea who he was other than his name was *Andy*."

"O… kay…"

"It turns out that I knew him in high school. In fact, he had been in our house more than once when we were working on projects together. You might remember him. Andy Bergstrom."

"Andy Bergstrom!" her mother exclaimed. "And he's with the police now?"

"The marine police."

"Well, I'm not surprised at all that he's in law enforcement. I always knew that boy was a protector."

Ivy opened and closed her mouth several times until finally sputtering, "Protector? How on earth do you figure that, Mom? Protector? Have you forgotten what he was like in high school?"

Her mother chuckled softly. "Of course, I haven't forgotten, sweetheart."

"Then don't give me any crap about how he really liked me but didn't know how to show it. That's as cliché as dipping a girl's pigtails in the inkwell!"

Her mother's chuckle turned into a full-bodied laugh. "Leave it to you to remember your Laura Ingalls Wilder books!"

"You know what I mean, Mom. Andy Bergstrom definitely did not like me. He had a chip on his shoulder, and somehow, it always seemed to be focused on me."

There was a prolonged silence, and her mother's lack of response piqued Ivy's curiosity.

"I'm sorry, Ivy. I guess I never realized how bad his attitude was toward you."

Shoulders slumping, she shook her head. "It wasn't that bad, Mom. He was kind of mean toward me, but I had too much confidence to let it get to me." She sighed. "Well, sometimes that wasn't true. It's hard enough being a smart girl in a world that values bubble-head bimbos. I certainly dealt with that in engineering school. Maybe I should thank him for making my skin thicker!"

"Did you ever see him pick on kids who couldn't handle his barbs?"

Ivy blinked, her mind cast back, shifting through the memories before sighing. "No. Never. In fact, he always seemed like he got along with everyone else. I was the only one who got in the way of his barbed, verbal arrows."

"Hmm." That was the only response.

"Seriously, Mom. That's it? I'm still curious why you saw him as a protector?"

"As a teacher in the school, I was privy to information about students that I didn't and won't share. But I'll say that he took on a lot of responsibility for his younger brother when he was very young. It was common knowledge that his mother was not in the picture, which probably colored his view of many things. But I had the chance to see through the bravado he projected. In fact, he often butted heads with female teachers, but that's not unusual for adolescent boys who don't have a mother in the home."

"Teenage anger and angst?" Ivy quipped. She snorted. "Like he was the only one with problems? The only one to have a burden to bear?"

"Don't underestimate teenage anger and angst! Anyway, I observed him. Sure, he was a big guy and had a swagger that I'm sure sent many a teenage girl into giggly fits. But he was kind to his brother and others who seemed a little lost. I could easily see him becoming a protector. So I wasn't surprised to hear he'd joined the military after high school and is now in law enforcement. I'd say he's fulfilling his destiny."

Ivy sighed heavily at the thoughts now swimming through her mind.

"Sweetie?"

"Yeah, Mom?"

"Honey, I'm not making light of the teasing he aimed toward you. Looking back, it was bullying, no excuses, and I should have done more about it then."

Ivy waved her hand dismissively even though her mother couldn't see the motion. "Oh, Mom, it's fine. Honestly, he didn't make my life miserable. I had a good childhood. I liked school. Clubs, chorus, running cross-country, good friends. He was even okay when he was here studying… or rather when I did the project, and he got to share the good grade. It was just that I could never understand his barbs slung at me. But who knows what makes some people do the things they do."

"Let me ask you this. When you saw him today, what was he like?"

Sucking in a quick breath, she let it out slowly as she remembered. "Well, the good-looking boy has certainly grown into a gorgeous man." She chuckled, then sobered, adding, "He was kind. He drove me home yesterday, then arranged to return my car and brought dinner tonight. He insisted on helping. He was… sweet. He told me that I had also saved the baby and probably the man on the bridge."

"And did he know who you were?"

"Yes! He realized that yesterday."

"Today was all after he knew who you were."

"What are you trying to say?" she huffed, her frustration spilling out.

"I'm saying that considering he jumped into the water for you, then came to find you, and once he knew who you were, he was still kind. I'd say that the man he is now isn't who you remember from years ago."

"That's what he said," she whispered, his words returning to her. "He said he wanted to apologize but that it wasn't the right time because I needed to rest."

"Well, then, the ball is in your court. What do you want to do about it? Hold on to the past and ignore him. Or see who he is now as an adult. Just keep in mind, honey, that there's no right or wrong decision. It's up to you whether you want to hear his apology… and perhaps his story."

With even more thoughts now swirling through her mind than before she'd called her mom, she sighed. "I love you, Mom."

"Oh, precious, I love you, too."

With goodbyes and promises to call the next day, she disconnected the call and tossed the phone to the nightstand. She slid under the covers and adjusted the pillow underneath her left arm. She closed her eyes, willing sleep to come. But her slumber was filled with the dark eyes of the teenage boy who'd sat at her table glowering as they morphed into the warm chocolate eyes of the man who'd smiled at her and then kissed her cheek.

Ivy walked into the CBBT Eastern Shore office, determined to do something today besides sitting around her house with her thoughts in disarray. *Order... I need order.* It felt good to dress in something besides sweatpants, although she was still more attired for convenience than fashion. Her plain black pants had been a struggle to zip, and she'd given up on a blouse with buttons, opting for a loose-fitting sweater that stretched over her cast. A headband kept her hair back, and it was clean, so she felt somewhat ready to face others.

Seeing her boss, Ethan Barker, in his office, she smiled and knocked on the doorframe.

He looked up and was startled. "Ivy, good God! Should you be here?"

"I needed to get out of the house and figured I'd come and see how far behind I was."

Ethan's gaze dropped to Ivy's wrist before he lifted his eyebrows and speared her with a hard stare. "Just because you want to get out of your house does not mean you're ready to come to work."

Duly chastised, she nodded. "I realize that, and that's why I'm not here officially to work." She glanced across the hall toward her office and shrugged. "I just thought I'd spend a little time in the office."

"I should kick you out," he grumbled. "HR will probably have a fit if you're here against doctor's orders."

"Actually, the surgeon said I can work as long as I'm not on the prescription pain meds. Although I'll be slow with the computer."

"You know, we were shocked at what happened the other day. When I looked at the surveillance video and saw you go over. Jesus…"

She pressed her lips together and nodded. She was trying to put it out of her mind but realized most people wanted to talk about it. "Well, I think I'll catch up on some emails."

Once inside her office, she sat at her desk and looked around. It was utilitarian, at best. Boring, actually. The gray metal desk, matching shelves, and filing cabinet made up most of the furniture. A metal table was pushed against the far wall. The cream-painted cinder block walls offered little in the way of personalization.

She had planned to bring a few pieces of artwork to hang on the walls to give the place some color. But everything was still packed from when she left her Richmond office. She walked to the ergonomic chair behind the desk and smiled. It and her computer equipment were the items that were perfect in the office.

Turning on her computer, she slowly began to see what she'd missed in the past few days.

For the next hour, she worked through the various programs with numerous interruptions from coworkers who stopped by to check on her. When she left at lunchtime, she was exhausted, but instead of feeling overwhelmed, Ivy felt like she was home.

12

Andy sat in the meeting at the station, his gaze riveted on the speaker Ryan had brought in. The man had presented to the North Heron sheriff's department and was now making his rounds to the smaller law enforcement stations. Today, he was hitting the Baytown Police Department, the local Coast Guard station at Baytown, and the Virginia Marine Police in a joint meeting.

"The Bloods had approximately sixty gang members on the Eastern Shore about eight years ago," Special Agent Markham said. "That number has now doubled. Their offenses have gone from distributing and running drugs to murder and weapons running up and down the East Coast from Florida to New York."

"They've operated mostly in my county," Liam Sullivan said. He was the sheriff of the other Virginia county on the Eastern Shore.

"But they've moved to be established in our county, as well," Colt added, his jaw tight. "And it's like getting rid of cockroaches… more keep coming in."

Agent Markham continued, "They are now using the Bay to transport, and that's where the VMP comes in."

Ryan and the other officers scowled. They knew drug gangs used boats on the Bay. Andy focused on the presenter, determined to absorb all the information he could to do his job more efficiently.

"In Miami, the custom of using mother ships where cargo ships drop anchor and someone on board drops drug packages to waiting gang members in speedboats has been a practice for a while. That practice has now made its way up the coast to the Chesapeake Bay. Unfortunately, the speedboats typically are built to outrun the Coast Guard or VMP slower boats. Last year, a Baltimore Marine officer boarded an unlicensed speedboat. She was beaten and tossed overboard as they got away. She stayed afloat and managed to get back to her vessel to call for assistance."

"Why the hell was she by herself?" Andy barked out.

The agent shook his head. "Fucked-up scheduling by their office, if I had to guess. But no matter the staffing limits, my advice is never to approach any situation with your guard down or alone. Especially when approaching a speedboat in these times." He looked over the group and added, "But don't be fooled. Not all are using these methods. Gang members transport drugs in the most innocuous ways possible. Keep an eye on the fishermen in the area. Any of them you don't recognize could be dealing in more than just fish, crabs, and oysters."

Colt added, "Liam and I have also noted a presence of Crips in our counties, but they tend to operate in

Maryland mostly. At least until they also started using the Bay to transport. The Bloods will dress almost exclusively in red and black. The Crips are known for their blue color. And we've got the Dead Man Inc coming down as well.

"Mostly Caucasian. They're not affiliated with any white supremacist group yet. But we believe they are infiltrating some of the local fishermen looking for ways to make money by transporting drugs, as well," Agent Markham said.

"We start looking at every possible boat on the Bay as a potential threat?" Andy asked, his brows raised.

Ryan nodded, his jaw tight. "We still maintain our relations with the fishermen we know, but we must be even more vigilant."

The presentation continued, involving multiple photographs on the wall screen showing gang tattoos, hand signals, and clothing to recognize. They looked at the boats used and the types of drugs and weapons transported. By the time their mini-conference was over, his head was spinning, and it was lunchtime.

Several of the group headed to the Seafood Shack, but he'd promised Brogan MacFarlane that he'd pick up the flyers for the next American Legion fundraiser from the pub and give them to his coworkers to distribute. Parking outside the pub, he walked in and sat at the bar. The scent of food made his decision to have their fish and chips platter just the meal to satisfy his hunger.

Brogan came over, and they clasped hands. "Good to see you, man. Here you go." He handed Andy the stack of flyers.

"Same to you. How's the family?"

Brogan's grin transformed his appearance. He was big, tatted, and sometimes fierce looking. Now married with a little girl, he'd battle the world to make sure they were cared for. "Fucking perfect," he exclaimed. Suddenly, his smile dropped, and he narrowed his eyes. "I don't know if I congratulated you the other day for the rescue that hit the news about that woman who saved the baby."

"Well, I wasn't the one who saved the day. You can thank Ivy Watkins. She's the one who stood out on the bridge for an hour talking to the man, calming him down, and making sure the baby was safe."

"Is she local?"

Before they had a chance to talk further, Brogan was called to the other end of the bar. Andy twisted around in his seat at the sight of a woman attempting to heft herself onto the tall barstool, having difficulty with a cast peeking out from a loose sweater. Jerking around, he looked up to see Ivy struggling to get into the seat.

"Ivy!" He slid from his stool and quickly placed one hand on her arm and the other on the back of the stool to steady her ascent into the chair.

"Oh..." Her mouth fell open as she blinked and looked around quickly as though to ascertain if she could make it to another seat, probably farther away from him. *Yeah, probably on the other side of the state.* Her inherent politeness caught up to her surprise, something he'd witnessed many years earlier.

"Andy... um... thank you." Her cheeks were pink, but

he had no idea if it was a blush from surprise at seeing him or the exertion from her barstool climb.

"How are you doing?" He wanted to know, but the desire to want her to stay in her seat almost overwhelmed him. His breath held as he awaited her response.

"Well… getting into the seat was harder than I thought it would be," she offered with a rueful chuckle.

"Should you be out today?" He slid back onto his stool next to her, his gaze never leaving her face.

"I'm not on the heavy-duty pain medication if you're worried about me driving." Her voice held a bite to it.

"No, no," he rushed. "That's not what I meant. I mean, yes, I'm glad you're careful about the drugs and driving. But it just seems so soon."

She shrugged, gazing down at her hands resting on the bar. "I wanted to go into the office and check things out this morning."

He opened his mouth to protest, then realized it wasn't his place. She looked only slightly more rested than when he had seen her a few days ago, but he had to admit the shadows under her eyes were lessened, and color had returned to her complexion. Her hair was pulled back with a headband, and she wore little makeup, probably to make the styling easy. And she was beautiful.

He winced, remembering the way they left the conversation. He wanted to say so much, but the time was not right. And even now, he had no idea if she wanted to listen. Refusing to take the coward's way out, he waited until she finally glanced up at him, her brown eyes holding his gaze. He used to notice that they had flecks of gold in them, and in the pub lights, the gold seemed to shine even more. Blowing out his breath, he blurted, "I hope when you're feeling better, Ivy, you'll give me that chance to apologize."

A wince passed over her face, and she waved her hand slightly to the side and shook her head. "There's really no need, Andy. My goodness, it was a long time ago."

Her pitch was higher than normal, and he wasn't sure if she was dismissing him or truly feeling that way. "Yeah, but my dad always said there was no expiration date on apologies."

At that, she scoffed before it morphed into laughter. Her face transformed from slightly pinched lines of pain to absolute, devastatingly beautiful. Nodding while still smiling, she said, "That's a great saying. I've never heard it before."

"Well, I can't swear that he made it up himself or read it somewhere. I just know I grew up hearing it. It's too bad I didn't take it to heart a long time ago."

Her smile faltered, and she looked back down at her hands. A server came by, and Ivy gave her lunch order. Casting a glance toward the server, he said, "Bring my lunch out at the same time, please." The server nodded, but Ivy tilted her head to the side as she stared at him. Shrugging, he said, "I don't want to squander this time or opportunity. I hope that's all right?"

She continued to stare for a moment as though taking his measure. Finally, she nodded, and her lips curved slightly. "Sure."

While the words weren't overly encouraging, the fact that she had smiled several times in the past few minutes gave him hope. Twisting in his stool toward her, he was glad she was next to the wall at the end of the bar. It gave him a chance to talk to her without others hearing. "First of all, I really want to apologize for all the times that—"

"Ivy!"

Andy jerked his head around at the same time she did and spied Katelyn MacFarlane Harrison walking toward them. Aiden and Brogan's sister was part owner but no longer worked at the pub. And her little boy was holding her hand as they drew closer.

"We were just in to grab some lunch to take back to Gareth, and I thought that was you. Sybil said you'd moved back. Her kids and Finn are good friends."

Ivy smiled down at the preschooler and exclaimed, "Hello, Finn! I know Ricky and Jessica, too. Do you like playing with them?"

"Yes!" the little boy screamed, throwing his hand into the air.

Katelyn rolled her eyes and laughed. "Believe me, his enthusiasm is real."

Brogan walked over with the two platters and set them down in front of Ivy and Andy while greeting his sister and nephew.

"This is Ivy Watkins," Katelyn said to Brogan. "The one who saved that baby on the bridge."

"Are you fuckin' kidding me?" Brogan asked, turning to Ivy. "Holy shit! Andy and I were just talking about you. Your lunch is on the house!"

Andy hated the interruption but couldn't deny that Ivy was certainly due her time in the spotlight. Turning toward her, he watched as she shifted on her barstool, her face blushing deep red.

Once again, she waved her hand dismissively. "I just happened to be at the right place at the right time."

Katelyn and Brogan assured her that what she'd done went beyond what many people would do. Pain lines bracketed Ivy's mouth, and Andy finally jumped in to say, "I think she needs to eat so she can get home to rest."

Katelyn nodded while trying to hold a bouncing Finn. "Of course! And I've got to get this little guy home, but we'll see you soon." She gave Ivy her phone number and added, "Give me a call, and we'll meet at Jillian's Coffeehouse."

"Sounds good," Ivy said, waving as they walked out the door.

Brogan headed down to the other end of the bar, and Ivy looked over at Andy and blew out a long breath. "Thank you for that."

"Well, I want to make sure you eat. Plus, you look tired."

"Yeah." She nodded. "I might have overdone it this morning. It's just that sitting at home was... I don't know..."

"Is it hard being there without your parents?"

Her gaze jumped to his, and she slowly nodded. "Silly, isn't it? I've been away from home and out on my own for years. Yet being back in my childhood home, it feels lonely to be there by myself."

He looked at his watch and knew he didn't have much longer in his lunch break. "I didn't expect to see you today, Ivy, but I'm really glad I did. I also didn't get to finish my apology. Would you consider having dinner with me?" His breathing slowed, and as much as he tried to adopt a casual air, the desire for her to accept seemed to pour off him in waves.

She held his gaze for another moment, her eyes searching his, and he hoped she could see his sincerity. Whatever she found, she must've believed him. She offered a little smile and nodded. "I suppose so. Yeah, sure."

It wasn't a resounding *Hell, yeah*, but he'd take whatever he was offered. He pulled out his phone and asked for her number. As she gave it to him, he typed it in and then sent a text. "Okay, you've got my number, too. I'm working late tomorrow, but how about the day after that?"

Again, she nodded, but this time chewed on her lip, and he was filled with uncertainty, wondering if she would change her mind.

"Andy, would it be okay if you came to my house for dinner instead?" she asked.

His mouth popped open at her suggestion. "Absolutely!"

"It's just that... well..."

"You don't have to give me a reason, Ivy. I'd love to come over."

She pressed her lips together, then nodded. "I agree that we have some things to say to each other, and it would be nice to have a chance to talk without anyone else around."

Even with her foreboding words, he was grateful she was giving him the opportunity and nodded enthusiastically. "But I don't want you to fix anything. There's an Italian restaurant in town, and they do takeout. I'll text you their menu, and you can tell me what you'd like. I'll grab it on my way home and come to your place."

Her smile returned, and her eyes appeared less pain-filled than they had. He tossed down enough money to cover both of their lunches, wanting to pay for her even if Brogan had said her lunch was on the house. "I'll call," he promised, gently patting her arm. He meant the gesture to be subtle, but the touch sent tingles through his hand.

A few minutes later, walking out of the pub wearing a wide smile, he hurried back to the station. The knowledge that in a couple of days, he'd have a chance to talk to her… really talk to her again had his heart pounding.

13

After boarding the boat they'd stopped on the Bay, Andy looked around as Jared checked the license and registrations. The three men stood nearby, their stances easy and casual.

"Nice day for boating," Andy said, not seeing any fishing equipment.

Before any of the men had a chance to respond, Jared looked at the driver and said, "This license is new, so I guess you and your friends couldn't wait to get out on the water."

The owner nodded, a wide grin on his face. "Been wanting a boat for as long as I can remember. Got a good deal and didn't want to wait until the spring. I've been out a few times but thought I'd bring some friends along today."

Andy kept a neutral expression as he looked over the group and then turned to Jared, a slight chin lift his only communication.

"All right, gentlemen. Enjoy your day," Jared called

out as Andy climbed back onto the VMP vessel. Standing outside the wheelhouse, he watched as the pleasure boat started again and took off slowly before building speed.

"Nothing?" Jose asked as he steered their boat farther out onto the Bay.

"Nothing I could see. No fishing license but then no fishing equipment."

"But?" Jose pressed.

"Christ, I don't know," he admitted as Jared walked over to them. "I'm starting to see gang members everywhere I look."

"I know what you mean. They looked too young to have a boat that easily cost fifty-thousand dollars." Jose sighed heavily.

"But there was nothing I could see. No big bags. No boxes. Granted, we didn't do a full search," Andy continued. "And that would only really show if they were carrying guns. Drugs? Could have had those stored in much smaller containers and still been profitable."

This was the fifth boarding Andy's group had made that day, and he knew the other teams were doing the same. When he'd first started with the VMP, he'd focused most of their stops and boardings on the fishing industry—illegal poaching, fishing, and catching. With the number of vacationers on the Bay near the Eastern Shore, boating licenses, laws, and regulations contributed to their stops. But adding in the drug and gang activity, they would soon need more officers.

"Ten thirty-eight, ten fifty-four," the dispatcher

called out, then added the location. Jose turned the vessel around, and they sped toward the scene of the accident. After five minutes, Andy spied the single boat ahead, and Jose slowed their vessel. The three men in the boat were all wearing lifejackets.

The cabin cruiser had extensive damage to the side. "Is everyone accounted for?" Andy called out as he and Jared floated alongside it.

"Yes! The fuckers hit us and then left!"

"We're going to bring you onto our vessel. The Coast Guard is on its way to tow your boat to the Baytown Harbor."

Two men bobbed their heads up and down with shock written across their faces. But the man he assumed was the owner was operating more on anger than fear at the moment. As soon as they drew alongside, the men crowded close, ready to climb onto the VMP boat. "Hang on, sir. Let us get tethered. Then you can come over safely."

He and Jared worked as a team as Jose expertly handled their boat. Once tethered, Andy reached out and helped the first two men. "Gentlemen, I'm gonna have you sit right here. You're safe now, and I'll take your statements shortly."

Turning back to the still-fuming man, he said, "Sir, let's get you over here, and then we'll proceed."

"They need to be caught! They need to pay for my boat! I want them arrested!"

"Sir, I couldn't agree more. But let's get you safely onto this boat, and then we need to take your statement."

"CG on its way," Jose called out.

Andy glanced behind him and saw the approaching Coast Guard boat, large enough to tow the cabin cruiser back to the harbor.

The owner finally crossed over with some assistance, still grumbling and cursing, but Jared settled him with the others. It took several more minutes for the Coast Guard to attach lines. Finally, as they pulled away with the boat in tow, Andy walked back to the three men sitting just behind the wheelhouse.

"Does anyone need medical attention?" he asked.

All three shook their heads, but he kept his eye on the owner, who was still red-faced and breathing hard. Nodding, he leaned into the wheelhouse and spoke low enough for only Jose to hear. "Have the Baytown Rescue meet us at the harbor. It may be nothing, but the owner looks like he could have a heart attack at any moment."

With a dip of his chin, Jose acknowledged, and Andy stepped back out of the wheelhouse and walked around to where the men sat. The air was brisk, and even though the men were dressed warmly and had not been in the water, Andy was concerned. "We have warming blankets or if you need to sit in the wheelhouse, that's fine, too."

The men shook their heads, so Jared began getting their names and identification.

Before they had a chance to ask for details, the owner, Bill Tudman, began shouting. "Those damn crazy men hit our boat. Just sideswiped us and kept going. I want them arrested!"

"Mr. Tudman, can you describe the boat or the

men?" Andy asked.

"It was sleek. Silver. Went too fast for me to get any ID on the boat, but I did see two men."

"What can you tell us about the men?"

"I don't know," he growled. "They had dark, heavy coats on. And they had knit caps pulled low. I couldn't even tell you what race they were."

The other two men were wide-eyed and shell-shocked, mostly nodding and muttering, "I don't know."

"Same thing."

"Two men, dressed in dark clothing."

"Did you hear them come upon you?"

"We weren't facing out that way. We had binoculars and cameras, watching for birdlife between where we were and the shore. I heard a boat coming out of the inlet but didn't think much about it. A flock of black pelicans was flying just above the water near us. We were taking pictures when I realized the sound was so close. By the time I turned around, all I could see was a larger boat near us. I yelled at the others but turned back toward the wheel, away from the men, to jerk us out of the way. Before I had a chance, we were side-swiped. We all went tumbling to the side, cameras flying out of our hands."

"So it wasn't an accident—"

"No way!"

"Absolutely not!"

"No!" all three shouted at the same time.

"Since you had cameras, is there any chance that you got a photograph of the other boat?" Jared asked.

The three men looked at each other, their brows

lowered as they pondered his question.

"My camera landed in the bottom of the boat when we got hit," one man said. "But it hadn't been pointed toward the other boat at all. I was only focused on the birds in the opposite direction."

"I'm afraid my camera is in the bottom of the Bay," another man moaned. "Almost a thousand dollars' worth of camera, lenses… all gone." He sighed heavily and shook his head. "Don't get me wrong, I'm glad I'm alive, but that's a hard pill to swallow."

"I understand, sir," Andy agreed. "So no one thinks they have a picture?"

Bill looked over, blinking as the creases in his forehead deepened. "I didn't have my camera with me right then. Since I was handling the boat, Carl and Matt took pictures. But I did have my cell phone out. It was in my hand when I turned to look at the noise of the approaching boat. But when we got hit, it went flying out of my hand and into the water, also." Suddenly, he jerked as though they had just remembered something. "Oh Lordy! I was on a call with my wife and was sending her the video! Can I get word to her that we're okay?"

"Absolutely, Mr. Tudman. Could you check with your wife to see if that video came in? Even if it's messy and grainy, if you can get that to us, we can see if we can pull any information from it to identify who hit you."

"I want those bastards arrested, so I'll do anything I can to help you!"

Jose turned the vessel into the Baytown Harbor and docked outside the station. Once tied off, Andy assisted the three men onto the dock and escorted them inside while Jared and Jose checked the vessel for the next time it needed to go out.

"What about my boat?" Bill asked.

Looking over his shoulder toward the harbor, Andy inclined his head. "The Coast Guard is bringing it in now. They'll look it over, make their assessment, and you can call your insurance company and let them know where it is. They'll send somebody out, as well, to do their own assessment of damages for your claim. We'll have a report by then for you to give them."

Once inside, they were met by not only Bryce and Ryan but also Zac Hamilton of the Baytown rescue squad and another EMT.

Turning to the three men, Andy explained, "Since your boat was in an accident, it's best to be checked out. Sometimes shock and adrenaline can mask an injury."

While the EMTs assessed the three men, Andy walked over to Bryce and Ryan, who met him in the conference room. He gave them the rundown of what happened and said, "We need to get Bill's wife on the phone. First, to let her know he's all right, but she may also have been sent a text with the video that could help us identify the other boat."

Bryce nodded and immediately went to the room where Mr. Tudman was being evaluated. After gaining the information about Mr. Tudman's wife's phone, Andy set up the interviews in the conference room. He, Jared, and Bryce interviewed all three men separately, and when one of their wives picked up the men, Andy found that all three reports were very similar.

Looking up as Jared came into the room, he asked, "Did she have anything?"

Jared nodded. "I had her send what she could to my email." Ryan and the others came into the room as Jared projected the scene taken from Mr. Tudman's cell phone. Just as he described, the video was of the three men looking at and taking pictures of birds along the shore. Their voices were heard, confirming their actions. Then the phone jerked around as one of the men yelled, "What the hell?"

Mr. Tudman could be heard cursing before the camera jerked back toward the front as he faced the steering wheel again, just as he said.

Jared went back, and they carefully watched the part of the video again where the oncoming boat was nearing. Silver. Sleek. A large racing boat. The front of the boat was lifted slightly, making it difficult to see, but two men wearing dark coats and knit caps pulled over their faces were visible.

"Shit. Doesn't give us much," Jared grumbled. "Looks like a racing boat. Almost like the old Cigarette boats."

"Play it again, and slow it down even more," Ryan ordered.

Andy leaned closer as Jared followed the instructions from their boss. Standing closest to the screen, he threw his hand up, exclaiming, "There."

Jared backed the video up for a few seconds and replayed it, stopping it right when Andy pointed again. On the front side of the boat, one letter and one number were visible.

Andy looked around the others and grinned. "It's not much to go on, but it's better than nothing."

With backslaps for a successful rescue, they headed back into the workroom to write up the reports and begin searching for possible boat identification.

An hour later, he was no closer to figuring out the information on the boat's registration, but his mind had slid to where he was going as soon as his shift was over. In truth, his thoughts had been on her all day. *Ivy*. She texted him her preference for dinner, and he'd already called it in. Now, anxious to see her again, he watched the clock slowly tick by. Finally, he and the others said their goodbyes, and he jogged to his SUV.

Only twenty minutes later, he pulled into the drive at her parents' house, his nerves making his stomach clench in a way he hadn't felt since he was a kid. *Maybe this is a mistake. Maybe I should just leave it at the apology I've already given, and she's accepted. Maybe I should cut my losses before walking in there.* He blew out a breath and sighed. *What the hell am I doing?*

A movement at the front snagged his attention. The front door opened, and Ivy stood, her head tilted slightly to the side as she peered out at him. For a second, he stepped back in time. He could still see her mother opening the front door when he arrived. She'd greeted him like he wasn't some poor, motherless kid or the dumb kid who needed her daughter's help to pass the class project. She was a good teacher, a good mom to Ivy, and never made him feel less than.

Suddenly, he knew what he was doing. *I want a*

chance to explain and to give Ivy a chance to rip me a new asshole if that's what she needs to move beyond the past.

For some inexplicable reason, he wished for more from the woman on the bridge, but if that was all he could get from Ivy, he'd take it, knowing he deserved it.

She wrapped her arms around her middle as she stood in the open doorway, and he bolted into action. Leaning over, he carefully grabbed the bag with their dinner and jogged to the front porch. "You shouldn't be out in the cold," he admonished, his gaze drinking her in.

She was dressed casually yet looked beautiful all at the same time. Leggings showcased her shapely legs, and an oversized soft pale-green sweater draped over her torso. He assumed it was easy for her to get dressed in something that didn't have buttons and zippers, and he had no complaints about what she was wearing at all. Her hair hung in long, loose waves that looked like she'd simply let it dry after her shower and run her fingers through it. Her makeup consisted of a subtle hint of blush and mascara and a swipe of lip gloss.

Her gaze followed him as he neared, but her expression was hard to read. She wasn't scowling, which he took as a good sign, but she wasn't smiling either. "Please, come on in." She turned and walked through the doorway.

He hastened to follow her inside, and as she closed the door behind him, he heard a slight gasp.

"Whatever you have in that bag smells amazing," she admitted.

He grinned and lifted it, dangling it in front of her. "I

got what you asked for, but I got a lot more. I thought we could try several different items from their menu, and whatever is left over will be easy for you to heat."

She held his gaze and then nodded slowly. "That was very thoughtful." She lifted her left hand and wiggled her fingers. "The swelling has gone down, and I can wiggle my fingers without too much pain, but still, easy to heat will be nice."

"Good, good. But you don't want to overdo it."

She offered a thin-lipped smile before leading him past the dining room and into the kitchen. Sweat rolled down his back at the thought that she regretted inviting him over for dinner, but it didn't escape his notice that she already had cutlery on the dining room table. Looking over her shoulder, she said, "I thought we could place the food on the counter to fill our plates and then take them into the dining room. But with so much food for us to sample…"

"You shouldn't have gone to any trouble," he hastened to say. "Um… we can just eat in the kitchen if you'd like." Secretly hoping for the informality of the kitchen table, giving the illusion of friends instead of the more formal dining room, he watched as a crinkle appeared between her eyebrows.

"Well, you were gracious enough to invite me to dinner and then bring it here. The least I could do was make sure we had a nice environment for our meal."

He made quick work of spreading out all the various containers. She watched, her brows lifting with each dish he set out.

"Maybe you're right, and the table here is easier," she

said, tucking a strand of hair behind her ear.

She turned to head into the dining room, but he stopped her. "You start fixing your plate, and I'll get the things from the dining room."

He made quick work of grabbing them and placing them on the kitchen table before she'd made it halfway through the containers. Lining up behind her, he loaded his plate. To fill the silence, he told her about the little restaurant where the food came from and some of the other new eateries in the area. He found the topic of food to be the universal conversation starter, and by the time they sat down, she was smiling with a more relaxed demeanor.

As she dug in, her moans of delight hit him right in his cock. He shifted slightly and grimaced. The last thing she needed to discover was that he had a hard-on just from watching her eat.

In high school, he'd never considered Ivy as a potential girlfriend. Inwardly rolling his eyes at the word *girlfriend*, he acknowledged he'd never had time for a serious girlfriend. But he'd never thought of flirting with or getting to know her. Since he'd become a jerk to her by the time they'd entered high school, she simply became the girl he dismissed in his mind. But looking back, he realized he'd been more of an idiot than he'd ever realized. She was beautiful. But more than that, she was sweet. As smart as she was, she could have lorded it over everyone. But she offered help when needed. He was fairly sure he remembered that she ran track, and a memory surfaced of her smiling face as she cheered on her fellow teammates.

The sinking feeling in his gut hit again at the thought that she might completely dismiss his attempts to reconnect. But maybe, as sweet as she'd been, she'd give him a chance.

Their casual conversation continued, mostly about the weather, people who still lived in Baytown, when she'd return to work full time, and his career with the VMP.

When they finished the tiramisu and leaned back in their chairs, she smiled as she patted her stomach. "I can't remember the last time I ate that much food!"

He laughed and agreed. "Everybody in town was really glad when they opened the Italian restaurant."

"Would you like some coffee?" she asked.

"Yeah, that'd be great." He was all for any excuse to stay longer.

They stood, and he offered to clear the table together while she fixed a pot of coffee. Once the dishes were in the dishwasher and the leftovers were in the refrigerator, the coffee was ready. "How do you take it?"

He was closest to the refrigerator and got the cream himself. Once they doctored their coffees the way they liked, he'd made a mental note that she liked sweeteners and so much flavored creamer that her coffee was more tan than dark. They stood in the kitchen, him leaning against the counter and her against the sink when she finally cocked her head to the side and said, "So when should we talk about high school?"

His stomach dropped, and suddenly the delicious food curdled slightly in his gut. Of course, that had been the reason for him wanting to get together... a heartfelt apology and a chance to talk. But now, seeing her serious expression while holding his gaze, it struck him that this might be the last time they had a convivial conversation. Blowing out his breath, he nodded. "Any chance we can get comfortable first?"

Her lips quirked upward. "Let's take the coffee into the living room. We'll be comfortable in there."

Once again, he let her lead and noticed she sat on one side of the sofa, twisting slightly, so it was easy for him to sit on the other side. He shifted so they almost faced each other.

Another flash of memory hit him from many years ago. "I remember sitting on this sofa, just like this, when you practiced your part of the presentation we worked on. Or rather, that you'd worked on. It was good. I remember that. I also remember thinking I would get a good grade because you were my partner."

She chuckled softly. "I remember that too. We sat just like this." She pressed her lips together and added, "Only not exactly like this. Back then, you looked like this was the last place in the world you wanted to be."

He dropped his chin and shook his head slowly, knowing her memory would be just as good, if not better, than his. "You don't pull any punches, do you?"

"No. But I figured this is your show, Andy, so I'll let you tell me whatever you need or want to say."

Blowing out another breath, he lifted his head, held her gaze, and nodded, glad her expression was open and not hostile. "Once again, let me start by saying I'm so sorry."

14

"Let me start by saying I'm so sorry."

Ivy heard Andy's words, but more so, she felt the emotion coming from inside him. It was strange because, in high school, it was hard to imagine he had any emotion other than an overblown sense of self. But now, looking back, that description could've counted for many teenagers. *Even myself. What does that say about me? I'm no better than anyone else!*

Suddenly, she didn't want him to feel the need to explain. "Andy, I accept your apology," she blurted.

He blinked, his chin jerking back slightly. "I know you said that, but—"

She shook her head and waved her hand. "I know I did, but it's important to let you know that you don't owe me an explanation. You don't have to delve into anything personal to explain your adolescent self. Quite frankly, I don't think any of us could stand up to much scrutiny when we look back at our teenage years."

He snorted and lifted a brow. "I can't imagine you have much to be ashamed of when you think back."

"We all have regrets," she said, shrugging. Her fingers fiddled with the bottom of her sweater before she finally linked them together in her lap. "I suppose some regrets are more hidden than others."

He nodded, thoughts moving behind his eyes. "Thank you for the acceptance, but can I explain anyway? I feel like I need this for me."

She pressed her lips together for a few seconds, then tucked another strand of hair behind her ear. "Absolutely, if that's what you want." Shrugging, she added, "I guess, in truth, I am curious. I could never understand what I did to earn your animosity."

He shifted quickly to face her more fully. "Ivy, that's the whole crux of the matter. It was nothing that *you* did. It all came from a place deep inside me that I didn't even recognize. And hell, even if I had recognized it as a teenager, I still probably could have or would have done very little about it."

Curious, she settled in deeper against the soft cushions. She was surprised by how comfortable it felt to have him sitting with her on the sofa in her house. The adult version of Andy was fascinating. And gorgeous. She would have to have been oblivious not to recognize the virility his presence gave off.

His dark hair was hastily swept to the side, as only a man who doesn't waste time worrying about his hair could look. The jacket he'd worn hung easily on the coat-tree near the front door. His muscles bulged against the long-sleeved Henley shirt. And that sight didn't come close to how his thighs pulled at the denim of his jeans. To ignore the adult version of him based on the adolescent version would have been impossible.

Refocusing on his words instead of his appearance, she picked up her coffee mug and sipped the warm, creamy brew before she gave him her full attention.

He was quiet for a moment and then scoffed as he shook his head. "I thought about what to say so you'd think I would be prepared. But suddenly, it's more frightening than I thought it would be."

"Frightening?" She stared at the uncertainty filling his face with the lines that now laced his forehead.

His shoulders hefted before falling back down. "Because the teenage me acted like I didn't care anything about your feelings. But I find that now, as an adult, just as we've barely reconnected, I care a great deal about how you might feel about me."

Her breathing became shallow, and she stared at his dark eyes, sincerity radiating from them. Speaking softly, afraid to break the fragile web woven between them, she whispered, "Then tell me everything."

"Do you remember—" He stopped and shook his head again. "I remember in eighth grade, I had your mom for a teacher. I had gone outside to wait for the bus, but one had broken down and was late. Many kids had to call their parents to pick them up because it would be late before they could get a bus back to the school to take us home. I sat out there and watched all these kids get picked up by their moms. Smiling faces. Hugs. Some even brought a snack with them. I knew my dad was out on the water, and I couldn't get ahold of Miss Sally, the neighbor who would've come, so I walked back inside. Your mom saw me and had me wait in her room." He snorted. "The fact that I wasn't doing very good in her class probably had something to do with it, too. She said I could finish some work, and I knew it would help my grade."

While he spoke, Ivy thought back to middle school. She loved having her mom as a teacher and never minded that they were in the same school together. And usually, she had activities after school while her mom finished her work. Afterward, she'd go to her mom's room until they came home. And even though it was a memory long forgotten, she remembered one day going in and seeing Andy sitting at one of the desks. Why she remembered that, she wasn't sure, but she remained quiet so he could share his side of the story.

"You came bouncing in, happy and smiling, and I remember looking over and seeing how your mom gave you a huge hug, kissed the top of your head, and asked how your practice had gone. I think it was chorus or band... something musical."

"Chorus," she breathed softly.

His top teeth dug into his bottom lip as he nodded, and she battled the desire to reach over and smooth the abraded flesh with her finger.

He continued. "I can't explain why, considering I'd just been watching a bunch of kids get picked up by their moms, but seeing you and your mother together, it was like something snapped inside me."

He winced, and Ivy's gut clenched at the sight. She

longed to offer him comfort but felt his story had just begun and wanted him to tell it his way and in his time.

He hesitated as he stared across the room for a moment toward the family pictures on the mantel, then jerked his gaze to her, and blurted, "My mom left when I was seven years old and never came back. Aaron was only two."

At that simple statement, Ivy gasped. It didn't matter that she'd already heard the information from her mom. Just hearing it from his lips and seeing the expression on his face, she felt agony to her very core. A mother walking away from her small children was unfathomable to Ivy.

"I hadn't really thought about it until years later, but even before Aaron was born, Mom was never involved with me." He shrugged. "Somehow, though, we're accustomed to the family we're born into and assume that's how everyone's family is. I guess when I was five and started kindergarten was the first time I really saw how different other moms were. But Aaron had some medical issues when he was born because he was premature. He needed special treatments, then physical therapy and speech therapy. I guess it was more than what Mom felt she could handle. Dad tried to placate her, but one day she told him she just couldn't take it anymore. One Saturday morning before Aaron and I got up, she packed a bag, told Pop she was done, and left."

Once again, Ivy felt gut punched. The lovely dinner that she'd enjoyed threatened to reappear. As her gaze roved over Andy's face after hearing his matter-of-fact telling of his story, she could see that even though he accepted his mom's actions, they'd marked him deeply. "Andy, I am so sorry that happened to you."

His lips curled slightly at her words. His shoulders hefted, but she wondered if the shrug was an attempt not to deflect the emotion. "Our neighbor stepped in and did a lot of things for us. My dad is the greatest man in the world. He worked all day but managed to keep up with Aaron's therapies in the evening and anything else needed. We had help—my grandparents pitched in, a couple of uncles and aunts, and our neighbors. And honest to God, I don't remember a lot about elementary school. I know I missed Mom... rather, I missed the idea of not having a good mom. But it wasn't until I started maturing as a teenager that her abandonment really dug in. Hormones. Puberty. Questioning myself. Questioning my family. Questioning adults in general. All of that started swirling by the time I was in eighth grade, and anger bubbled just under the surface."

"I don't remember you being a troubled student."

He shook his head. "I kept a lid on it. I didn't take any time to analyze it. Hell, what thirteen-year-old boy does?"

"Why do I get the feeling this is about to tie into the day you were in my mom's classroom?"

He grimaced again and shook his head. "Because this is where my stupidity grew by leaps and bounds and somehow centered on you. I sat there with no one able to come to pick me up, no mom to greet me at the end of the day, and suddenly, you and your mom were in front of me. You two were the only ones in the world for a few minutes. Love. Affection. Things I couldn't even describe at that time, but looking back, it was nothing more than a beautiful bond between a mom and her child. But something inside me just cracked. I think it was right after that, Pop and I were at the drugstore, having to get some calamine lotion because Aaron had gotten into poison ivy. I stood there and looked at the words on the box, and your name came to mind. I chuckled, thinking what a funny nickname it would be just to be mean. Christ, I was such a dick."

Ivy recalled all the times she'd heard him call her "Poison Ivy" and how angry it made her. But she'd simply narrow her eyes and cast a glare in his direction or pretend she hadn't noticed. She knew whatever he felt for her wasn't from a misguided attempt to flirt but from a dislike she would never understand. And at that age, she was determined she didn't care to understand. But now, years later, when the taunts carried no residual barbs, she found that seeing the hurt child who became an angry teenager made her ache for him, not at the verbal lashes he'd delivered.

He shifted his large frame again, this time moving closer. His gaze bore straight into her eyes. "In case you're wondering if it was easy to come to my realization, it wasn't. While I didn't pick on other kids, I struggled with some female teachers. Especially the ones who had a sharper way of speaking. I barely managed to keep from lashing out at them, too."

"You heard your mother in their voices, didn't you?"

"Yeah, I guess I did. I sure as hell didn't realize that as a teenager, but she always had a demanding way about her. I reckon I projected that onto some of the female teachers. Believe it or not, I actually had a coach jump down my throat about it more than once."

"You seem so self-aware now," she said, leaning a little closer toward him. "I'm curious how that came about."

He barked out a laugh, but she knew the sound didn't come from anything amusing.

"That happened in the military. I had a female Chief Petty Officer who hit my trigger, but my military discipline won the day and kept me from getting booted out. She got in my face, though, and told me, "If you've got fucking mommy issues, figure them out, or your ass is out of *my* Navy." He chuckled ruefully at the memory.

"Oh..." Ivy said, her brows lifting to her hairline. "I'm glad she gave you another chance."

"Hell, me too! She could have booted me down in rank or booted me out."

"What did you do?"

He offered a nonchalant shrug, but she could see the memory still haunted him. "I was so angry. At her. Mostly at me. I called my dad. I guess I thought he'd be sympathetic, but he nailed my ass to the wall. Told me that despite Mom leaving, I was a better man than mouthing off to someone. Told me that, if nothing else, *he* taught me better than to behave that way. I walked away from his phone call, pissed as hell, but it slowly sank in. As much as I felt like a pussy, they were right. I had fucking issues."

She chewed on her bottom lip, desperate to ask him more and not just because she was curious.

But now that he was forthcoming with his tale, he seemed willing to share it all. "One of the things the military provides is counseling. I felt like a complete loser when I went, but I told myself I had no choice. I guess, in reality, I didn't."

"I'm assuming it helped."

He huffed. "Yeah. Overall, yeah. I didn't really get into talking about my issues, but mostly, it helped me identify that my anger at my mom's indifference did shadow my behavior. I didn't go to military counseling. To be honest, I didn't think they'd understand or care. Let's face it... the military is all about duty and service, which works for them, but it's not so great if you have an individual need. I found a counselor in the town where the base was located, and we hit it off. I only went for a couple of months. Mostly, he just let me talk. And as dumb as it sounds, that seemed to be what I needed."

"A nonjudgmental place to unburden."

He grinned, his body relaxing as some earlier tensions seemed to leave. "Oh yeah. Anyway, I'm dragging my story out a lot longer than I meant to. You probably don't care about all this shit."

She leaned forward, finally giving in to the urge to place her hand on his. "Please. Take your time. I want to hear."

He held her gaze for a long moment, and she wondered if he was finished. But then he squeezed her hand and continued.

"Anyway, we unpacked most of the shit that was in my head. He helped me see how my mom's attitude and abandonment had shaped me as a young man. And then, essentially, I had to decide whether I was going to keep letting her control me or if I was going to forge my own path and become the man who my father would've wanted. There was no doubt. No question. I wanted to be like my dad and move forward in life. Be the kind of person he was. Be a decent man, a good brother, a good son. So I let her go."

"I can't imagine that was easy."

He scoffed. "To be honest? At first, it was fucking painful. I really hated talking about her. I hated giving her more headspace. But then, I realized I'd been giving her headspace all those years. After a while, it was easier and easier to let go of her."

She breathed easier when she heard his confession. The pent-up frustrations she'd had with him as a teenager dissipated like the fog lifting from over the Bay once the sun rose. "Thank you," she whispered, her gaze pinned on him.

"Ivy... I don't..." Clearing his throat, he shifted closer. "Shit, my thoughts are all over the place."

"I'm not going anywhere. Take your time."

He smiled, but tension tightened his shoulders and jaw again. "I'm not going to lie and tell you that I thought about you since high school."

His honesty brought a smile that turned into a chuckle. "Aw, I'm heartbroken," she teased.

"Smart-ass," he groused, his demeanor more lighthearted. "But something happened when I saw you on the bridge. I had no idea who you were. I hadn't seen you in twelve years. But seeing you give everything you had to help a child you didn't know and try to keep a man from making his mistakes worse, I was... shit... fuckin' ensnared while watching you. I had you in my sights with the binoculars, and at first, I was struck by your beauty. Then with your voice coming over the police radio, I was captivated. Then you went over the edge. Christ, I would have jumped in for anyone, but I knew I had to go for the woman who was still giving everything she had. From that moment on, I wanted to get to know you. I wanted to spend time with you. I couldn't think about anything or anyone else."

His impassioned words delved deep inside, making it hard to breathe.

"And when I realized it was you... aw, fuck. I was both thrilled that I knew you and fuckin' horrified that you'd hate me because of our past."

"I think *hate* is way too strong of a word, considering how long ago high school was." She sighed. "Anyway, I never really hated you, Andy. Frustrated. Irritated. But you know, I never saw you pick on someone weaker than yourself. You were nice to other kids, especially those who seemed to struggle."

"I suppose being Aaron's brother and my father's son, I'd learned something good. And honestly, you always seemed to blow off my taunts." He leaned back against the cushions, but his hand continued to hold hers. "Jesus, I am so sorry. If I could take back all the fucked-up shit I used to say, I would do so in a heartbeat. It was mean. It was wrong. And I wouldn't blame you if you kicked me out right now and never wanted to see me again."

Every preconceived notion she'd ever had about Andy faded, replaced with awe and admiration. "And the cute teenager became a gorgeous man," she whispered.

He blinked, his chin jerking slightly. "What?"

Her cheeks burned, suffused with blush. "Just something I thought of when I realized who you were." She choked back a snort. "Let's face it... you were a really cute high schooler. And you've grown into a really good-looking man. But someone who owns up to past mistakes and even apologizes... well, you've shot straight to gorgeous."

He threw his head back and laughed.

15

Andy couldn't believe what he was hearing. Hell, he couldn't believe he sat in Ivy Watkins's living room years after being a teenage jerk. Her forgiveness washed over him, freeing the ache in his chest. And the way she stared at him made him feel like he had a chance. A chance to take her out. A chance to learn more about her. A chance to get to know the adult version of her. A chance to discover how she'd found the bravery inside to go up against a stranger on the bridge.

And the way her gaze kept dropping to his lips, he wondered if he'd get a chance to kiss her. That thought bolted through him, and his fingers twitched as they held hers. She looked down at the slight movement, and the moment was gone. Disappointment and relief hit him at the same time.

Clearing his throat, he said, "Well, that's it, I guess."

"That's it?" Her chin lifted, and her gaze hit him once again.

"Um... well, I apologized. And tried to explain my

stupid adolescent attitude that you bore the brunt of. Um..." He suddenly felt lost when he realized he had no idea what was supposed to happen now. He couldn't figure out where his confidence fled to in the presence of Ivy. Wincing, he could only imagine how ridiculous he must look as he tried to figure out what to say.

"Well, I was kind of hoping that the apology and explanation weren't going to be the end," she said, her eyes searching his.

Her words planted a seed of hope in his chest, but he wasn't about to make any assumptions. So it was soon replaced with uncertainty. He waited to see what else she would say.

Her head bowed as her gaze flickered at their still-connected hands. "When you asked me to dinner, I knew it was so we could talk about the past. There was a lot to unpack, so to speak." Her tongue darted out, licking her bottom lip, snagging his attention.

"Adolescence was a long time ago, and for me to hold on to the past no longer felt like a good thing to do. You coming here tonight and telling me your situation and reasons was really brave."

Shaking his head quickly, he refuted her words. "Ivy, if anyone was brave, it was you."

She hesitated again, and his breath halted as he waited to see what she would say next.

"Do you think that maybe we could get to know each other more as we are now?"

Seeing doubt move over Ivy's face and how she shifted back ever so slightly away from him, he squeezed her fingers, drawing her gaze back to his. "I would love nothing more than to see you again. How about dinner out next time?"

She smiled and nodded. "Yeah. That would be lovely."

"Don't get me wrong. This was wonderful. The fact that you invited me here and opened your home so we could have a private discussion is more than I could've ever hoped for. But I would love to have the chance to take you out." He reached over and gently tapped her cast. "When do you go back to the doctor?"

"I have an appointment with the surgeon in a week. They'll put me in a removable brace if all looks good."

"And you can go back to work full time?"

"He said I could have up to two weeks off, more if I needed. But I don't want to wait that long. I've only been at the job for a few weeks, and I don't feel right taking that much time off if I don't need to. The pain is minimal, and I only take over-the-counter medicine when needed. I don't have to do any lifting— just get used to going slower using the computer keyboard and mouse. I'm going in for half days for a while."

"I've got an idea. The American Legion is hosting a winter dinner and dance fundraiser this weekend. I was going to stop by to show my support, but I wasn't going to stay very long. Would you like to come with me? You can meet so many people from the area. Hell, some of them you'd probably remember from high school."

"Are you telling me you didn't already have a date?"

He snorted. He couldn't remember the last time he'd had a real date. He hadn't met a woman he'd wanted to spend more than a night with, and to be honest, those one-nighters had definitely slowed since he'd left his twenties behind. The idea of taking someone to the fundraiser dinner hadn't occurred to him—not until Ivy. "No, I didn't."

"Well, good, because I wouldn't want to break the hearts of any jealous Andy-girlfriend-wannabes."

He rolled his eyes. "I'm afraid my dating life isn't very exciting. I go out some, but not nearly as much as I used to. I haven't had a relationship that lasted more than a month or so. And even those should've ended before they did."

Her brows lowered as her unasked question hung in the air.

Hoping he didn't sound like an ass, he rushed, "I only say that because as soon as I knew they weren't long-term relationship material, there wasn't any reason to drag it on."

"Do you think your mother's problems with marriage and motherhood affected your dating as well?"

Her question surprised him. Not because he hadn't thought of it himself but because she'd refused to dance around the topic. He remembered that about her from school. Inquisitive. Always wanting to learn things. He could still see her bent over the science lab counter as she dissected the frog in their biology class. Now, he suddenly felt sorry for the dead frog who had no secrets left. Or maybe he admired the frog because it had her undivided attention. Jerking slightly at the turn of his thoughts, he nodded, shifting a little closer to the sofa. He couldn't deny that her instincts were right.

"I think I'd be foolish not to consider that the nonrelationship I had with my mother affected more than just my adolescence." As soon as the words left his mouth, he was slammed with another thought, this time shooting fear through him. He rushed to add, "I don't want you to think I can't commit. I think I successfully faced those devils a long time ago. But once I realized there was no staying power with a woman, I didn't have it in me to keep trying to make something work that wasn't right to begin with."

He couldn't figure out why he continued to talk, babble, and explain to her. Hell, he gave her more about his background and thoughts than anyone else in his life other than his dad, Aaron, and his counselor. But something about Ivy made him trust that she would take the parts of him from his past and not hold them against him.

She offered an enthusiastic grin, and his heart pounded at the sight. A sight he hoped he had the opportunity to see a lot more often.

"Andy, I would love to go."

A strange sensation hit him in the chest, and he couldn't remember the last time he'd felt this way. Certainly not when picking up a woman in a bar. Not even back in high school, when girls chased him as soon as he hit his growth spurt in ninth grade. And not when in the Navy and women hung around the bars thinking that banging a serviceman gave them some kind of status. No... this sensation came from the anxiety of asking someone he respected to spend more time with him in public and wondering if she would agree or shoot him down. Her ready acquiescence sent his heart into overdrive, and a wide smile slid across his face.

"I'm honored, Ivy. Really. I'll check with one of my coworkers who will be going with his wife to find out any details."

"Like what I should wear, I hope?"

"Yeah, I'll find out. But it's not fancy."

"You said it was a fundraiser?"

"Yeah. The American Legion hosts it, but anyone in the area can buy tickets. We use the money for the sports programs and other activities we support in the community."

"I think that's wonderful," she said, and once again, her praise made him want to howl with excitement that Ivy Watkins held him in esteem.

The old clock on the mantel chimed, and he glanced over, stunned at the time. His lips curving downward, he sighed. "I hate to leave, but it's much later than I realized, and I've got an early shift in the morning."

Her expression fell, and he was thankful she seemed to hate the idea of their evening ending as much as he did.

"Thank you so much for bringing dinner over, Andy. And you're right about the Italian restaurant. Their food was amazing."

"Then we'll go in and eat sometime soon," he offered, already calculating when he could take her. Standing, he reluctantly started to let go of her hand, but she quickly jumped to her feet as well, holding fast to his fingers. He glanced at her, but she seemed unaware that her actions kept them connected. It was perfectly natural to her. And once again, a strange shifting in his chest occurred.

She walked him to the door but made no move to open it as they stood in front of each other, their gazes locked and their fingers still entwined. There was a shy but hopeful expression on her face, and he prayed he was reading her right. When her gaze dropped to his mouth, he leaned forward slowly, giving her plenty of time to put distance between them or to say no. But instead, she placed her cast on his shoulder and lifted to her toes.

With their mouths now a whisper apart, he said, "I'd like to kiss you."

Her lips curved, and her breath wisped across his cheeks. "I'd like to be kissed by you."

He loosened his fingers from hers so that both hands could slide to her waist and offer steadiness. Bending, he eliminated the minuscule distance between them, barely touching his mouth to hers. The attempt to keep the kiss light backfired when their lips touched, and a tiny moan slipped from her. The slight sound hit his ears like a thunderbolt, and he angled his head to deepen the kiss.

Her soft, pliable lips molded to his, and she opened her mouth, welcoming his eager tongue. Sweeping his tongue over hers, he reveled in the sensations rocketing through his brain. The taste of coffee and tiramisu. The press of her hand as it slid from his chest up to his shoulder. He pulled her closer and now felt her soft curves. The feel of her tongue as it glided over his. The sound of another moan. The sight of her eyelids fluttering before she closed them tightly. The light sting of her fingernails as they dragged along the skin at the back of his neck.

Everything about this woman called to him. Her beauty. Her kindness. Her bravery. And right now, the way her body responded to him.

No more thoughts moved through him as he gave himself over to the physical sensations of their kiss. He slid his hands to her back, one low, where his fingers danced along the top of her ass, and the other moved higher, pressing between her shoulder blades. With their bodies aligned, his cock swelled. He fought the desire to press his hips into hers to seek relief.

But somehow, in the middle of their desperate kiss, she'd straddled one of his legs, and he felt her hot core pressing on his jeans-clad thigh.

He knew the nerves firing between their kiss and his cock were on overload, and if her actions were understood, the same was happening with her mouth and core. The desire to strip them both and plunge deep inside her sex made him pull back regretfully, sucking deep breaths into his oxygen-deprived lungs.

She'd leaned forward with her eyes tightly closed, her lips still seeking his, until with a furrowed brow, she blinked her eyes open. Flaming red blush hit her cheeks as she settled her heels back to the floor and started to push away.

He kept his arms in place, not willing to let her step back, especially if her reaction was due to embarrassment. Her hair fell around her shoulders, her lips slightly swollen, and her chin was pink from where his beard had rubbed. "Christ, you're beautiful," he said, still trying to catch his breath.

Her tongue slipped out to moisten her lips before she pressed them together. With her still held tight, he added, "I'm only stopping the kiss because if I don't, I'm liable to take this way further tonight than you deserve."

She tilted her head slightly to the side. "I'm not sure if you're telling the truth and being honorable or if you're telling me a line because you think that will make me feel better."

He pulled her closer, but their bodies were already flush from knees to chest. Dipping his head again, he smiled. "You will only get the truth from me, Ivy Watkins. You are someone I want to spend time with, and I want to do this right with you."

He kissed her lightly this time, forcing his hands to loosen their hold. "I'll call you as soon as I know more about the fundraiser."

"Okay," she whispered with a smile as she stepped over to the door and opened it.

With a final good night, he walked out, his heart light with how the evening went while his inner battle raged to turn, head back in, and kiss her until the sun came up.

16

The cold air whipped past Andy's face as their vessel moved over the Bay. With Bryce at the wheel, they headed to the oyster beds about ten miles north of Baytown.

Jose's brother was an oyster fisherman who worked for Chesapeake Bay Seafood Company, and he'd called in a sighting the VMP wanted to check out. Hustling so they didn't waste time, Bryce pushed the vessel faster than their normal patrol speed.

Slowing as they neared, they drifted in closer to where several men were standing in chest-high water near their flat-bottomed boats. Seeing Jose's brother, he grinned at their similarities. Only a year or so apart, they could pass for twins.

Andy called out, "Hey, Jimmy!"

Jimmy waved at Andy, then tossed a two-fingered salute toward Jose, who'd turned the wheel over to Bryce. Jose approached Andy, closer to the oyster boat.

"What happened, bro?" Jose asked.

"We were out here when a fuckin' silver speedboat came blasting by. I know there ain't no law against it, but it was fucking dangerous."

"Can you tell us anything about them? Boat? Driver? Where they came from? Which direction were they going?" Andy bit out.

If the rapid-fire questions surprised Jimmy, he didn't show it. Instead, he nodded and said, "They came from the Parker Inlet area. Can't swear they left out from there, but that's where we first spied them. They must not have been expecting us to be right here because they came damn close before jerking out toward the Bay's center. They were hauling ass."

The fisherman next to him nodded. "Two men. Dark coats and knit caps. Can't tell you anything else 'cause they were covered up. Don't know if it was because of the temperature or not to be seen, but that was all I got."

"Don't suppose you had your phone out calling Mom and got a picture, did you?" Jose asked jokingly.

Jimmy scowled. "Fuck, man, if I had been, Mom woulda heard me cussin' a blue streak."

Andy's hands landed on his hips as his head dropped and shook with laughter. It was a fucked-up situation, but having met Jose and Jimmy's mom, he knew she would have been in the front row of their church, praying for her two sons.

After thanking the fishermen, Jose returned to the wheelhouse and guided them toward Parker Inlet. Andy and Bryce carefully scanned the area, paying attention to each lot that backed up to the water, especially those with personal docks. But they didn't find anything untoward or suspicious.

Radioing in their lack of findings, he looked at Bryce. "Do you think it would be worth checking up on each of the homeowners in this area? Especially if any of them have seen a silver speedboat they haven't recognized."

Bryce nodded. "Good idea. Bring it up to Ryan. If he's willing for us to partner with the sheriff's department, that might just be a way to cut through some of our searches and actually find what we're looking for."

"Of course, we're assuming that the silver speedboat from today is the same as the one from the other day's incident and that it's gang members running drugs and guns. That's a pretty big leap to make."

"Yeah, and we could be totally wrong. But then, on the other hand, can we afford to ignore any leads at this point?"

Grimacing, he knew Bryce was right. While they had little to go on and no way to catch a speedboat once it got out into the Bay, he still wanted to shut down the movement of gangs in their area. With a hand signal toward Jose in the wheelhouse, they turned and headed back out of the inlet. Once docked at the station, he walked inside to talk to Ryan, who agreed it was a good plan and said he'd bring it up to Colt.

Walking out of Ryan's office, he stopped and turned. "I've got one other thing, Captain. Believe it or not, I have a date for the AL fundraiser tomorrow night. I know it's not super fancy, but do you happen to know what Judith is going to wear?"

Ryan's brows lifted, and it was all Andy could do to keep from squirming. But at least Ryan didn't make fun of him. Instead, he grabbed his phone and pressed a number. "Judith? Andy wants to know what you're wearing tomorrow night. He's got a date, and he told her he'd find out what most of the women are wearing."

"A date?" Judith's voice came through the phone.

"That's what he said."

"Well, he certainly waited until the last minute to let her get ready! Anyway, tell him he's in luck. The men will be in suits or just slacks, shirts, and tie. And the women will just be wearing casual dresses or skirts."

"Okay. Thanks, babe. Love you."

Judith laughed. "Love you too, sweetheart. And tell Andy I can't wait to meet his date."

Ryan disconnected and grinned over his desk toward Andy. "You got that?"

"Yeah, yeah, I got that. Thanks, boss."

Walking back outside since he was spending the afternoon on boat maintenance, he texted Ivy. It had only been a day since he'd seen her, but they had already texted several times. *Hell, I didn't do this in high school!* Thinking about high school had him wince, and he shook his head, glad she'd accepted his invitation. His phone vibrated, and he looked down to read her text.

Good. I can do casual. Can't wait.

With a grin, he shoved his phone in his pocket and headed down the dock.

Ivy glanced toward the driver's side of the SUV where Andy sat, her mind a muddled mess. At the age of thirty, she thought the idea of butterflies on a date had long since passed. But seeing him in navy pants and a pale blue shirt with a matching tie, she tried to slow her breathing so he wouldn't notice her hyperventilating. They certainly hadn't coordinated outfits, but her blue dress, a deeper color than his shirt, made them look very much *together*. She'd paired her dress with black heels and a black coat to ward off the chill.

She couldn't understand why nerves were zipping through her. She'd certainly been to events over the years, especially formal evenings for the engineering company she used to work for. And it wasn't that she wouldn't know anyone at the fundraiser, considering she was slowly meeting a few people in town.

No, my nerves come from my date. She glanced to the side again as he pulled into the parking lot of the community college. It was the only facility in the area that could hold such a large gathering. Before she knew it, he had taken her hand, and they hustled through the cold to the doors and entered the building. Once inside, she was divested of her coat, smiling to see Andy hand it to the young man at the coat check and immediately tuck the ticket into his pocket.

Looking around, she was impressed. The room was decorated with greenery and poinsettias, signaling the upcoming holidays. Laughter and chatter filled the room as people greeted friends. On one side, the caterers put the final touches on the buffet, and in the center, couples danced as a band played on the stage.

"Are you okay?" he asked, leaning close as his hand held hers.

She nodded and offered a smile. "I'm fine. I feel a little nervous in unfamiliar settings, but I recognize a few people already."

Grinning, he jiggled their hands slightly, and she smiled in return.

"Don't worry. It won't be long before you consider many of these people your friends too."

She leaned her head back and stared at him for a moment, studying the angles of his face and the thick, trimmed beard that bracketed his smile. It was almost hard to imagine him as the teenager she had known. But in truth, she'd always been fascinated with his dark eyes, and right now, staring into them again, she was just as mesmerized. Nodding, she dragged her gaze away from his face. "Well, okay. I'll let you lead the way."

He was right, and soon she was saying hello to some of the people she'd already met, and some she remembered their names from high school. Tori and Mitch Evans, Grant and Jillian Wilder, Callan and Sophie Ward, and Zac and Maddie Hamilton. The MacFarlane siblings—Katelyn, Aiden, and Brogan MacFarlane—and their spouses. Most had been juniors or seniors when she was only in eighth grade. But she'd been awestruck then and was surprised to realize they'd returned to Baytown as adults and were all still friends.

"I remember your mother was my eighth-grade English teacher," Mitch said, drawing the attention of the others, and they soon joined in. Everyone loved having her mother as a teacher, which didn't surprise her. They also remembered her father since many had attended the Baytown Elementary School.

"Are they still around?" Jillian asked. "I haven't seen them at the coffee shop in a long time."

"They're actually in North Carolina right now. My grandmother has dementia, and they're settling her into a memory care facility. And then they're going to have to take care of her house. I'm staying at their place here until they return, and then I'll look for something."

She met more spouses, but Zac's wife pulled her to the side while Andy chatted with the others.

"I know this is the wrong time," Maddy said, her eyes full of concern. "But if you have any trouble processing what happened on the bridge, please call. I'm a counselor in town. I know what you did was amazingly brave, but all trauma can come back to hit us at a weird time."

Ivy smiled and reached out to take Maddy's hand in hers. "Thank you. The nurse at the hospital said the same thing to me. I seem okay now, but if I need you, I promise I'll call."

At that, Maddy handed her a business card from her purse and then pulled her in for a hug. Ivy felt her body relax at the acceptance she'd received.

Eventually, everyone moved toward the food lines, and she found herself in front of Andy with his hand on her shoulder. He leaned down and said, "I don't want you to carry anything too heavy. If you pick out the food you want, I can carry your plate."

She looked over her shoulder and smiled at his offer.

"I'll be fine. I can balance the plate on my wrist, but if I decide on too many desserts, I'll let you carry those."

He laughed, and his hand squeezed her shoulder. Such a simple gesture was casually offered yet taken to heart.

After finding a table, Andy introduced her to another couple, Belle and Hunter Simms. She remembered Belle as having only been two years older when they were in high school. And her husband worked for the sheriff's department.

"It's so lovely for you to move back," Belle said, smiling shyly. "I've always lived here. Never left. By the way, I heard what you said about your grandmother. I'm a nurse at the local nursing home here. We don't have a specialized memory care unit, but we do have a number of patients with dementia. It's so hard for them and the families."

"I know my parents are struggling with everything they're having to go through."

"Did they ever consider having her come here to live?"

"I don't think so. At least not right now. While my grandmother has dementia, she still recognizes some people. And she has friends from her church in North Carolina who visit. At some point, they might be able to move her closer here."

"Well, if you ever need any assistance, let me know."

Offering her heartfelt thanks, she smiled, now understanding what Andy meant when he said she'd soon have a lot of new friends. Looking at the other side, she spied Andy and Hunter with their heads together, deep in conversation. Turning back to Belle, she lifted her brow.

"Oh, I'm sure those two are talking work. The sheriff's department works closely with the marine police," Belle explained. Clearing her throat loudly, Hunter and Andy turned, and both had the good sense to appear contrite. Hunter bent and kissed his wife, whispering an apology.

As Andy slid into his seat, he reached for her hand. "I'm sorry. I never meant to ignore you."

She laughed and leaned into his shoulder. "Believe me, I didn't feel ignored. I've enjoyed having a chance to meet so many people."

Another group came to their table to sit, and she met his coworkers and their wives. Joseph and Shiloh, Callan and Sophie, Jared and Billie, and Ryan and Judith. The laughter abounded as she heard stories and was drawn into conversations. By the time they'd finished, Andy leaned in and said, "I need to talk to Ryan for a moment. Is that all right?"

"Of course," she agreed readily. As she watched him step to the side, Ryan and Hunter joined him.

"Ivy?"

Hearing her name, she turned to see the deputy that had taken her statement in the hospital walk over. Standing, she smiled and shook his extended hand. "Hello, Deputy Jenkins."

"It's Josh. Good to see you, too. How are you?" He looked down at her wrist. Several people moved past them in a crowd, and he drew her toward the middle of the room.

"I'm much better, thank you."

"I went by the hospital the day I thought you were being discharged, but they said you'd already left. I was sorry to have missed you."

She recalled Andy showing up and how she'd initially thought it was the deputy coming. Her surprise at realizing it was the officer who'd rescued her and what Andy was now becoming caused a smile to cross her face. Suddenly, a gentle pull on her hand brought her attention back to the deputy standing in front of her.

Josh met her smile with one of his own. "Let's dance."

"Oh, well, I—" She looked around but didn't see Andy. Seeing no reason to be rude, she maintained a distance between their bodies but placed her hand on his shoulder.

"I saw you come in with Andy Bergstrom."

"Yes. We knew each other in high school—"

"Oh," he said, his eyes widening. "Good. I thought maybe you were together."

Heat infused her face as she tried to think of what to say. She and Andy weren't *together*, or at least nothing had been said that officially defined what they were. *Jesus, we just shared one kiss. I'm sure, for him, that hardly qualifies us as a couple.* She wished the last thought didn't cause her heart to sink.

"I remember you now from Baytown High. You were a couple of years behind me. A real brainiac. What do you do now?"

She sighed at the non-endearing term. "I'm an engineer."

"No shit? Smart but boring, right?"

She blinked, her feet jerking to a halt. "Excuse me?"

"You know… smart girls in those kinds of brainy jobs. Pretty boring."

"Are you referring to the job or me?" she asked, her eyes narrowing.

"Both, I guess." He laughed. "Anyway, enough about that, what do you say about going out on the water with me sometime? I've got a boat and go fishing just about every weekend."

Blinking furiously, she shook her head as she tried to come up with a polite refusal in the face of his rudeness. "I… I…"

"Her fishing dates will be with me."

Josh jerked, and she looked over to see a tight-jawed Andy standing next to them. He reached out, and with no hesitation, she immediately placed her hand in his, feeling the tingle from his touch. As she looked into his now almost black eyes that pinned Josh to the spot before they turned toward her and warmed, an unbidden smile curved her lips.

17

Andy knew he shouldn't have stepped away from Ivy but seeing her surrounded by good women who he knew would become her good friends, he'd taken the opportunity to speak to a couple of the other law enforcement leaders who were also a part of the American Legion. *I shouldn't have mixed business with pleasure!*

When he turned around and spied Josh's hands on Ivy as they danced, white-hot jealousy raced through him. And for a second, he was hit with doubt as his old feelings roared back. Josh was a couple of years ahead of them in high school but had belonged to the more elite crowd. His dad had owned a string of gas stations up and down the Eastern Shore. Even when times were hard, people needed gasoline, so the Jenkins family always had money. Josh had had the air of someone who was better than others, and now with a badge, it seemed he maintained that same opinion.

For a second, the old insecurity reared its ugly head. *Why would Ivy Watkins want to be with me?* But he quickly pulled his head out of his ass as he saw her use her casted wrist to push slightly against Josh's shoulder to create space between them.

Battling the urge to knock into people as he pushed through the crowd heedlessly, he made it to their side just in time to hear Josh insult her and then invite her to go fishing. From the look on her face, Ivy was trying to find a polite way to decline. Pissed that Josh had insulted her and then was trying to set up a date with her made red flash across Andy's vision.

He held out his hand to her as he approached. "Her fishing dates will be with me." It was a bold statement he wasn't sure she'd back up. They'd only shared one kiss. Okay... one incredible kiss that had him rethinking everything he'd ever thought about a kiss being the precursor to sex and not an entity of its own. But he'd seen it in her heavy-lidded eyes that the kiss had affected her as well. But now? What would be her response to his caveman pissing contest?

The relief spreading across Ivy's face as she turned and smiled at him caused him to battle the heavy sigh of relief that wanted to rush out. And when she placed her hand in his, easily allowing him to draw her away from Josh, it felt as though long-lost parts of him clicked together again.

Determined to maintain a professional facade, he wrapped his arm around Ivy and looked at Josh. "Thanks for keeping my beautiful date company while I had some business to attend to, but I've got it from here." Without giving Josh a chance to reply, he turned and, with Ivy tucked under his arm, walked toward the bar.

"Now I remember," Josh called out, drawing their attention back to him. "You used to call her Poison Ivy." Josh cackled as though the memory was hilarious.

Andy felt Ivy's body stiffen next to him. Turning, he stalked over, barely aware of her arm pulling him back and his friends moving forward.

Not stopping until he was in Josh's space, he growled, "I was a punk-ass prick in high school when I said that. Not an excuse, but that was then. I sure as hell know it and have apologized. And I'm grateful to my very bones that Ivy had the grace to accept that apology. But to bring that up as an adult? What's your excuse for being a punk-ass prick now, Josh?"

Turning around, he was aware his friends had closed rank, probably to keep him from ruining his career by doing something like putting his fist into Josh's face. He didn't stop until he'd wrapped his arm around Ivy's shoulders again.

"Sorry…" Josh called out behind them, but Andy didn't turn around. Instead, he kept Ivy tight against his side as they walked to the bar.

After ordering two glasses of wine, they moved through their groups of friends. More introductions were made, more congratulations were sent her way, and she received offers for getting together from many of the women. He pushed Josh out of his mind, enjoying the evening with the beautiful woman on his arm.

When Ivy excused herself with several others to go to the ladies' room, Callan and Joseph closed ranks.

"Josh is a prick. Always been," Joseph commented, shaking his head.

"I thought you handled that well, man," Callan added.

Andy offered a rueful chuckle. "I wanted to rearrange his face." He sighed heavily. "But then, honestly, it was my fault. I should have never walked away to talk about business and left Ivy alone. Hell, I did it twice tonight. Shit. She's probably in the ladies' room telling the others what a fucked-up date I am."

"You didn't leave her alone. You left her with friends, and she was having a good time chatting. I saw Josh walk right up and pull her away. She looked surprised," Callan added.

"And I don't know if you noticed it, but she looked fuckin' happy when you showed up." Joseph laughed.

He smiled, but on the inside wanted to throw his arms up and yell with testosterone-infused pride. *The beautiful, smart, sweet girl wants to be with me!* Instead, he simply offered his friends a chin lift, then made sure he waited on her at the end of the hall when she and the other women emerged.

Offering his bent elbow, he winked at her. "Wanna dance with an old sailor?" If he'd had any doubts that she was glad to be with him that night, the smile on her face erased them.

"I can't think of anything I'd rather do more than dance with you," she said, her face beaming. As one hand slid around her waist with his fingers splayed over her lower back and the other hand gently pressing between her shoulder blades, she made no attempt to push him away as she had with Josh. Instead, she wrapped her good hand around his neck, and her injured hand rested softly on his shoulder. And then she pressed in tightly.

And the testosterone-infused pride roared to life again. They moved in slow circles, and then she rested her cheek against his chest. Once again, the pieces he didn't even know were missing clicked into place.

"I haven't told you how beautiful you are," he whispered against her hair.

"You did," she refuted. "When I opened the door, and you first saw me tonight, you told me I looked beautiful."

"That was just about your appearance, which, in case you didn't know, took my breath away."

She leaned back, and he grinned as a crinkle of confusion settled between her brows.

"This is about *all* of you, Ivy. Not just how beautiful you are to look at any time, or tonight in that dress, but all of you."

She pressed her lips together as though to keep from smiling, but the crinkle between her brow remained.

"I'm not as eloquent as some men would be. But I think everything about you, especially who you are inside, is beautiful."

She lost the battle, and her lips curved into a wide smile. "I don't think I've ever been given such a sweet compliment by a man before."

"Then I'm honored to be the first."

He pulled her back to his chest, and they continued to sway to the music. He blocked out all other thoughts and all other people as this woman in his arms filled his senses.

By the time they'd said their goodbyes and drove back to her place, it was late. At her door, his heart pounded as he waited to see her safely in, but he didn't want the night to end. She turned and looked up at him, her lips curving. "Would you like to come in?"

Blowing out his held breath, he grinned. "You don't mind?"

"I wouldn't have asked if I didn't want you to."

She opened the door, and he eagerly followed her inside. After she tossed her purse onto the dining room table, he walked behind her to assist with taking off her coat. Gently sliding it over her cast, he hung it on the coat-tree. His jacket quickly joined hers.

"A woman who knows what she wants. But then, you've always been that, haven't you?" He moved closer, and she leaned her head back to keep her eyes on him, their sparkle drawing him in.

"Always."

He wrapped his arms around her and held her close. They began moving slowly to the music playing only in their minds. After a moment, she leaned back to hold his gaze again, and this time, he bent to take her lips.

It was only the second time they'd kissed, but their mouths molded together as their heads angled to make the most of their contact. So perfectly in sync, it was as though they'd practiced this maneuver for years.

His arms tightened, and with her body pressed impossibly close to his, he felt the blood rush to his cock. She shifted her hips slightly, rubbing against his erection, and he groaned. "Shit, Ivy," he mumbled against her lips. "You feel so fuckin' amazing."

"Do you want to stay the night?" she whispered, her lips skimming over his.

"Yes. God, yes." He threw his head back and stared at the ceiling, groaning. "But no."

"No?"

At her one-word question that dripped with surprise, he dropped his chin and held her gaze. "Christ, Ivy, I want to. I want to take you upstairs. I want to watch this dress hit the floor and discover the treasure underneath. I want to take my time and unwrap the gift that you are."

"Okay... that all sounds good to me," she said, a hopeful specter in her eyes.

"But I want more. Or rather, I want to give you more."

Her nose scrunched. "More than sex?"

"Hell yeah, Ivy. More than sex."

She tilted her head to the side but remained silently waiting. And he prayed he was getting the words right.

"I realized tonight that when I stepped in when you were dancing with Josh, I was pissed at him. But while you were my date for the fundraiser, I wanted you to be more. I wanted to claim you as not only my date but..." He sighed. "I'm not very good at this, am I?"

"I don't know, Andy. I think you're doing a good job so far. But I have my own confession to make."

Now it was his turn to hold her gaze, waiting to see what she wanted to say.

"I had no interest in dancing with Josh and realized I

should've let him know immediately." She grimaced. "I hate social situations when it's awkward to be forceful to get someone to back off. Some women are so good at doing that, and you'd think I would be, as I'm in a male-dominated career. Anyway, he mentioned seeing me arrive with you, and when I told him that we'd come together, I realized that that wasn't the same as *being* together." Shaking her head slightly, she blew out a heavy breath. "I swear, this is why I never date. It's so freaking complicated!"

He barked out a laugh, relieved at her confession. "I know. There's only been a couple of women I've been interested in over the years, but the timing wasn't right, or they weren't right, or I wasn't right."

She clutched his shoulders as she enthusiastically nodded. "Yes! Been there, done that."

"Ivy, I'm really interested in you."

"I'm really interested in you, too. And I don't know about you, but this timing seems perfect."

He sucked in a quick breath, his gaze never wavering. He needed her to say exactly what she was thinking. No room for doubt. No room for misunderstandings. No room for error. "So…"

"If you want, I really hope you'll spend the night. I'd love for you to see this dress hit the floor." She grinned.

Now the air rushed from his lungs as he shouted, "Oh, hell yeah. Nothin' I want to do more." He lifted her and swung her around before he started for the stairs. He kissed her smiling lips as his fears that she didn't feel the same melted away.

Her legs wrapped around his waist, and his arms

tightened around the precious cargo he held. At the top of the stairs, he mumbled, "Bed...room..."

"Umlefmm..." She pointed to the left, and he moved in that direction. Without looking around, he stopped at the center of the modest-sized room. She took the hint when he squeezed her waist and slowly lowered her legs. He held her close so her front pressed against his aching cock when her feet finally touched the floor.

He didn't want the kiss to end but forced their bodies to separate, wanting to take all of her in. His eyes had been filled with her since the moment she opened her door earlier in the evening. From the top of her shiny auburn hair and delicate makeup to the beautiful dress that hugged her curves and gave a hint of cleavage, he wanted to explore in detail, down her shapely legs all the way to her black heels, which he decided he wanted her to keep on for a while.

They stood barely apart, and he watched, his breath shallow, as she untied the belt at the side of her waist. It hadn't dawned on him how she'd gotten dressed until he saw that there was no zipper, so she had been able to wrap the dress around her body and tie it at the waist. As the material parted, she shrugged slightly, and it slid slowly down her back and off her arms, snagging slightly on her cast before dropping to the floor.

If he thought her beauty in the dress had taken his breath away, it was nothing like seeing her stand in a pale blue satin bra and matching panties and black heels. As his gaze rove from head to toe and back again, taking time to appreciate and begin to memorize the curves in front of him, he watched as she lifted her hand

and tucked a strand of hair behind her ear, her confident expression wavering ever so slightly.

The women he'd been with over the years had quickly stripped and flouted their assets, waiting for him to go straight for a condom.

But Ivy was different. Unique. A mixture of confidence and uncertainty. He wanted her confidence to overflow and her uncertainty to disappear. Stepping closer, he placed his hands on her shoulders and glided them down her arms, reveling at the petal-soft skin underneath his fingertips. "Christ, Ivy, you're perfection."

At that, her eyes widen slightly, and her grin spread across her face, taking her from perfection to sublime.

"You're not bad yourself, sailor, but it's hard to tell under all those clothes."

He laughed, but the sound died in his throat as she stepped closer and began undoing his tie. Once it was loose, she slid it slowly from around his neck. Then she moved on to unbuttoning his shirt. He didn't want her wrist to hurt, so he took over and was soon divested of his blue shirt, and it landed on the floor next to her dress.

Now it was her chance to run her gaze over his chest, her perfect white teeth showing as she bit her bottom lip. Her palm glided over his pecs and abs, and appreciation glowed on her face.

Her fingertips trailed to the waistband of his pants, and she fumbled slightly with the belt buckle. Like the buttons, he took over and, after toeing off his shoes, shucked his pants to the floor. He almost pulled his boxers off at the same time but wanted this evening to go at her pace. And since she was still in her underwear, he left his on as well, for now. But he didn't need to look down to know that his erect cock tented the front of his thin boxers.

He was ready, but he was willing to wait. Anything for Ivy.

18

Ivy had no issues with her body or her sexuality. But standing in front of Andy Bergstrom with only a bra, barely-there matching panties, and her high heels with his gaze raking hotly over her had her unnerved.

She had no doubt his sexual experiences were vast compared to hers. Even in high school, she'd hear the whispers of girls who got cute guys to go under the bleachers with them. Not her... no siree. The only thing the guys in high school seemed to want to do with her was to add her to their study group. College wasn't much better, considering she avoided frat and keg parties. Engineering had been hard, and if she wanted to make the cut, she had to be as competitive as the other guys in her major. The few women engineering students banded together, giving her a friendship group that made it easier to get through.

As an adult, her sexual encounters were with men she'd gotten to know, thought a relationship was possible only to find out it wasn't, or the occasional meet-greet-fuck that scratched an itch but left her feeling a little despondent when it was over.

But this... Andy standing in front of her, as disrobed as she, and from the bulge in his boxers, just as turned on as she.

He stood still except for his chest moving with each breath. *Waiting.* Then she realized he was giving her control. Waiting for her. She stepped closer until only the barest hint of space remained between them, erased if either of them inhaled deeply.

She placed her cast-covered wrist on his shoulder and allowed her fingers to dig in slightly to keep her from teetering on her heels. Her free hand flattened against his chest, the feel of his heartbeat underneath her fingertips giving her strength. His skin was satin over steel, smooth over hard. And oh, so warm.

She wanted to explore each muscle, but the desire to kiss him again overtook all other thoughts. Gliding her hand up to his neck, she eliminated the space between them and pulled him forward as she lifted on her toes. Just as their lips met, she teetered slightly, and his arms wrapped around her back. One hand slid down to cup her ass, and the other slid upward, gliding through her hair, then fisting the tresses, angling her head.

Their bodies pressed together from knee to chest, soft curves against hard planes. She'd taken control with her initiative, but now she handed it back to him, eager to follow where he led them.

With their lips still locked together, he lifted her slightly and walked toward the bed. His hands now met in the middle of her back, where he deftly unhooked her bra, then gently pulled the straps down her arms to free her breasts. The cool air caused her nipples to bead in hard peaks, and as he leaned back and dropped his gaze, his eyes flashed with pure lust.

He cupped the weight of her breasts in both hands, palming the mounds as his thumbs circled her nipples. She sucked in her breath and dropped her head back, closing her eyes as she gave herself over to the sparks that zipped along her nerves between her nipples and her core.

He bent and lifted her breasts, then suckled one nipple deeply while still palming the other. Then he switched breasts, and for a moment, he moved back and forth until her panties were soaked, and she pressed her hips forward, desperate for the friction only he could provide.

Her fingernails dragged through his hair, lightly scratching his scalp and the back of his neck. He hissed, the sound dragging through his teeth as his cock seemed to swell even more. Patience flew out the window as she pressed her hips against the bulge, rubbing up and down. The low growl from deep within his chest sent shivers throughout her body.

No longer willing to wait, she dropped her hands to her hips, slid her thumbs under the elastic of her panties, and bent. She slid them down her legs. His hands remained on her shoulders to keep her steady as she stepped out of her panties. Looking up, her face was directly in front of his cock, and she leaned forward, pressing a kiss against the soft cotton of his boxers, feeling the hard length of him against her face.

The next growl that left his lungs was loud enough to reverberate through the room, and she shivered as his fingers dug into her shoulders.

Straightening, she tilted her head to the side. "Shoes on or off?"

He replied with a guttural "on." His hands on her shoulders gave a gentle nudge and pushed her to sit on the edge of the bed. He jerked his boxers down, freeing his impressive cock. As it bobbed in front of her, she stared as he snagged his wallet out of his pants. He tossed several condoms onto the comforter next to her, but she was barely aware of anything other than the drop of pre-cum on the end of his cock.

Leaning forward, she licked the pearl and grinned as he hissed once again.

"Oh no, babe," he said as he continued to push her shoulders until she was lying back on the bed. "There will be a time for your mouth on my cock, but right now is not that time. I'm barely hanging on as it is. And I've got things I want to do to you first."

His words made it hard to breathe. She knew there was no label on them as a couple yet, and if she only had tonight with him, she'd go for it and tuck it away in her memory box under the label of fan-fucking-tastic.

He knelt next to the bed and lifted both legs over his shoulders. Placing kisses on her inner thighs, she sucked in a breath that hitched, unsure there was enough oxygen in the room to keep her from passing out with anticipated pleasure. He didn't make her wait any longer as he licked her folds. She whimpered as her fingers gripped the comforter. Her left wrist twinged, and she grunted.

He lifted his head, his eyes narrowing on her face. "Are you okay? We can stop—"

"Don't you dare!"

He chuckled but shook his head. "Babe, I don't want you to hurt in any way."

She lifted her head and speared him with a narrow-eyed glare. "Andy! My wrist just twinged when I bent my fingers. It's fine. I'm fine. You're more than fine. Do. Not. Stop!"

His grin widened. She stared for a moment, thoughts rushing through her. The cute boy grew into a gorgeous man. And thinking of the cute boy, she no longer remembered a past that included her being furious and him being envious. It was just that they had a past. Maybe that was missing with the other men she'd tried to date. There was no anchor.

"You okay, babe?"

She blinked and smiled. "Oh yeah." As he dove between her thighs again, she flopped back and stared at the ceiling, her smile still in place but now given over to the sensations of his tongue, his teeth nipping at her clit, and his beard dragging along her skin. Her hips bucked upward, and he spread his hand over her tummy, his fingers splayed, pressing down to hold her in place. The coil tightened inside, and with only a few more nips and his finger thrusting deep inside, she cried out her release. Forget stars and fireworks... she might have just heard choirs of angels sing.

The feel and taste of Ivy's release were still on his tongue as Andy slowly kissed her mound, over her belly, feasted between both breasts, nipped at the fluttering pulse point at the base of her neck, and then continued along her jawline until his lips found hers again. Her legs had fallen boneless to the side, and as he trailed his lips over her body, he rested his bulk on his forearms, now planted on either side of her shoulders.

Her eyelids blinked open as though Sleeping Beauty was awakening from a deep dream. Once again, his world seemed to click into place in the presence of this woman he wanted to mark as his own.

As their lips molded together again, his tongue thrust inside her mouth, sweeping along the surfaces, tangling with her tongue, tasting her sweet scent, and allowing her to taste her essence from him.

She moaned as she pulled him closer, and he swallowed the sound, feeling it deep in his chest. As her legs regained their strength, she bent her knees on either side of his hips, squeezing, bracketing him in. As much as he hated to stop, he lifted slightly and peered down into her eyes. "We can stop now, Ivy. We don't have to do anything more tonight than we've already done."

Her eyes shone in the pale light of the lamp beside the bed. Her fingers clutched his shoulders tighter, and she whispered, "I want you. I want this. And if I need to make myself absolutely, utterly, and unconditionally clear… I really want your cock buried deep inside me."

With his chest lightly pressed against hers, every

nerve fired where they touched, and when he began to chuckle, her tempting breasts rubbed against him. "Well, I'll take that as your definitive yes."

She grinned. "You'd better!"

He shifted upward so he was knees bent and ass to heels, grabbing a condom lying next to them. With a quick rip, he rolled it over his cock, anticipation building with each second. Tossing the wrapper off the bed, he leaned forward and planted his hands on either side of her shoulders. With his cock lined up at her entrance, he pressed forward, inch by inch, until he thought he would go mad with the need to plunge.

Her tight but slick channel accommodated him, and soon he was pressed to the hilt before dragging back out and thrusting again. She was tight, and the sensation made his cock swell even more. Sucking in a quick breath, he was determined not to unman himself by coming like an untried teen. He quickly fell into a rhythm that not only created friction he knew she wanted, but his pelvis also dragged along her clit, eliciting more moans from her lips. Her breasts bounced with each thrust, and he bent his elbows so he could pull a taut nipple into his mouth.

Her hips rose to meet his, and they thrust in time, faster with each plunge. His senses heightened, and he noticed everything. The light floral scent of her perfume as it swirled around him and mixed with the musk of their combined ardor. The glow of reddish-gold highlights in her hair. The sheen of perspiration that covered her satin skin. The curves that cushioned his body.

Her short fingernails dug into his shoulders, and the sharp nip drew his attention to her face. Her head was thrown back, her eyes were squeezed shut, her neck was taut, and her top teeth dug into her plump bottom lip, making it even redder. Her knees tightened on either side of his waist, and her heels dug into his ass. He felt his cock swell even more as her inner core spasmed, and just as she cried out her orgasm, he thrust through his own release, coming so hard he saw pinpoints of light dance behind his eyelids.

The ability to breathe fled as he emptied himself deep inside her. As his muscles quivered and his arms shook, he couldn't remember ever coming so hard in his life. Knowing he could not hold himself up, he managed to slide his hands under her shoulders and roll her slightly to the side as his arms gave out, and he fell to the bed. *Her cast!* He barely managed to determine that he'd rolled the correct way so that her casted wrist was on top. Lying side by side, they gasped, trying to drag in oxygen. Her sweat-slick breasts crushed against his chest, and neither spoke for a long moment as their arms held tight and their legs tangled.

He lost track of time passing as they lay together, neither speaking as their heartbeats slowed and their bodies cooled. Their eyes were now opened, staring at each other, and he prayed she could see deep inside where everything that he felt for her was growing.

Her lips curved slightly, and she whispered, "Wow."

Surprised he had the energy to chuckle, the sound rumbled up from his lungs. "Yeah, wow."

He smoothed her sweat-slicked tresses from her

face, gliding his thumb over her silken cheek. "That was more… that was better… that's nothing like I've ever felt before," he finally managed to say.

She nodded, her smile widening. "Ditto."

"I don't want to share you with anyone else."

At that declaration, she blinked, lowering her brows in confusion.

"What I mean is that that wasn't just sex. I want us to be exclusive. I really want to take this as far as it will go. I want to give us a chance."

"Take it as far as it will go," she repeated softly. "And what if it keeps going?"

"Then it keeps going. We keep going."

She nodded, a smile gracing her lips. His chest clenched as he stared at her smile. It was the most beautiful thing he'd ever seen in his life.

19

After their round of what was undoubtedly the best sex she'd ever had, they got out of bed and went downstairs long enough to get water bottles to take back upstairs. Then a shower started to become shower sex until Andy called a halt on that particular activity since her cast wasn't supposed to get wet. Plus, he was afraid if she slipped, she'd end up with an injury on top of her injury. So they dried off, started kissing in the bathroom, and barely made it back to the bed for round two.

Finally exhausted, she rested her head on his chest, listening to his breathing deepen and his heart beat against her cheek. He tucked her body close as little puffs of breath danced across her forehead, and she closed her eyes, hating to miss a moment of their time together.

The following morning, she stared at his face as soon as her eyes blinked open and awareness filled her. Her forefinger hovered over his face, and she air-traced and memorized each angle. A few minutes later, he woke, and there was no awkwardness. Just more kissing until their stomachs growled. "I make a mean breakfast. Interested?"

"Babe, I wouldn't care if you served me runny eggs and burnt toast."

She laughed as they rolled out of bed. As she dressed, he walked over and helped her step into her comfy sweatpants, sliding them up her legs and hips. "You seem to be taking your time getting my pants over my ass," she quipped with a grin.

"Babe, I'll help you get dressed any time, although getting you undressed is still my favorite. But I'm not about to squander a chance to get up close and personal with your ass."

She couldn't think of a more perfect way to start the day as they headed downstairs, where they made breakfast together. Soon the sizzle and scent of bacon filled the air. Plating the crispy goodness with non-runny scrambled eggs and perfectly toasted bread, they sat at the table, eating and chatting easily. Once cleanup was complete, he sighed heavily.

She was surprised at how much she hated to see him go, but he needed to go home to change before driving to Sunday dinner at his dad's house.

"Come with me," he begged, making big, sad, puppy-dog eyes at her.

Laughing, she walked him to the door. She was tempted but didn't want to rush anything. "You go be with your dad and Aaron. You and I can spend some time just being us before we add family."

She threw open the door at the same time his lips hit hers, and his tongue swept through her mouth. It shot straight to a goodbye kiss to rival all goodbye kisses. Pressing their bodies together, he banded his arms tightly, holding her in place even though wild horses couldn't drag her from his embrace. Or his lips.

"Uh-hum."

At the sound of someone clearing their throat on the front porch, she jumped back, her eyes wide. Gasping, she shouted, "Sybil!"

"Damn, girl. I go on vacation, and you move home, end up in the news doing some crazy-ass rescue, and then I get here and find you in a lip-lock with—" Now the gasp came from Sybil as her gaze landed on Andy. "Holy shit! Andy Bergstrom? Jesus, Ivy! Are you suffering from amnesia after toppling into the water?"

"Oh... well, um... yeah. Me and Andy. Um..."

He chuckled and squeezed her around the waist. "I'll leave you to explain, babe." With another kiss, he ducked past Sybil and nodded. "Good to see you, Sybil."

She shot a narrow-eyed glare at him, then turned her intense gaze back to Ivy.

"Chicken," Ivy grumbled as she watched Andy jog to his SUV, then reached out to grab Sybil and pull her into her house. "Come on in. I guess I have a lot to explain."

"I'll say you do!" Sybil agreed, tossing her purse to the table before pulling off her coat. "And you could begin by telling me how you ended up with the boy who used to make you miserable, calling you Poison Ivy?"

Linking arms with her oldest friend, she led her back to the kitchen. "Don't I at least get a hello hug?"

Sybil rolled her eyes and grinned as she pulled her in for a tight hug. "I'm so glad you've moved back here. Now, pour me a cup of coffee and start dishing on all the dirt. I need to know what the hell is going on around here!"

"Do you want the condensed version?" Ivy moved behind the counter and poured a cup of coffee for both of them. After liberally adding sweetener and cream to each cup, she pushed one to Sybil.

"I'd like to say no and that I want the full-length version. But Steve and the kids will not get any vacation laundry done unless I'm at home supervising. So you'd better give me the short version. But," she added with a lifted brow, "I expect a girlfriend date with all the details as soon as we can arrange it."

Ivy leaned her hip against the counter and inhaled the savory brew with her fingers curled around her mug. Blowing across the top before taking a sip, she finally turned toward Sybil, thrilled to be so close to her best friend again.

"Andy was the one who jumped into the water and rescued me."

Sybil's mouth dropped open, and her eyes widened. "No shit!"

Shaking her head, Ivy said, "No shit. He dove into the water and pulled me out when I was dragged off the bridge."

Sybil's eyes watered. "I still can't believe that happened to you."

Ivy reached across the counter and grasped her hand. "I'm fine." Glancing down at her wrist, she amended, "I'll soon be fine."

"Okay, I get the whole rescue thing, but there had to be other officers around. It could've just as easily been someone else, and would you be in a lip-lock with them?"

"Are you gonna let me tell my story or not?"

Offering an exaggerated huff, Sybil nodded. "Fine, my lips are sealed. Go for it."

Ivy snorted but took another sip before plunging back into her story. "I didn't know who he was because he looked so different. But he came the next day to the hospital and offered to take me home. Honestly, he didn't know my name at that time, either. When we pulled into the driveway, he obviously realized where we were and then realized who I was but said nothing. It wasn't until he brought my car the day after that I realized who he was."

She waited to see what Sybil would say, but true to her word, Sybil kept her lips pressed tightly together.

"He told me he wanted to apologize." Ivy grinned when Sybil's brows shot to her hairline. "And he did. He apologized and explained a lot of things about his life when he was growing up, which I won't get into because they're his story. But let's just say that I realized while it wasn't an excuse, there were reasons he was so angry back then. He apologized profusely, and I accepted."

Seeing Sybil about to bust, she laughed. "Okay, you can unseal your lips."

"You just accepted? You didn't make him grovel, beg, plead, lie prostrate on the floor in penitence?"

"You goof! No, I didn't. His apology was sincere, and if I didn't accept it, what would that say about me? Anyway, we had dinner together, and we started talking. We went to the American Legion fundraiser last night, and then—"

"Holy shit, he *has* been making up for lost time! And then he obviously stayed the night! That's moving kind of fast, don't you think, Ivy?"

"Maybe. I mean, granted, I don't usually move quite so fast, but…" She set her cup on the counter and leaned forward, her fingers wrapping around Sybil's again. "I discovered that I really like the adult Andy. The teenage Andy doesn't exist any more than the teenage you or me. But the adult version? Damn, I really, really like him."

Sybil stared for a long moment, then her lips curved. "When you put it like that, none of us are what we were like in high school."

Her grin widened, as well. "Well, we just decided to be exclusive. Neither one of us wants to date anyone else right now. And who knows? We're gonna see how far we go with this."

"You were always the smartest person I knew, so if you trust him, then I do too. And it's obvious he's making you happy." Sybil slid from the kitchen stool and walked around the counter to pull Ivy in for a deep hug. "I've missed you so much. I know your parents have, too. We've got to get together soon for a much longer visit."

"I met many of the local women I know you're friends with when I was at the dance last night. They all want to meet for coffee, so we'll do that as soon as we can make the arrangements."

"Well, as much as I hate ending this girl talk, especially as fascinating as it's been, if I don't get home and referee between Ricky and Jessica and help get the laundry started, my house will probably collapse!"

She walked Sybil to the door, waited as she slid on her coat and grabbed her purse, then hugged her friend again. Waving as she left, Ivy closed the door behind her.

Her phone had indicated a message came in while Sybil was there, and she walked back into the kitchen to grab it off the counter. Looking down, she grinned at the text from Andy.

Are you surviving Sybil's inquisition? I hope so. I don't want you to doubt us.

She fumbled as she texted with one hand. **I survived and convinced her that you and I are together, and it's a good thing.**

The three dots appeared, and soon she read, **Thank God! Getting ready to head to my pop's house. I'll talk to you tonight.**

She sent a heart emoji and then curled up on the sofa, settling in to read the newest book on her e-reader, knowing the romance hero couldn't come close to Andy.

Ivy sat at her desk, her gaze pinned on her screen. Her finger clicked on the mouse to move the images from one to the other as she monitored the status of the bridge. Curt Cellini, Director of Maintenance for the CBBT, radioed, "Do you see sector 42?"

"Yes. I've got it pulled up right now."

"Take a look at the wear and tear of the joint near pylon 276."

"Got it. Can you also take a close-up and send those to me?"

"No problem. I'll come to your office before you leave at lunchtime and show you the cameras located underneath."

"Thanks, Curt. That would be great."

She continued to scan through the images, loving the complex camera system the CBBT had for not only monitoring the traffic near and in the tunnels but also the cameras mounted underneath the bridge for checking to see areas of concern. Curt and his crew checked the bridge each day in all weather. But as a systems engineer, she was also involved in the process of determining when others might need to be brought in.

As she leaned back in her chair, her mind drifted to Andy. Specifically, the night he'd spent at her place. *Well, my parents' house. In my old bedroom.* An unbidden snort slipped out at the memory. *I need to find my own place to live!*

It had been a couple of days since she'd seen him, but she was going to his house tonight. Well, dinner first and then to his house. He'd told her to pack an overnight bag. Grinning, she thought of how she hoped their evening would end—amazing sex and then curled up together sleeping.

"Are you still coming in half days now?" Ethan asked from her doorway.

She startled and looked up. "Sorry. I was… looking at the images Curt sent," she lied smoothly. "And yes. I go to the surgeon on Friday and should be cleared for full days. He'll take this cast off and give me a removable splint to wear."

"Good. I know you'll feel better having a splint that you can take on and off when needed. I remember when my eldest boy broke his arm. He had to have a cast on for six weeks. And when it itched, he stuck a coat hanger down under the cast. Used to drive my wife crazy." He chuckled.

She smiled and nodded, glad she'd only had to endure her cast for two weeks.

Inclining his head toward her computer monitors, he said, "The cameras are great, aren't they? Once we installed more than just the traffic cams and added the specialized ones for close-up work on the structures, we can get more detail before Curt has to have his team go under the bridge."

"Curt's going to stop by before lunch to review a few of the latest figures with me, and I'll run the concrete stress analysis tomorrow."

"Sounds good. I appreciate the work you've already put in, but I don't want you to overdo it."

A flash of her and Andy *overdoing it* ran through her mind, and she quickly shook her head, trying to dislodge the thought before it became evident on her face. "Well, next week, I should be back full time."

"Just remember to bring whatever you can from the surgeon and turn it in to HR."

"Will do."

He headed back to his office, and she continued to work for another half hour until Curt appeared at her door. She'd only officially met him one other time but was thrilled to be working with him. He'd spent his twenty-year career so far providing maintenance on the CBBT. As far as she was concerned, he knew more about the bridge-tunnel than anyone else.

"Staring at the cameras becomes addictive, doesn't it?" he said, chuckling.

"I'm so glad to hear you say that! I could spend hours just flipping through all the various camera angles. Even the traffic cams are fascinating, but the cameras mounted under the bridge are captivating."

"Guess what we're getting next?"

She held his gaze as she shook her head. "I have no idea."

"Thermal infrared beam cameras for under the bridge to heighten security."

"No way," she gasped, her smile wide.

"Yep. It's in the budget for next year."

He pulled a chair next to her desk, and they sat side by side, going over some of the data she would need to perform her test the next day. When they finished, he stood and walked toward the door, then halted and turned. "I'm really glad to have you on the team, Ivy. I've been pushing for us to get a systems engineer for several years. I'm glad to see the higher-ups finally saw the wisdom."

She smiled. "Thank you for your vote of confidence. Now, if we can just make sure the CBBT Board continues to like the work that I do."

"I have no doubt they will." With that, he tapped on the doorframe as he walked through, and she heard his footsteps go down the hall. She had only meant to work half a day, and it was almost noon.

Looking back at her screens, she was drawn into the camera shots, especially since she could control where some of them were angled. Deciding to spend a few more minutes experimenting with the program, she watched small fishing and pleasure boats move in and out of the Bay underneath the bridge. Jumping to the area at the first tunnel, she watched as a cargo ship heading toward Baltimore passed over the tunnel. The line of sight she had made her feel as though she was almost standing on the ship.

Flipping back to the cameras underneath the bridge, she continued to look at some of the stress points Curt had pointed out. A fishing boat moved underneath the bridge, so clear that she could see the woman and two men bundled against the weather as they cast their lines into the water near the pylons where fish would gather.

"You're supposed to be gone!" Ethan yelled from his office across the hall. Wincing, she knew she needed to leave. Closing down her computer, she grabbed her coat and purse, waved goodbye to him, and hustled to her car. Most people might be thrilled to have days off, but she was anxious to return to work full time.

But first... dinner and a night with Andy.

20

Andy met his brother and Detective Sam Shackley at the sheriff's department, glad Ryan had assigned him to go with them to check on the properties that backed up to Parkers Inlet.

"On one side is Pineview Lane, and on the other side of the inlet is Harvestdale," Aaron said, pulling out of the parking lot. "There are eleven residents on Pineview and eight on Harvestdale."

While Aaron and Sam knew what the properties looked like from the road and even knew some of the residents, Andy knew the waterside. "Not all of them have docks or boats. I know of three with docks where I have never seen a boat and at least nine that do have boats."

Anxious to get started, they stopped at the first house on Pineview. Letting Aaron and Sam take the lead since they were the law enforcement for the area, Andy was brought into the conversation with the owner as he held out the pictures he had brought with him. Several photographs were of speedboats, mostly silver, but also white and black. He also had the picture taken from the cell phone that showed the silver speedboat with the two men in dark clothing aboard.

The property owners' reactions varied. Some were immediately nervous when they opened their front door and saw three men in uniform on their front stoop. Others knew either Aaron or Sam and greeted them warmly. But they made their way to the seventh house on Pineview without anyone recognizing that boat specifically.

"We used to go boating all the time," said one of the residents, "but it got so expensive. Maintenance. Insurance. The kids grew up, left home, and even though we could take it out when they visited with the grandkids, they don't make it home often enough to make it worth all the money."

Another resident stood with wide eyes as he looked at the pictures and said, "I've got a boat kind of like this. Do you want to take a look at it?" They agreed, and the owner walked him around the backyard, down through the trees to where he'd docked his boat.

Andy stood on the wooden planks of the dock and looked at the boat up on the dry dock, out of the water. "How long has it been up?"

"Since October," the resident admitted. "We only take it out in the nicer weather. Once it gets cold, my wife doesn't like going out. Honestly, I don't much like the cold weather either."

Andy's practiced gaze let him know the man was being truthful, and with a quick shake of his head toward Aaron, they walked back to the house. At the last house on Pineview, they were taken to see another boat, which the owner still used. It was evident to Andy that it also wasn't the one reported by the fishermen as the one that came too close to them. As they left, he commented to Aaron and Sam, "He only has a single engine, and what we're looking for will have four."

Several residents weren't home, so Sam made a note to return later. Andy also made notes of those homes so he could come back by water and look at the docks from the waterside again.

The last houses on Pineview were met with similar results of residents not seeing or hearing anything. Sam sighed heavily. "I can see why. Some of these people sit on their back porches, and with the woods growing close to the water, they don't get a good sighting of what's in the inlet."

"No, and it's even worse on Harvestdale," Andy said, knowing the thick brush that grew close to the water's edge.

It had taken several hours to make their way to the end of Pineview, where the inlet met the Bay, and then they climbed back into the sheriff's vehicle and drove to the other side of the inlet to Harvestdale.

"My guess is that the boat isn't stored at somebody's dock. It's brought in specifically when there's a drug shipment to go out, and that would keep it from being seen just sitting around."

Sam nodded. "That makes sense. Even if you were a resident, you wouldn't think anything about seeing a boat going in and out because not everyone who boats on the inlet actually lives here."

The residences on Harvestdale had more acreage, giving them more space and privacy between the houses. The first several they visited, the residents responded almost verbatim to the ones they'd talked to earlier in the day.

At the last house, the front driveway was longer, keeping it from being visible from the road. After Sam rang the bell, the door swung open, and a beautiful blonde dressed casually in jeans and a sweater stared back at them with wide eyes.

"My goodness, officers, what's going on?" She leaned her head out and looked from left to right as though she were expecting someone to jump out. When her gaze swung back to the three of them, she looked them over and placed her hand over her chest. "Is there a problem? Should I be concerned?"

"Ma'am, we're checking the properties along the street that back to the inlet. We're interested if you or any resident of the house has seen a silver boat that looks like one of these?"

"Oh, please don't call me ma'am. That makes me feel old. I hope you don't mistake me for someone old!" She smiled widely, her long, fake eyelashes blinking. "I'm Roberta."

Andy stepped up and showed the pictures to her. "Roberta, if you'd please look at these and let us know if you've seen a similar boat in the inlet."

She spent a great deal of time perusing the pictures before she finally looked up and shook her head. "I'm afraid I'm not in the backyard often and can't say I've seen any boat like this." She laughed. "Plus, I don't know one boat from another."

"Is there anyone else who lives here who might be able to identify having seen a vessel like one of these?" Sam asked.

She tossed her hair over her shoulder, and her gaze passed over Aaron and Sam, landing on Andy. "Well, my husband is never home, and when he is, boating just isn't his thing, either. We don't own one, and I'm not sure he's been down to the dock since we moved in."

"And do you and your husband own this property?" Aaron asked.

"Just renting. We wanted to get a feel for the area before buying a vacation home. But everything around here is so... well, not very nice if you know what I mean. I prefer the other side of the Bay."

Not having a response that would be polite, Andy simply nodded as he stepped back and let Sam offer their goodbyes.

"Oh, it was all my pleasure, I'm sure." She smiled.

As the three walked toward their SUV, Aaron grumbled, "What the fuck is someone doing out here who hates the area?"

Andy knew the Eastern Shore wasn't for everyone. But for him and his brother, it was home. "I don't know. Some come here thinking it will be a hot vacation spot on the Bay. If they did any internet searches, they'd know that's not true."

As they left Harvestdale, Andy vowed to return to

the inlet by boat to look at the area from the water again.

They drove back to where Andy left his SUV at the sheriff's office. Hunter met them in the parking lot as Sam gave him an update on their investigation. Just as Andy was ready to leave, Hunter looked over and said, "Belle liked talking to Ivy the other night. Said she remembered her from high school."

"You married a good woman," Andy replied honestly. "I know Ivy needs friends out here, so I was glad she hooked up with Belle." He chuckled. "I'm not sure that her best friend from high school is my biggest champion. I should have Belle put in a good word."

Hunter narrowed his eyes in question.

"High school shithead antics," Andy replied with a shrug, causing the other men to laugh.

"Damn." Hunter's mirth slowed, and he shook his head. "At least you can blame it on fuckin' teenage hormones and idiocy. Me? I was undercover when I met Belle a couple of years ago, fucked up big time, and nearly ended us before we had a chance to get together."

Sam added, "Then I guess the moral is, do your dumb shit in high school and give them a chance to forgive you later, right?"

"That's what I'm counting on," Andy agreed.

As the last miles churned back to town, Andy looked out the window, smiling as he thought about seeing Ivy in a few hours. And he thanked God she was giving him a chance.

Roberta watched the officers leave and pursed her lips. Once they'd turned off her drive and back onto the road, she pulled her phone out of her pocket. With the push of a button, she dialed. "The police were here. Yeah. Looking for a silver speedboat." She didn't let the other person finish before she jumped in. "Yes, I know. But that's not all. They have a photograph of you. It's not clear, but you must have been sighted sometime on the water."

Closing her eyes, she grimaced. It wasn't the first time she'd regretted getting involved. "Of course, I didn't say anything. But tell them to be more careful. Showboating on the Bay is the way to get noticed… not the fucking way to fly under the radar!"

Speaking sharply to him was risky, but then he was the one who took orders from the man she was with. It didn't give her much power, but she'd take the modicum of authority she could get. Disconnecting, she called the next number.

"The police came by. Ty, where are you?"

"Baltimore. What the fuck did they want?"

"Just questioning everyone in the area, I suppose. But, Ty, they have pictures. The new crew you've got is sloppy out on the water. What the fuck is wrong with—"

"What kind of pictures?" he roared.

"Just pictures of a silver boat. And one that shows two men. They are all covered up, and it looks grainy, so there's no way to ID them. But this could be a disaster."

"Don't tell me my business. You're there to make sure the transfers take place and be my eyes and ears."

"And you don't mind sharing when it suits you, do you?" she bit out, thinking about the last time the local gang leader, Linc, stopped by. She could still see the bruises on her arms.

"You know what you need to do to make these transactions go smoothly," Ty growled. "And you live a fuckuva lot better than being on the streets."

"Fine, but you need to rein him in. I tried, but he won't listen. Give the gangbanger a fast boat, and suddenly, he thinks he's Mario Andretti."

"That's a racecar driver, stupid bitch." He laughed.

Pinching her lips together, she grimaced. "Whatever! Just know that if they keep acting like fools on the water, they will get stopped."

He was quiet for a moment, and she wondered if she'd pushed him too far. Holding her breath, she waited. For an ex-hooker, this was a pretty good living, and she needed to learn how to keep her mouth shut. Just when she was about to apologize, he spoke.

"You're right. I'll talk to Marcus, and he'll bring Linc in line. Maybe I'll have Marcus come stay at the house with you for a few days."

Softening her voice, she said, "I'd rather it be you."

He chuckled. "I'll be down this weekend. Until then, keep Marcus happy."

He disconnected, and she sighed heavily as she walked back into the kitchen and stared out over the Bay. From the house, she could view the glorious sunsets over the Bay or walk through the woods to the dock on the inlet.

And she wondered how she'd gotten to this place in life. It sure as hell wasn't the life she'd envisioned when she was younger. Turning quickly, she walked away from the beautiful view.

21

"I haven't been here in a long time," Ivy said, looking around the restaurant. They were seated in a large, round booth in the corner of the Sunset Restaurant. And the evening view provided a perfect sunset over the Chesapeake Bay. The restaurant managed to be both upscale and family friendly.

As soon as she'd gotten into Andy's SUV when he picked her up, her attention had focused on the dark pants he wore that made his thighs and ass look amazing. The gray shirt fit his torso although she wondered about the strength of the material as it strained over his biceps. A leather jacket completed his outfit, giving him the gorgeous, casual, confident look he sported so well. Then she spied the sheepish expression on his face.

But before she could ask, he'd immediately blurted, "I hope you don't mind, but Aaron and my dad are going to crash our dinner."

"What?" Her eyes widened, but before she had a chance to speak further, he continued.

"I'm sorry! I know I should've spoken with you earlier, but they really, really want to meet you. I suggested we wait till a Sunday dinner, but Pop said he'd be nervous if his first time meeting you was over some of his homemade chowder."

"Well, I'll have to tell him that I can't wait to try his homemade chowder."

Andy's relief was palpable, and she reached over to squeeze his hand. "Granted, you surprised me, but I'm fine with meeting your brother and dad."

When he helped slide her coat from her shoulders, he'd leaned close and whispered, "Talk about gorgeous. Ivy, you're beautiful."

Blushing, she'd smiled at his words before sliding into the booth. Now, ensconced in the beautiful restaurant, she relaxed against the leather booth cushions. "I think the last time I was here was when I came for their Mother's Day buffet." As soon as the words left her mouth, she winced and jerked her gaze over to Andy.

He caught her expression, and his smile faltered. "Ivy, it's okay to talk about mothers. You don't have to feel bad for me."

She sighed heavily and nodded. "I know. It's just that... well, now I know how difficult it was for you."

"Yes... the operative word here is *was*. Past tense. You have a wonderful mother. A lot of my friends have wonderful mothers. It's okay. My *mommy issues* from my teenage years are behind me."

Her raised brows must have hit him because he quickly amended, "Okay, so I realize I have to deal with them, but they no longer make me an insufferable prick."

At that, she laughed and nodded. "You are definitely not an insufferable prick!"

"Are you sure about that?"

The question came from the side, and she swung her gaze around to see two men standing nearby.

"Aaron. Pop. Glad you could meet us here," Andy said, rising to shake their hands and receive back slaps in greeting.

Ivy wiped her palms on the napkin already in her lap before stretching her hand out as well.

"This is Ivy Watkins. Ivy, this is my pop, Arthur Bergstrom, and my brother, Aaron."

"It's lovely to meet you both," she said, her gaze moving among the three men, seeing the obvious familial similarities.

"I think the honor is all ours," Arthur said. "And you can call me Pops."

She blinked, wondering if he knew she and Andy had just started seeing each other. "Uh…"

"Don't worry," Aaron jumped in. "Everyone calls him Pops."

"Oh… okay." She smiled at the younger brother noticing that a look was shared among all three men but had no way to decipher its hidden meaning. Before she had time to worry, the server came to take their drink orders.

"I met your dad quite a few times," Arthur said, leaning back against the cushions. "Back when Aaron was in elementary school. Good man. Liked him a lot.

He and Aaron's teachers all made sure my boy had what he needed."

Her smile widened at his praise. She knew her dad was wonderful, but it was nice to hear someone in the community say the same. "Thank you." She wasn't sure if Aaron knew that Andy had told her a little about him, but he needn't have worried. It appeared the Bergstrom men had little to hide.

"I was a preemie," Aaron said with a smile. "Underdeveloped lungs and muscles. Needed a lot for years but eventually, my body caught up to my superior brain."

Andy snorted and almost spat out his sip of beer. "As you can see, my brother suffers no problem with his ego."

Laughing, she immediately felt at ease.

"Now, what were you saying about my brother being an insufferable prick?" Aaron asked, taking a bite of the crab dip appetizer that had been served. "I need to hear all about this."

Andy swatted at Aaron's hand. "Manners, bro!"

Arthur sighed. "Ivy, let me go ahead and apologize for my boys. It seems my lessons fell on deaf ears when I was raising them."

"I think you did a wonderful job," she assured, her smile still firmly in place. The concern that she'd feel awkward with his family had already disappeared.

Arthur grinned at her praise and glanced back and forth between his two sons. "Heard you two got to work together today."

"Too bad we had no luck with the drug-running boat we were searching for," Aaron grumbled.

Andy looked over his shoulder, but no other patrons were seated near them. Shaking his head, he said, "I just wish we had a better system of seeing the watercraft on the Bay. It would make it easier to catch the gangs running drugs with boats."

Ivy had taken the opportunity while the men chatted about work to scoop some crab dip on her plate, but at Andy's comment, she shot her gaze toward him. She wasn't ignorant of the crimes in the world but had never really considered gang activity or drug running on the Eastern Shore. Swallowing, she asked, "Is that prevalent?"

Andy hesitated, then shrugged. "More than most people realize."

Aaron winced. "I'm sorry. I shouldn't have mentioned it. Occupational hazard, I guess."

"Are you in law enforcement also?" she asked.

"Sheriff's department," Aaron replied.

"Proud of my boys," Arthur said, his warm smile beaming, and she couldn't help but smile in return.

At that, the conversation halted as their main courses were delivered to the table. Each exclaimed over their meals as well as looked at the other delicious plates. She'd ordered the stuffed shrimp, which she loved, but she had to admit that Aaron's sizzling steak smelled tantalizing. Arthur had the fried oysters, and Andy's seafood platter with rockfish, shrimp, scallops, and clams also held her attention.

The Bergstrom men had no problem keeping a conversation going, and by the time the meal ended, she was stuffed with excellent food and loved getting acquainted with Andy's family. Seeing the three men interact gave her an understanding of the strong bond they shared that wasn't diminished without having a maternal influence. Leaving the restaurant, she offered and received heartfelt hugs from Arthur and Aaron before Andy assisted her into his SUV.

"I really liked your family."

Andy directed his smile toward her before turning his attention back to driving. "They liked you, too."

"Can I ask about your work?"

"Sure. As long as I can share, I will. Specifics in an ongoing case, I can't. But then, usually, our cases are short-term with what the VMP works on."

"I guess I never thought much about gangs in the area. It seems so… I don't know… inner city? Not really out here on the shore."

"We're becoming a link from the drugs coming in from Florida and heading up the Highway 95 route to the northeast. To avoid possible detection on the major highways, gangs bypass Richmond and DC by using the rural Eastern Shore. Now, they're even using the Chesapeake Bay to transport drugs, guns, and humans by water."

"Oh…" she said, shocked at his words. "I feel rather foolish that I had no idea."

"Most people don't. Although, some arrests and trial cases have been written up in the local newspaper. Last year, two members of the Bloods were arrested on charges of violence in two separate incidences. One of them was a known leader in this area. The sheriff's department is trying to keep an eye on another one, but he's elusive."

"I have a bird's-eye view of the Bay where I work, but it's only at the bridge. And, of course, it would be too ponderous for someone to try to monitor all the smaller boats that move over the Bay every day."

"Yeah," he agreed, then turned on his blinker, and her attention shot to a house at the end of the driveway.

A small, pale blue, two-story house with an attached two-car garage sat back from the street. Trees were in the backyard, and a few were scattered in the front and sides. The shutters and front porch were painted white. It was darling but, at first glance, didn't seem like the kind of house she would have pictured Andy in. "Oh my, is this your place?"

He nodded after casting her a sideways, nervous look. He climbed down and walked around the front of his SUV to open her door, and her gaze followed each step of the surprising man who now captured her attention. Assisting her down, he linked fingers with her, and they walked to the front.

Once inside, she was even more surprised. It was as far from a bachelor pad as she could have imagined. They walked straight into the living room, and the wood plank floors were worn but clean, covered with a blue and green rug. A dark-blue sofa sat facing the fireplace with a wide-screen TV mounted over the mantel. Two chairs flanked the sofa, both covered in blue and green plaid. The whole effect was warm and inviting. It appeared so homey, she changed her mind and decided it looked exactly like what Andy would want... and deserved.

"Come on, I'll show you around," he said, leading the way as she eagerly followed.

The space was bisected by the hall and staircase at the back of the living room, which took up the entire front of the house. He led her down the hall toward the back of the house, where there was a beautiful kitchen with new appliances, white cabinets, and a green and blue backsplash. The other side of the space opened into the eat-in kitchen, where an oak table, matching chairs, and an antique pie safe cabinet sat. "This is lovely," she gushed.

He blushed and shrugged. "Ms. Sally, Pop's neighbor, had this in her house for years. I used to love it because she'd keep pies and cookies in it all the time. When I bought this place, she insisted on giving it to me. Said I needed to fill it with goodies. I'm afraid all I've done so far is use it for storage."

She squeezed his hand before he continued the tour. The dining room and kitchen area opened to a deck at the back of the house, shaded from the evening sun with some trees.

Still entranced with all she was seeing, she barely missed him walking through the kitchen and opening another door. "This is the pantry and where the washer and dryer are," he said. As she followed him, she peeked inside and smiled. Going back toward the front, he pointed out the small half bathroom before they rounded the bottom of the stairs and began their ascent.

Upstairs, there were three bedrooms, two small ones, and the owner's bedroom, which was larger.

A bathroom sat at the end of the hall, and the owner's bedroom also had an updated bathroom with white tile and dark-blue cabinets.

Delighted with the entire house, it hadn't registered in her mind that they were now standing in his bedroom. "Andy, I'm stunned!"

He appeared to startle, his brows lowering as he stared back.

Realizing her comment could've sounded rude, she rushed to say, "It's not that I thought you were going to live in a bachelor pad, but this place is so quaint and homey."

He chuckled and nodded, his shoulders relaxing at her explanation. "Aaron gave me a lot of shit when I bought this place. I assure you that I had nothing to do with the renovations or decor. I just happen to be at the right place at the right time."

She wanted to hear the story and, once again, followed as he walked over to the bed, sitting so they could face each other.

"I knew I wanted a place of my own. I didn't want an apartment or a condo. I wanted a house but had no idea if I could afford anything in the area. By the time I got up my nerve to contact a real estate agent, they were very excited because a young couple had inherited this house and paid to renovate it. He was working in Virginia Beach and traveling over the bridge every day, but just when they moved in, he got transferred to some state out West."

Ivy listened, eyes wide.

"They had just contacted the same real estate company and wanted a quick sale. Since they inherited the house, and his company was going to be supplying them with a place in Colorado, they weren't trying to make a killing off this place. So I bought it for a reasonable price and even negotiated for them to leave some of their furniture. The living room and dining room are compliments of that young couple. Everything upstairs is mine."

"Wow... that's an amazing stroke of luck. To get this cute house and so much furniture. And the place had been renovated!"

He nodded enthusiastically. "I've only had it a couple of months. Kind of felt bad for Jared. He bought a house about the same size right before me, but he has to do the renovations himself. So far, he's done a great job, and I've gone over to help out."

"It's hard to imagine you guys having house envy." She laughed.

"Does that mess with my street cred?"

She snorted, then clapped her hands over her face, shaking her head. "That's embarrassing!"

"Snorting? Nah, it's endearing."

She peeked between her fingers, blushing. "Endearing?"

He reached over and gently pulled her hands down. Leaning closer, he said, "Don't cover your beautiful face."

Her breath caught in her throat as she stared at his eyes, now so close to hers. Hyperaware of the crackling sexual electricity firing all around them, she wondered if he could feel it, too. She felt sure he did as he leaned closer and cupped her cheek with one hand, dragging his thumb over her lips. The oxygen in the room seemed to disappear the closer his lips came.

Just when his mouth sealed over hers, she squirmed around to straddle him. And he fell back on the bed with her landing on top of him. Their bodies were a messy tangle of arms, torsos pressed together, and legs tangling. The kiss might have been equally as sloppy, with bumping noses and teeth, but their lips never separated.

He reached to the side and grabbed a small remote on the nightstand. Holding it out, he pressed the button, and the lights went out while the overhead fan began to twirl slowly. Grinning, she mumbled against his lips, "That's a neat trick."

Still kissing his now smiling lips, he mumbled in return, "Hang on, babe. I've got a lot of neat tricks."

And as the night continued, she discovered just how many tricks he had. And loved every one of them.

22

Andy went back to Parker Inlet with Jose in a small fishing boat. He'd received permission from Ryan to investigate the inlet further, but to do so in a private boat with their VMP uniforms covered by their outer coats. Appearing as a couple of fishermen, he wanted a closer view of the docks on the inlet.

Nothing suspicious was to be determined even though he carefully looked over the private dock at the end of the house where he, Aaron, and Sam had questioned Roberta.

"You know what we need? Remote cameras at the entrances to some of these inlets," Jose said.

At first, Andy chuckled, but he had to admit Jose's idea, in a perfect world where law enforcement didn't have to worry about gathering evidence illegally, would've been a great notion.

Jose continued. "I'm not talking about anything we'd use against anyone in court. But just to give us clarity on where to focus."

Suddenly, Andy jerked and looked back at Jose as a memory hit him. "Dylan Hunt, the police chief in Seaside, and his wife, Hannah Freeman-Hunt, the chief in Easton, did something very similar! It was when I was working for the Manteague Police Department with Joseph's brother, Wyatt, that I heard about it. They installed cameras on the Seaside public harbor to catch drug runners using that little harbor."

Jose nodded, then he sighed heavily. "I know this was my idea, but now that I'm thinking about it, how would we do it? It's not like a small harbor with light poles."

As they maneuvered back into the Bay, Andy scoured the shore. "There are plenty of trees." Turning back to Jose, he said, "Why don't we run it by Ryan and see if we can do anything."

"Sure as fuck beats not being able to do anything with these gangbangers."

Heading back to the station, Andy was excited about possibly moving their investigation further for the first time in weeks.

Ryan called a departmental meeting after Andy and Jose talked to him. Andy looked at the others around the table and said, "I know whether or not we can do it is above my pay grade, but if we could have some closer-to-shore cameras near some of the inlets that we know may have drug runners, it would help us know where to keep a closer eye out." The others gave their enthusiastic agreement.

"Okay," Ryan began, rubbing his chin. "We can use

cameras to monitor parts of the Bay without having warrants. They won't be aimed at anyone's specific property but at the point where the inlets meet the Bay. Let's look at the map and determine where they'll work the best. And then I'll requisition the cameras from the state."

"Oh God, that'll take forever," Bryce groaned.

"We have money earmarked for shutting down the gangs," Ryan said. "We just need to get our hands on it."

"Ivy mentioned that the CBBT has cameras on the bridge, some underneath, to monitor the structure, but she said she can see boats that go under the bridge all the time. It made me think that we could approach the CBBT police to find out if there's a way to use their system also," Andy added.

Ryan grinned. "I've already been in touch with Mac Davenport, Chief of Police of the CBBT. He's checked with his superiors and the Board. As long as it does not take away from their duties, if they come across camera footage that would be helpful to us, the Virginia Beach Police, the Coast Guard, the US Navy, or the VMP, they can share that information with us."

"Hot damn!" Jared called out as Andy leaned back and grinned.

"And there's more," Ryan said, gaining everyone's undivided attention. "The Baltimore Port and the Norfolk Port have agreed with the DEA that the tugboats in the Bay can also provide information."

"We're tightening the noose," Callan said.

"It's a lot of areas to cover, but we're certainly

starting to work toward a partial solution," Ryan agreed. He looked around the table. "Jose, go to the equipment room and round up all the cameras that we have so far. I'll call my contact in Richmond and get more. Andy, stay here and work with Callan and me on the best locations that will work legally for the cameras. Jose, join us once you've checked to see how many cameras we have. The rest of you are back on patrol. Later today, I'll talk to Mac to see if it's possible to access his cameras to see if the boat passed underneath the bridge when our cameras pick up suspicious activity."

With renewed energy, the group dismissed. For the next two hours, Andy worked with the others as they studied the maps, specifically the land that bordered the entrance to an inlet and the Bay. Ryan called Colt to let the North Heron sheriff's department know what they were doing, and soon, Sam Shackley arrived to assist. Jose walked back in and reported, "We have seven cameras that can be attached to trees."

Andy grinned. "I called Dylan Hunt to see what he and Hannah used a couple of years ago. They gave me the name of the store." Looking at his captain, he added, "I thought I'd head there when we're out and grab a few more."

Ryan nodded. "I'll get a requisition ordered."

"When is the best time to get these up?" Callan asked.

The group debated the merits of various timing to have the least number of eyes on what they were doing, knowing the fewer people who knew the cameras were up, the less chance the drug runners might know they were there. Finally, they decided on the early evening after the fishermen had usually headed back to their docks and harbors, and the drug runners would have made their early morning runs but not their middle-of-the-night runs. With no shortage of volunteers, Ryan finally decided on Jose, Bryce, Andy, and himself.

"With four of us, we can get the job done quicker and more efficiently," Ryan had declared.

Andy leaned over and fist-bumped Jose, both grinning at the excitement of the evening's plan.

Ivy smiled as she drove to work, glancing down at her now splinted wrist. She'd just left her two-week checkup, and the surgeon had declared her wrist was healing the way he'd expected. It had been shocking to see her wrist after the half cast was removed, but the sutures had dissolved, and the scarring was not nearly as bad as she had anticipated. While he was pleased with her mobility, he prescribed physical therapy for six weeks. She made the appointment before leaving the hospital and drove the hour-long trip back to the CBBT.

As she passed the turnoff for Baytown High School, her mind drifted to days gone by. And in truth, most of her memories were good ones. She thought of the chorus she'd participated in, remembering when they had traveled to Richmond for the state competition. She remembered running cross-country, loving both the singularity of the sport as well as the team spirit. She loved the math and science clubs and participated in a local university's camp for future women in engineering. Looking back, she had friends but not a lot of romance, which was fine.

Snorting, she shook her head and wondered how many guys Andy might have chased away with his stupid nickname for her. And while she'd been angry at the time, she could not deny the attraction she felt for the adult Andy.

With that came the realization that his high school memories might not have been nearly as wonderful as hers. Wincing at that thought, a heavy sigh escaped for the boy whose mother had simply walked away.

As she passed the turnoff for Baytown, her mind now drifted to the friends she was starting to make. She and Sybil were going to a meeting of the AL auxiliary, and she was excited to once again have a group of women friends, something she hadn't had since college when the women majoring in engineering banded together.

Approaching the first toll gate at the CBBT where her office was located, she thought of Andy at work, wondering if he was out on the water. And if he was safe. It had only dawned on her with their latest conversations about the drug running on the Bay that she realized how dangerous his job could be.

By the time she walked into her office, her mind was in turmoil with the tangled thoughts that had flung themselves at her for the past hour.

"I hate to do this to you when you've just walked in," Ethan said, "but we have a staff meeting with section heads, and I want you there as well. Since you're directly under me and technically a part of the construction, maintenance, and management information systems divisions, you need to attend this meeting."

"Give me just a moment, and I'll be ready." She pulled off her coat and hung it on the back of her door. Grabbing her laptop, she turned and followed Ethan down the hall.

Once there, she recognized most of the people in the room. Sitting next to Ethan, she shot a smile across the table to Anne Baxter. Anne worked for the management information department and had welcomed Ivy on her first day of orientation. Bradley Carpenter, the head of the cybersecurity section, winked at her from the other side of Anne. Curt was there, as well as Mac Davenport, the head of the bridge-tunnel police force.

The first part of the meeting dealt with budget items, and her mind wandered. Not that she wasn't interested or didn't understand the significance, but her wrist had begun to ache after the doctor's manipulations. Her phone was on silent mode, but her laptop alerted her to a message from the physical therapist. Her mother also sent a message, and Sybil's message was ranting about the preschool sending her daughter home due to a "runny nose."

She swallowed a sigh over the distractions and refocused her mind on the meeting as Mac moved to the podium.

"Gonna keep this short, folks," he began. "While not

changing our operations, we will provide any surveillance information we receive from our cameras to the state police and other law enforcement. Do not misunderstand me. We are not actively searching for video surveillance on illegal activities that cross under or over the CBBT, but if asked for specific time or date information based on legitimate concerns, we will comply. My department already receives the video from all the various cameras, although we only spot-check them other than for specific needs. Officer Ronald Jeeves is a new hire from Baltimore City Police, and he'll be in charge of following up with more requests." A young man with a killer smile and dressed in a uniform looked around the table and offered a friendly wave.

As Mac returned to his seat, Ivy's gaze whipped around the table, surprised that no one else seemed overly interested. *I guess it's because I know what's probably behind the request with the drug runners moving under the bridge to get in and out of the Bay.*

As the meeting finally ended, she greeted several others before falling into step with Anne as they walked out. Anne was pretty, with thick blond hair and delicate features overshadowed by her large, dark eyeglasses. They gave her an owlish appearance, but she worked it, managing to look cute and quirky at the same time. Ivy had never acquired a personal style, often just dressing to suit the occasion.

"God, that was boring, wasn't it?" Anne asked, dragging Ivy from her wandering thoughts.

"Yes. Budget meetings suck all the energy from a

room. But I am curious, will Mac's surveillance request come to you?"

Anne crinkled her nose. "According to my boss, we won't change anything we're doing. The cameras still feed into the information systems. If we get asked for something, we'll provide the video. I guess the new part will be with that new police officer." She grinned. "Cute, huh?"

Smiling in return, she nodded. "Yes, he's cute." What she didn't say was that while Ronald Jeeves certainly filled out his CBBT officer uniform nicely, he didn't hold a candle to Andy.

"I brought my lunch since I didn't know how long the meeting would last," Anne said. "I thought I'd eat on this side of the Bay if you're free."

Anne's office was on the Virginia Beach side of the CBBT, and Ivy was thrilled to be able to share lunch with her. Entering the workroom, they settled at a small table. Anne looked down at Ivy's arm resting on the table. "Oh my goodness, you got your cast off!"

"Yes, just this morning. It already feels so much better."

"Have you seen the handsome cop again?"

Her smile slid over her face, and before she could reply, Anne laughed and pushed her glasses up on her nose. "I guess that answers that question! Two weeks. Damn, girl, you move fast."

"Well, it's not like we've declared undying love after only two weeks," she retorted. "But we are dating."

"I don't suppose he has any single friends, does he? Although, I might give Ronald a whirl."

Ivy thought about a few of the single men she'd met at the AL fundraiser but had a feeling Anne might be a little bit of a maneater, and she wasn't sure she wanted that drama. "I'd say if you have your eyes set on Officer Jeeves, you've got your hands full."

Anne laughed and nodded. "Well, I don't have a date with him yet, but I'm working on it."

The lunch was soon finished, and she waved goodbye to Anne before returning to her office. It was the first time in several weeks that she had worked a full day and found that by midafternoon, she was tired. Forging ahead with several projects, she sent a group email to Ethan, Mac, and Bradley, asking about integrating the security and IT systems, wondering if the process could be streamlined for assisting other law enforcement. By the end of the day, she received replies, giving her the go-ahead to pursue the project.

She felt a modicum of guilt that during the last thirty minutes of her day, she simply flipped through various camera angles from the equipment underneath the bridges to see what could be tweaked that would not interfere with the maintenance department's work.

As pleasure and speedboats made their way from the Atlantic Ocean into the Bay, she couldn't help but think of the information Andy had given her about drug running. Before, when she looked at the boats, she was simply fascinated with the people's lives and what they were doing. Now, it was hard not to view each one with suspicion.

Hearing Ethan shutting down his computers across the hall, she quickly did the same. She walked out, looking forward to another evening with Andy when she received his text. He was going to be working late, and as she climbed into her car, she considered the merits of going home alone or making a detour.

With a wide grin, she detoured and headed to Sybil's house.

23

Andy and Jose used an expandable ladder leaning against a tree trunk to attach a small camera with movement sensitivity. Ryan and Bryce were on the ground, testing the equipment. They'd selected four inlets north of Baytown and two south of town to focus their attention on until more supplies came in.

Using hand signals previously agreed upon, Andy silently asked Ryan if he was getting a signal on the camera reception. As soon as Ryan offered a thumbs-up, he climbed down the ladder and glanced over to where Jose had set up another one at a slightly different angle. This was the last inlet they would work on for the evening. The sun had almost set, and they would soon be unable to see what they were doing safely.

So far, they'd managed to avoid being seen by anyone while they worked on the ladders. Any fishermen or residents who saw them while they were in the boat, or even just on the shore, wouldn't have wondered what they were doing since it was a common sight.

Once they were all back on the boat and heading to the station, he turned to Ryan and asked, "Any chance we can get eyes on the dock that Aaron, Sam, and I are suspicious of? I know it would be on private land, but I wondered if Hunter could get permission from that lot owner across the inlet."

"I'll talk to Colt," Ryan said while nodding. "If so, that would need to come from him. What we set up were on trees that were technically on the Bay's easement."

He checked his phone and spied a message from Ivy saying that she'd gone to Sybil's for dinner and for him to come by. He hesitated, having no doubt that Sybil would be gunning for him. *But she is one of Ivy's oldest friends, and if she and I have a future, then Sybil will have to accept me eventually.*

With that in mind, he followed the address Ivy sent to him. Soon, he knocked on their door, surprised when it flung open, and a pint-sized princess wearing a Wonder Woman top paired with a frilly pink tutu stared up at him. Grinning, he squatted so that he would be on her level. "Hi there!"

"Are you the man who Auntie Ivy is dating?"

"Yes, I am. I'm Andy."

A little boy bounded beside the Wonder Woman princess and eyed him suspiciously. "Are you a cop?"

"Yes, I'm a police officer."

It didn't miss his attention how carefully he was

being eyed by both of them, and he wondered if they had a career in interrogation.

"Are you gonna marry Auntie Ivy?" the little girl asked.

At the same time, the boy asked, "Do you have a badge and a gun?"

Caught by surprise, he decided to answer the boy first. "Yes, I have a badge, and I also have a gun. But I only have the badge with me right now." He'd secured his weapon in his SUV but wasn't about to impart that tidbit of knowledge.

"Can I see it?" the little boy asked.

"Are you gonna marry Auntie Ivy?" the little girl repeated louder, obviously unhappy about being left out.

"Well, I think that's something I should talk to Ivy about first, don't you?"

She pondered, then nodded. "Yeah. If you're going to get down on your knee, you need to do it when it's just the two of you. 'Cause if she says no, then you'd be embarrassed."

"Why would she say no?" the little boy huffed. "Who wouldn't want to marry a cop?"

He barked out a laugh and shook his head. Hoping a response wasn't needed, he stood.

"My mom says that you weren't very nice to Auntie Ivy in high school."

He grimaced, then nodded. "You know, your mom is right. But I've learned a lot since then. I've learned that it's not nice to make fun of other people. We don't like it when people make fun of us, do we?"

"Jessica! Ricky! Let the man in!"

Andy spied a man walking down the hall toward the front door with his hand extended, glad to see a welcoming smile on his face.

"You must be Andy. I'm Steve, Sybil's husband. And you've just been grilled by Jessica and Ricky. My son is probably only interested in you as a policeman, but my daughter has been raised by my sweet but gossipy wife, Sybil, who I understand, you know. Come on in. You might as well get the worst part out of the way."

He stepped in and whispered, "How bad is this going to get?"

Steve appeared to think about the question, then shrugged. "Well, Sybil's had three glasses of wine so far. I'd say that gives you a fighting chance."

He'd barely had time to steel himself to meet the Sybil firing squad when the sound of female laughter met his ears. He followed Steve into the family room to see Ivy with her head thrown back in laughter. She was always beautiful, but with her face filled with easy laughter and pure bliss, she took his breath away. She looked over her shoulder and graced him with a smile that caused his heart to skip a beat. Without paying attention to what anyone else was doing, he walked straight to her, bent, and kissed her. He wanted to take it deeper, longer, fuller but managed to pull back when he heard a little giggle and knew that somewhere close by, a Wonder Woman princess with marriage on her mind was lurking.

"Hey, babe," he muttered against her lips.

"Mmmm, hey," she replied.

As he slid onto the arm of the chair next to her, he looked down. "Babe! Your splint. What did the doc say?"

"He was pleased, and I can now start physical therapy."

He lifted her hand and kissed her fingers lightly. "I know you're glad. Congratulations, Ivy."

The sound of a throat clearing across the room caused him to shoot his gaze upward, seeing Sybil curled up on the sofa, her gaze pinned on him.

"Sybil, thanks for letting me come by."

She pinched her lips together for a second, then nodded. "Well, I was prepared to give you hell, but after seeing the way you greeted my best friend, I have to admit that perhaps she was right about you."

Lifting his brow, he said, "I'm almost afraid to ask. What did she say about me?" With his arm around Ivy's shoulders, he gave her a little squeeze as he waited to see what Sybil would say.

"She said you're very different from what we remembered years ago. But then, considering we all are, I really shouldn't be surprised." She smiled as Jessica and Ricky bounced into the room and up on the sofa. Once she'd kissed her kids' heads, she lifted her gaze to him again. "I'm glad you could come, too."

He'd been holding his breath so long to see what she would say he felt his lungs burning. Now with that comment, the air rushed out as he smiled and squeezed Ivy tighter around the shoulders. Steve walked in and handed him a beer.

"I'm afraid we've already eaten, but there are some delicious leftovers," Sybil offered.

He hesitated, but Steve said, "A lot of things I can say about my wife, and a good cook is one of them. She did a mighty fine roast beef. How about I make you a sandwich?"

Nodding, he said, "I'll take you up on that. It has been a long day."

He and Steve headed into the kitchen while Ivy and Sybil rounded up the kids and took them upstairs to get ready for bed. As he took the opportunity to chat with Steve, he discovered he liked a lot about the big man. Steve was muscular but with a little girth in the middle and didn't seem to give a fuck about counting calories. Andy had a feeling that Sybil would bust Steve's balls if his cholesterol went up. He also had a feeling that Steve would be able to handle his wife no matter what.

"Virginia Marine Police, huh?"

"Yeah. I was at the Seaside Police Department before that. And before that, the Navy."

Steve nodded as he handed Andy a plate with a massive roast beef sandwich and chips on the side. Digging in, Andy groaned in appreciation. As soon as he swallowed, he nodded. "Yep, Sybil can cook a mean roast beef."

Steve chuckled. "Sounds like she's relenting on giving you a hard time." Shaking his head, he said, "I met her in college. Honestly, if I ragged on her about all the shit she used to get up to, she'd have my head on a platter. My girl's a good woman, but damn, she was a hell-raiser back then."

"I can see that. She was a ballbuster in high school, but I deserved any darts she threw my way back then."

"No sense in living in the past," Steve said.

It struck Andy that with Steve's sage advice, he completely agreed. Whatever residual anger he'd had toward his mom had long since burned out with the realization that she'd given up getting to be with a good man and knowing her two sons. Hearing Ivy laughing upstairs with Jessica and Ricky, it hit him that if they one day married and had children, his mom had also given up that future as well. But he, Aaron, and their pop still had that in their future. Finishing the sandwich while enjoying a conversation with Steve about the Baytown High School sports teams, he grinned when Ivy walked back into the room.

She slid her arms around his waist and pressed her head on his shoulder. Kissing the top of her head, he whispered against her hair, "You ready to head home?"

She nodded, and they said their goodbyes to Sybil and Steve. Once in the driveway, he stood at her driver's door. "Which house? Yours or mine?"

She hesitated and then crinkled her nose. "Honestly, I like yours more. I still feel like I'm sneaking a boyfriend over when we have sex at my parents' house."

He laughed. "Do I want to know how many boys you snuck over?"

She play-slapped his arm. "Seriously? How many do you think had the nerve to date Poison Ivy?"

At that, he deflated, his expression falling. "Oh, babe, I'm—"

"No!" she rushed, grabbing his shoulders. "I'm sorry."

"You're sorry? What do you have to be sorry for?"

"It was years ago, and you apologized. For me to

keep bringing it up is wrong. I really didn't mean it the way it came out, but I'm sorry nonetheless."

He drew her close, holding her gaze. "Ivy, you were joking, and that's fine. You weren't throwing something in my face. You weren't trying to drag us backward. It's okay."

She sucked in her lips, then slowly smiled as she stared at him. "Okay. But in answer to your earlier question, I never snuck a boy into my parents' house."

"I was your first sneaky rebellion?"

Her laughter rang out as she nodded. "Yes. Tell you what, I'll stop by my house and grab some clothes. Then I'll come straight to your place."

He kissed his reply before assisting her into her car. Watching her drive away, he walked to his SUV and then glanced toward Sybil's house, seeing her standing in the living room window with a wide smile. Chuckling, he pulled out of her driveway, his heart light.

He managed to get home and had time to toss his dirty clothes into the laundry before changing into jeans and a Go Navy T-shirt. Hearing Ivy at his front door, he pulled it open and drew her inside. Kicking the door shut, he immediately pulled her into his embrace. Just before his lips landed on hers, he said, "In case you were wondering, I've never had a woman over here. You're the first in my house."

She jerked in his arms, her eyes wide. "Really?"

"When I bought this place, I knew it was my *home*. A special place where one day I hoped to have a wife and kids. I didn't want it tainted with a… well, with a one-nighter."

Inhaling quickly, she blinked, and he spied moisture gathering in her eyes.

"You brought me here," she whispered.

"Yeah. Ivy, you're special. A special person and special to me. I know we're in the early days of our adult relationship, but I'm not sure my heart knows that 'cause it beats differently just when I hear your voice. And my breath gets stuck in my lungs when you smile or laugh. My mouth automatically smiles when I get a text or see your number on my phone. And when you stand in this house, it feels right."

A tear slid down her cheek, but her smile showed that she liked his words.

"Do you know what I want to do right now?" she asked, her eyes bright.

He shook his head, no longer trusting his voice.

"I want you to take me upstairs. To your room. To your bed. And I don't want to leave there until we pass out from exhaustion."

His heart stumbled but quickly recovered. "Damn," he rushed, then scooped her into his arms. He'd never mounted the stairs faster but made sure he didn't whack her head on the banister. And when he lowered her feet to the floor next to his bed, he knew he held the prize in his arms. He'd known he wanted her since the moment he'd seen her standing on the bridge. Ivy Watkins… brave, smart, beautiful, loving… and his.

24

Standing in Andy's bedroom with the lights low and Ivy's eyes filled with nothing but him, she wondered if she was crazy. Two weeks. In the span of the centuries, two weeks was a dot in time, yet she knew this was the man she wanted to be with.

Staring up at him now, she could still see him leaning over her as she lay shivering in the bottom of his boat. Scared, in shock, in pain, and cold to her very marrow. But she'd stared into his dark, warm eyes and was mesmerized. Water droplets dripped from his dark hair and beard, but he'd wrapped her in blankets and gently pushed her wet hair from her face. Unconcerned for himself, he gave all his attention to her. And it enveloped her as much as the warming blankets.

Those obsidian eyes had kept her grounded as she'd listened to him tell her that she would be fine. And she'd believed him.

And now, holding his gaze, she still believed him. Whatever Andy had been as a boy, the man was everything she wanted. Time seemed to stop as they remained still, neither moving, neither speaking, their breaths and heartbeats in sync.

Her fingers gripped his shoulders as nerves threatened to weaken her knees. His hands stayed steady on her waist, and she relished the feel as well as the knowledge he'd catch her if she fell.

"It's crazy," she whispered as the words came unbidden from deep inside. Seeing his brows lower slightly, she swallowed deeply. "The way I feel. It's crazy."

A crinkle in his forehead joined the lowered brows, and she lifted a hand, soothing her fingers over the crease and then downward to cup his jaw. "Two weeks ago, I fell off a bridge, and you rescued me. Two weeks ago, we didn't even recognize each other. And now?" She dragged in a shaky breath, the air heavy between them.

"What about now?" His words were low and raspy, and she felt fear coming off him in waves.

"Now... I've fallen for you."

He jerked slightly, and she had no idea how to interpret his actions, considering his expression didn't change.

"It's true." Her gut clenched, but she nodded slightly as though the movement would emphasize her words in case he was in doubt. "It might not be logical. Or the way I thought it would be. It might seem too fast or too impulsive. Or maybe, it might seem as though I'm just reacting to the events of the rescue." She slowly shook her head. "But it's what I feel... what I know." Swallowing deeply again, she pressed her lips together and shrugged. "I just wanted you to know before... well, um... before."

"Before?"

"Before we sleep together again. It doesn't seem right for me to hope that what we're doing would lead to expectations if you aren't inclined the same way. At least without letting you know in case... uh...." Her words trailed off, sounding ridiculous to her ears, and she could only imagine how they sounded to him. She closed her eyes, feeling the heat rising off her face.

"Ivy," he whispered as he cupped her face. "Look at me."

She shook her head. "I feel stupid and have just messed things up, haven't I?"

"Look at me. You're too brave a person not to look at me."

She forced her eyes open at that, now wishing she was a wimp to go along with being a fool.

"You haven't messed anything up at all. Instead, you continue to be brave."

Inhaling quickly, he caught her off guard with his words, but she had no idea what he meant. Biting back the urge to ask, she remained quiet, held in place by his dark eyes.

He cupped her face with both hands, his thumbs gently caressing her cheeks. "You're brave because you honestly spoke what was in your heart. But you don't need to worry that your feelings are one-sided."

She blinked and pressed her lips together, a kernel of hope planted but too nervous to let it bloom.

He bent so that his face was directly in front of hers, his dark eyes holding her captive. As he spoke, his breath puffed gently over her face. "I've fallen for you, too."

Her heart pounded loud enough that she was sure he could hear it. He smiled and said, "Breathe, baby. I don't want you to pass out before we have a chance to make love."

Dragging in a breath that hitched on its way into her lungs, she tried a second time, finally inhaling without choking. A smile curved her lips as moisture gathered in her eyes.

"It looks like you're smiling and crying at the same time," he commented, his brows lowered once again.

She nodded. "I think I am."

"Why?"

"Because I'm happy."

His smile joined hers, and he closed the distance so their mouths were sealed together. The kiss bypassed sweet and launched straight to wild. Noses bumped and teeth clashed as all finesse flew out the window.

His arms banded around her waist to lift her, and she whipped her legs around him. Her brace kept her from moving her hands the way she wanted, but she gripped the back of his head with her good hand, dragging her nails along his scalp. She quickly swallowed the groan that erupted from him, and she hoped it was only the first of what would be many groans she elicited from him that night.

With one of his hands now on her ass, she ground

herself on his crotch, the need for friction overpowering all other desires.

He walked them to the bed and bent forward, lowering her onto her back. His body lay on top of hers, and she welcomed the weight. Continuing to shift her hips against his, she didn't care that she was dry-humping him to seek release.

He pushed upward, forcing their lips to separate. She hated to let go but was desperate to get rid of their clothes, and it seemed he had the same feeling as his hands went to the bottom of her shirt. With some difficulty, she rolled back and forth so that he could drag it up over her breasts, getting it snagged first on her chin and then in her hair. Finally, when the offending material was tossed to the side, she was grateful her bra had a front snap and was quickly divested of the scrap of satin.

Her hands darted to where his shirt was tucked into his pants, and she managed to pull it free. Unable to do much more, she smiled as he shifted to his knees, now resting on either side of her thighs, and whipped his shirt over his head with much more finesse.

Her gaze dragged over his torso, her fingers dancing lightly over the warm skin and tight muscles. Fascinated with the ridges highlighted in the light of the single lamp, she couldn't wait to taste every inch.

He shimmied back off the bed, his hands going to her shoes, which quickly joined her shirt on the floor. He leaned forward and kissed her belly as his hands snagged the waistband of her leggings, and he began to inch them down over her hips. His mouth followed the path as he kissed her mound, then each exposed thigh and calf. When he'd discarded her pants and panties, and she lay completely exposed, she reveled in the appreciation of his gaze traveling slowly over her body.

"You are so beautiful," he said, with reverence dripping from his words.

His intense, worshipful stare made her heart sing. It didn't feel like a pickup line. It didn't feel like something he felt he *should* say. With his eyes moving over her body before settling on her face, she felt his words deeply.

Bending over the bed again, he continued to kiss from her belly upward, his tongue swirling around each hardened nipple before drawing it deeply into his mouth. She hissed as she drew air through her gritted teeth, forcing her body to lie still when all she wanted to do was grab him and hold on.

Suddenly, she felt the cool air move between them as he stood again. His hands moved to his belt, and the click of the buckle and the leather dragging through the belt loops sounded out in the quiet room. He shifted from one leg to the other as he pulled off his boots.

His hands moved to his waistband, and before she could blink, he'd shoved his pants and boxers to the floor, shifting from one foot to the other to kick them away.

She leaned up and rested on her forearms, allowing her gaze to peruse every inch from his beautiful face down his gorgeous body, settling on his long, thick erection.

It wasn't their first time. And this wouldn't be their

last time. But if the words they'd said earlier were true, he would be the last and only man she made love with. And that thought didn't scare her at all. She lifted her arms and wiggled her fingers, beckoning. "I want you. Right now, all of you."

He crawled over her again, but instead of settling between her legs, he lay on his side, facing her, with his elbow crooked and his head resting on his palm. He glided over her body with his free hand as he worshipped her curves. By the time his fingers ended up at her sex, she was wet and more than ready. With his thumb pressing circles on her clit, he inserted two fingers, and the scissoring movement sent her hips bucking up off the mattress. He leaned forward, and his tongue swept through her mouth, mimicking the thrusts of his fingers.

So ready for him, she felt the coil tighten deep inside, and closing her mind to all thoughts other than pleasure, she bucked her body again as her release exploded. His kiss stole her breath as much as her orgasm, and while she hated to lose his lips, she was almost glad when he kissed a trail down her throat so she could drag in oxygen.

He pulled out his fingers and brought them to his mouth, sucking her juices off before leaning over to kiss her again. Tasting her essence was not something she'd ever experienced before, but like everything he did, she found the eroticism overwhelming.

Her foggy mind was still floating on a sea of bliss when she felt him shift again. When she opened her eyes, his dark stare penetrated her as his cock lined up with her eager sex. She wrapped her legs around his waist and, with her heels, urged him on, surprised when he suddenly stopped.

"Wha—"

"Condom," he growled.

Her hands gripped his shoulders. "I'm clean. I was just tested as part of the physical for the new job. I can show you on my phone." She hadn't planned on saying the words that blurted out but had no desire to take them back.

He held her gaze for only a second before replying, "I'm clean too. The department also requires us to get tested."

"I'm also on birth control. I understand if you wanna get a condom, that's fine—"

"What I really want is to be inside you with nothing between us," he confessed.

The ball was in her court. He was giving all control over to her. She hesitated briefly but knew she trusted this man with her life. Her lips curved, and her heels dug into his muscular ass again. "That's what I want, too."

He held her gaze for a few seconds before grinning. He kissed her with a smile on his lips, causing her to smile, also. And with the thrust of his hips, he was fully sheathed inside her waiting body. He continued to plunge, slow at first, then building to an almost pounding pace. But with every thrust, she clutched him tighter, urging him on.

In the past, sex had always been almost polite and somewhat functional. But this was raw. Wild. Animalistic. But with more emotion than anything she'd ever felt in her life.

He hooked a forearm under one leg and lifted her knee, allowing him to go even deeper, which she wasn't sure was possible. Clutching his shoulders again, she gasped. "I'm close!"

He buried his face in her neck, and just as her release hit deep inside, he roared out his orgasm as they came together. She lost track of how long they lay, gasping and panting, heartbeats radically pounding, and sweat-slicked bodies slowly cooling.

Eventually, she became aware of the weight of his body pressing her down, and as though it just hit him simultaneously, he lifted off her chest, keeping his weight on his arms.

"Sorry, babe. I didn't mean to crush you. Damn, I wasn't sure I was able to move."

Still holding him tight, she laughed. "I didn't want you to move. Not after that."

As his smile held her captive, she was struck with the realization that his smile wasn't filled with a sense of self. Some men like to boast after sex as though they just gifted a prize to the woman and expect songs of praise to erupt. Instead, Andy's smile was gentle, almost thankful.

And he proved it when he said, "You're amazing, Ivy. I'm so humbled you're in love with me."

Her chin quivered as she felt tears gathering once again. Unable to keep one from sliding down her cheek, he captured it with his thumb before leaning forward to kiss the next one away. He kissed her lightly on the lips, then slid off the bed and moved into the bathroom. He returned with a warm washcloth, wiping her gently. Crawling back into bed, he pulled the covers over both of them and tucked her in tightly.

Not wanting the night to end without making sure he knew her feelings, she whispered, "I do love you, Andy."

"And I love you, too, babe."

She lay enveloped in his arms, cheek resting on his chest. Two weeks. She'd always thought love would take longer to experience. But she had no doubt. All it took with Andy was two weeks. With that, she closed her eyes and drifted off to sleep.

25

Roberta walked down the stairs and stopped at the landing, surveying the scene before her. Allowing a private grimace to mar her expression, she then wiped her face clear of disgust and continued descending the stairs. At the bottom, she turned toward the sunroom, but Ty's voice halted her.

"Hey, we're hungry!"

She wanted to argue that she wasn't their cook and maid, but she hardly had a job description. Swallowing her pride, she nodded and proceeded into the kitchen to prepare sandwiches. It wasn't fancy, but with the way the men in the family room were snorting coke, she figured they wouldn't care what she handed them.

"Here you go," she announced, trying to infuse her voice with a level of enthusiasm. As long as Ty was happy with her, she'd keep her position as his main woman. But the gang was volatile, and she knew that position rested on a knife's blade. He'd found her in a cheap brothel in Baltimore, decided he liked what he saw, and brought her into the Blood's fold. *Well, as much as any woman could be.* Bringing her with him to this house, which was nicer than any place she'd ever lived, had been a dream come true. But with some of the local gang members, she was uncertain where she stood with them. As long as they knew she had Tyrone's eye, she was protected.

She returned to the kitchen and grabbed some beer bottles, setting them on the table, as well. Serving Ty first, she smiled when he wrapped his arm around her waist, holding her in place for a moment. "You need anything else, baby?" she asked.

He patted her ass and nodded. "I'll have you make a call in a few minutes."

She walked back into the kitchen, putting away the sandwich fixings after nibbling on the ham and turkey, forgoing the bread. Ty said he liked her curves, but she noticed he would sometimes fuck skinny girls. There was no room for jealousy. Her feelings were purely selfish. *Gotta keep my position as long as I can.*

Her dream had always been to make enough money to be able to have her own life somewhere away from the easy drugs and easier fucks. It would take forever for that to happen in the brothel, but with the money Ty was giving her, she figured she could make it to a place where she could get a job working as a receptionist in a salon, then train to be a stylist. That had been her goal since she first looked at hairstyles in the magazines her mom gave her to keep her quiet while she entertained her *gentleman callers*. She snorted at the memory—*only my mama could make turning tricks sound fancy.* Sighing, she wondered if she was more like her mama than she wanted to admit.

She moved to the counter to hear what was being said in the next room, knowing they must be planning another shipment.

"Fuckin' po come around, so gonna make a change for this one."

"Hell, one comes when I'm here, gonna take care of his ass."

"Linc, you ain't gonna do a goddamn fuckin' thing. You fuck this place up, and I'll fuck you up," Ty growled. "You got me?"

"Yeah, yeah, man. Chill."

Roberta held her breath. Usually, Tyrone was careful with what he did, but lately, Linc had been getting bold. He was the local leader, and she wondered if he was chaffing under Tyrone's control.

"We've got another boat coming in this evening. They're not coming here. I've told them to go to the north drop-off," Ty said. "Roberta?"

She hustled into the room. "Yeah, baby?"

"Make your call. Tell them tonight, and you'll let 'em know the exact time once we know it."

"Sure thing, Ty." She walked out of the room smiling until she was at the bottom of the stairs. Then she allowed her grimace to reappear from the comments about her coming from Linc. And even though Ty claimed her, he wouldn't defend her. His brother Marcus came the closest to being someone who seemed to care about her, but he was subservient to Ty.

Once inside the bedroom, she pulled out the burner phone and dialed.

"Hey, sweetie," she said when the call was answered. "Tonight. I'll text when we know the time."

"Got it. Let me know as soon as you can about the time."

"Absolutely."

Disconnecting, she walked to the window that overlooked the lawn, and she could see the Bay in the distance. She placed her hand over her heart at the scene's beauty before her. Sucking in a deep breath, she curled up in the comfy chair near the window and allowed her mind to drift to a place where she felt safe and able to make life her own. And wondered if it would ever happen.

26

Andy spent the morning on patrol, then the afternoon on maintenance of their vessels with Bryce in tow as he trained the former Navy medic on diagnosing problems with their boats instead of diagnosing human ailments.

An eager and fast learner, Bryce quickly became an asset to the VP of Baytown.

"I think some others are heading to the pub after work," Bryce said. "You going?"

As tempting as it was to spend time with friends, he shook his head. "I'm going to look at the camera footage from last night. I've been trying to do it each morning, but with a call out early, I didn't have a chance."

Bryce shook his head. "You've got to spread this around, Andy. I know Ryan didn't mean for you to take the burden of trying to do it all yourself."

"I know. I just find I've gotten sucked in, and it's hard to let it go."

"Then why don't we make sure that somebody's available to look at it in the mornings, and if that's not you, then someone else. That way, you're not working late trying to play catch-up."

He agreed and thanked Bryce. Heading into the station, he stopped by Ryan's office. "Hey, Captain. I didn't get a chance to look at the camera this morning, so I'm gonna take a look now."

Ryan sent a sharp glare his way. "I want to put everyone on rotation so that this doesn't fall completely on you."

Chuckling, he nodded. "Bryce just said the same thing."

Ryan's expression relaxed. "Good. Let me know if you find anything."

He entered the workroom and fired up the computer where the camera motion sensor feeds were sent. Quickly, moving through the various shots taken when wildlife crossed the camera angles paths, he could also see fishermen, recreational boaters, and even a few kayakers who braved the cold coming out of the inlets.

Finally, his attention was captured by a long silver boat that came into Hangars Inlet at 9:17 p.m. At 9:52, it left the inlet. It was dark, but two people were visible in the boat. Both wearing black. Calling for Ryan, he wasn't surprised when Callan walked in along with their captain.

They reviewed the video footage again, and then Ryan called Mac Davenport. "Mac, I've got Officer Bergstrom with me. We found suspicious activity last night that could possibly put someone passing by the bridge between ten and ten thirty."

"Damn," Mac said. "I'm not in the office today. But

I'll call Officer Ronald Jeeves, who's on duty right now. I'll give him the okay to talk with you."

A few minutes later, their phone rang, and Andy picked up. "Officer Jeeves? I've got you on speaker."

"Yes, thank you. Captain Davenport told me that I would be your liaison for now. Can you give me the information?"

Andy repeated the information they'd given Mac with the time and boat information they could provide.

"Okay. Give me a few minutes, and I'll go through and see what comes up. What's the best number to call?"

Andy gave him the office phone, then also his cell phone. "You can call anytime," he offered. "Station or my personal cell. We just appreciate having you work with us."

"My pleasure. Captain Davenport told us what was going on, so I'm excited to help."

Andy disconnected and glanced at the time. Looking toward Callan and Ryan, he said, "Since nothing can be done today, don't feel like you have to stick around. If Ronald can see them pass under the bridge, then we'll know that our camera system works. If not, we'll just have to tweak it more to try to catch them."

"Sounds good," Callan said, clapping him on the back. With a nod, he and Ryan left the room, and Andy reviewed his camera footage while he waited for the call. He noted that they didn't use Parker Inlet. Scrubbing his hand over his face, he sighed heavily just as his phone vibrated, and he grinned when he read the text from Ivy.

I'll meet you at your house. I'll fix dinner!

He leaned back in his chair, the heaviness pressing on his chest from his job stress easing at the thought of Ivy in his kitchen. While he'd never expected her to cook for him, the domestic scene in his mind still filled an empty place deep inside. A scene he wasn't sure he'd ever see.

His phone rang, and he spied Ronald Jeeves's number. "Man, I hope you can give me some good news." A heavy sigh was heard from the other end, and his stomach dropped. "That doesn't sound good, Ronald."

"It's not," Ronald agreed. "I have no idea how this happened, but I was going through all the under-bridge camera angles, as well as the ones angled for over the tunnels. Two cameras were turned in weird directions, then went offline."

Andy sat up straight, his body jerking slightly. "Went offline? What do you mean?"

"Just that. For about ten minutes, both of those cameras were nothing but static. Then suddenly, they came back online. But the timing was from ten twelve to ten twenty-one."

"You have got to be fucking kidding me?" Andy bit out.

"I have no idea what the hell happened, but I'll talk to Mac. In fact, I'll send him something now, and we'll meet first thing in the morning. I'm really sorry, Andy."

He disconnected but sat for a few minutes, wondering how gangbangers could have managed to interrupt the camera signals to keep them from being visible when they passed from the Bay out into the ocean. He didn't have a clue, but he bet he knew who might, and she was currently in his kitchen.

Firing off a text to Ryan, he shut down the computers, waved to the night dispatcher, and headed to his SUV.

As soon as he walked into his house, the sight of Ivy stirring something in a pot on his stove caused his feet to stumble to a halt, and all thoughts of work, cameras, and drug gangs flew from his mind. He barely remembered his mother in the kitchen when he was little, and then from the time he was seven, it was either his dad or Ms. Sally. His hand lifted to rub his chest as he blinked away the moisture gathering in his eyes.

She looked over her shoulder, and as soon as her gaze hit him, she smiled. "Hey," she called out softly.

His feet became unglued from the floor, and he was at her back in a few steps. His arms encircled her, and he nuzzled her neck. She tilted her head to the side, offering more silky skin for him to kiss.

"Damn, babe, something smells good."

"I didn't go to the grocery store, but you had a jar of spaghetti sauce, and I had a few vegetables at my place. So I'm turning your grocery spaghetti sauce into my own creation."

"That sounds fucking amazing, but that's not what I'm talking about. What I think smells even better is just you."

She laughed and turned in his arms, placing her hands behind his neck. "I think I'm gonna have to call bullshit, Andy. I've been at work all day and haven't had a shower. I hardly think I smell good."

"And what you don't get, babe, is that I just like your scent. It doesn't have to be sweet or perfume. It just has to be *you*. And you here in my house is the best place you could possibly be."

With each word, he watched her eyes grow bigger and brighter, and when her gaze dropped to his mouth, he took the invitation, kissing her deeply. He'd just angled his head and thrust his tongue into her mouth when the buzzer on the oven sounded, and they both jumped.

"Shit, that scared me," she said. "I hate to end that kiss, but I don't want the bread to burn."

He stepped back, and while she finished dinner, he grabbed the plates and cutlery. Soon, a simple, home-cooked meal was plated, and as they sat and ate at the table, it was as though all the scattered pieces from his childhood fell into place. She was doing what his mom never had, and it meant more to him than she could possibly know.

He kept his thoughts to himself but was determined to prove to her tonight how much she meant to him when they made love.

"Anything new from the cameras?" she asked.

Jerked back to reality, he nodded and wiped his mouth. "Funny you asked because I wanted to get your take on something." He went through what he found with his cameras and his call to Mac. Then he relayed what Ronald had told him. With each comment, he watched her brows lower, confusion etched deeply in her expression.

Her mouth opened, but nothing came out for a

moment. Then she suddenly shook her head. "Exactly when someone would be passing under the CBBT, the camera went offline?"

"That's what he said."

She leaned back in her chair, her brow scrunched, still shaking her head. Finally, she met his gaze. "I honestly don't know, Andy. I mean, that's not my department or my program, but I work to provide continuity between the various systems of the CBBT. My suspicious nature makes me wonder if that was done intentionally, but I have difficulty understanding how someone could have made that happen on their own without others knowing."

"What are you thinking?"

Pressing her lips together, she finally sucked in a deep breath and let it out slowly. "There are always coincidences, but usually, the percentage is much greater that human manipulation was the reason. Now, whether by purpose or mistake? I can't say."

Her words were strong, but her tone edged on strident. Lifting his brow, he waited, reminded of her having the same expression on her face when they sat at her parents' kitchen table working on a project. He knew if Ivy was still like she was as a teenager, she would ponder a problem, continually searching for a solution. He didn't care back then, figuring her inquisitiveness would gain a good grade for him, but now he was fascinated as she quietly analyzed.

"In the realm of all possibilities, there are multiple explanations. It could be that someone who has access to the cameras has tampered with, re-programmed, or otherwise made a temporary change when they want the passageway to be obscured or completely taken out of commission. It could be that there is some kind of device the drug runners have that allow them to jam the camera signals, but that seems unlikely unless they have access to someone on the inside as well."

Ivy leaned back and sighed, her gaze focused off in the distance. He remained quiet, then finally reached over and placed his hand on her arm. "Babe?"

She startled, and her gaze snapped back to him. "Sorry!"

Chuckling, he shook his head. "Don't be sorry. It's just that I didn't mean for this conversation to take over the wonderful meal you cooked."

Her shoulders relaxed as she beamed another smile toward him, and he could swear the room was filled with light. Leaning closer, they met halfway and kissed. Sweeping his tongue inside her mouth, the taste of the tangy sauce, wine, and simply her caused his cock to twitch. When he leaned back to adjust himself, her eyes blinked open as though surprised, and a small kitten mewl escaped from her perfect lips.

He knew what she wanted and chuckled since it was the same thing he wanted also. "We've got time for that, but first, I want to make sure you eat, babe."

At those words, the room grew even brighter with her smile.

27

"Anne? Hi, it's Ivy. I've got something I want to ask you about, but I'd rather do it in person."

"Oh, that sounds mysterious." Anne laughed.

"I'm just trying to figure out an anomaly, and I think you're the best person to help me determine what happened."

"You can come anytime you want. I don't have any major items to work on today. It's mostly just system maintenance."

"Would it be possible for me to come at a time when no one else is in the office with you?"

"Oooh! This sounds even more mysterious. I love it! I was actually getting bored today." Anne laughed. "You can always come at lunch. My two officemates and I usually head down the road to one of the restaurants near the Virginia Beach toll gate. But it just so happens that today I brought a sandwich because I looked in the mirror and realized that too many taco lunches were going straight to my hips."

Ivy laughed. "Perfect. I brought my lunch also. I'll tell my boss that I'm going to have lunch with you so that we can review a couple of programs."

Disconnecting, she continued to work on maintenance analysis, then, at lunchtime, she grabbed her purse and lunch bag and stepped into the hall. Seeing Ethan at his desk, she stopped at his door. "I'm heading across the bridge to have lunch with Anne. We're looking at a possible anomaly. I thought we'd do it and have lunch at the same time."

"Anomaly?" Ethan asked, looking up from his computer to where she stood at his door.

Inwardly wincing, she wished she hadn't said anything. *I suck at lying!* "Not so much an anomaly... um... just seeing how we can work on the camera angles for security and maintenance without compromising either one." Seeing him about to question her again, she cursed her inability to lie creatively. Her stomach knotted, and she waved her hand dismissively. "That's why I'm going at lunch. It's nothing right now other than me seeing if certain things are possible. Um... sort of exploration." Starting to walk away before she blabbed anymore, she prayed he didn't see through her ridiculous excuses.

"Let me know how it goes. I'll be interested," he called after her.

Glad to escape, she hurried to her car and drove over the bridge. It was now weeks since her accident, but this was the first time she'd been on the bridge since then. Wondering if she would be hypersensitive, she couldn't help but look at the area on the other side of the north bridge where she'd first encountered Larry and the baby. *And, just below, where I first met Andy again.*

Driving turned out not to be traumatic. In fact, just like always, she relaxed on the trip, fascinated with the sea birds. It also hit her that since working for the CBBT, she was more intricately in tune with the physical structure than ever. Twenty minutes later, she reached the other end, where she pulled into the building off to the side of the toll gates on the Virginia Beach side. Walking inside, she scanned her ID and was glad Anne met her at the entrance.

"I know you were here when you were first hired and doing initial training," Anne said. "But I figured you might've forgotten where my office was, so I thought I'd come." Leaning closer, she whispered, "My officemates have gone to lunch, so we have the place to ourselves."

They walked into the work area that held three desks and multiple computers. Glad they were alone, she noticed Anne went so far as to close the door.

"Okay, I'm pulling out my chipped ham and swiss cheese sandwich, and I'm going to eat while you tell me what's going on because my curiosity is about to explode!"

"I want to know if someone can alter or tamper with the cameras on the bridge?"

At Ivy's question, Anne halted as she brought her sandwich toward her mouth. Her owlish eyes behind her glasses were wide, and her mouth hung open. "Huh?"

"Sorry. I guess I just kind of dropped that on you."

"You think? Jesus, Ivy! Way to give me a heart

attack." Anne dropped her sandwich on her napkin. "Okay, what are we talking about? Because if you're giving me definite information, this could be huge."

"No, no, it's not definite. I just want to know if someone can jam the cameras."

Anne stared, her eyes narrowing slightly. "What are you not telling me?"

Sighing, Ivy leaned back in her chair. "You know from our staff meeting that the local law enforcement are working with Mac's office, and... completely unofficially, so you can't tell anyone... when they tried to check on a couple of cameras, they appeared to be offline."

Anne's brow lowered as her chin jerked back. "Seriously?"

Ivy hefted her shoulders. "I know there can be many reasons, but I just wanted to hear from someone who might be able to tell me what they think."

Anne blew out a long breath, then leaned back in her chair. "Well... one of the things that the maintenance crews have to do constantly is to check the cameras. Wind. Weather. Damn birds. Occasionally even a dumbass pilot of a boat that shouldn't be on the water but can't drive worth a shit bumps into the pylons. And, of course, that's not even considering something going offline due to connectivity issues. Although, when that happens, we should get an alert."

Nodding slowly, Ivy had already thought of all those possibilities. "Okay, that makes sense. And, um... human error... here?"

Blinking, Anne chewed on her bottom lip. "I don't

really see how." Her gaze jumped to Ivy's. "I'm not just saying that because it's the department I worked in. But, if I'm honest, I know anyone can make a mistake. I just can't figure out how it would be done. Someone would have to specifically go into the program and make a change. Then change it back."

"And if that happened, it would have to be someone in this department? No one has access?"

"Right... well, mostly."

"Mostly?"

"Well, we each have our specialties. This office works with the toll equipment, the auto pass system, the customer advisory signs, and the data advisory equipment. But there are more employees in the department who work in cybersecurity, the computer network, and radio and telephone communication networks. Bradley is the head of that area. And the CBBT police officers, while a different department, have access to the camera equipment."

"I didn't realize that." Ivy nodded. "And is it possible for an outside source to try to jam the system?"

Anne shook her head, then sighed. "I'm sure anything is possible. I just hate like hell to think about it. If what you're suggesting happened, that's an act of terrorism. Let's face it, the CBBT provides access to the Chesapeake Bay. While we're not the gatekeepers for all points north, including Norfolk's port or the Naval base, or Baltimore's port, we are certainly used by the Navy and Coast Guard as a point of entrance and exit for ships from all over the world."

The two women sat silently for a moment, and Ivy tried to wrap her mind around the possibilities.

"Look," Anne said, fiddling with her napkin. "Are you telling me something needs to be reported?"

"No," Ivy said, shaking her head. "I know the police are just checking on all possibilities, and I wanted to understand for myself. Whatever happened, Mac and Ronald know and will handle things from here. As the systems engineer, I need to be aware of all the various ways the systems integrate. I'm learning but still have a ways to go in my training."

"Good, because I now want to enjoy my lunch!" Anne laughed as she picked up her sandwich again and, this time, took a huge bite, groaning with appreciation.

Ivy didn't feel the same sense of ease but pretended to enjoy her lunch, as well. Once finished, she gathered her items and slid her coat on. "Anne, thank you so much. I hope I haven't made things awkward for you."

"Hell, no! This gave me some excitement, girl!"

Anne offered a hug, and Ivy walked back to her car. This time as she drove back to the other side of the Bay, she couldn't help but stare at the bridge with a different feeling. *Could there be someone on the inside who's assisting drug gangs?*

Andy looked at Ivy, incredulity filling his being. That, and anger. "Are you crazy, Ivy? You need to stay out of the investigating and leave that to us!"

Her eyes narrowed, and her hands landed on her

hips. "I'll have you know that I was careful and only talked to Anne. I wanted to know if someone could do what you think happened."

Andy's fists were firmly planted on his hips, and he dropped his chin to stare at his boots for a moment. In truth, he knew what Ivy said made sense, but having already seen her in danger once when she wasn't his, he couldn't stand the thought of something happening again now that he had her in his life.

She stepped forward, her hands landing on either side of his waist, and he lifted his head to look into her eyes.

"The problem, Andy, is that I didn't really find out anything. All the cameras are necessary for the safety of the bridge and tunnels. Like any piece of equipment, they're not infallible. There can be connectivity issues, weather, mechanical difficulties, and even birds and boats interfere. While Anne didn't completely deny that someone on the inside could have purposely altered the system, she admitted it wouldn't be easy to go undetected. As far as someone jamming it, that would be a much more serious issue."

He forced his arms to relax and wrapped them around her back, pulling her close. Resting his chin on the top of her head, he breathed in her calming scent. "So if we disregard all the non-purposeful reasons, do you know how it might be possible for someone on the inside to make that happen?"

"Multiple people have access to computer programs that deal with the cameras. It's not as though just one person sits in an office and handles everything. Even the bridge police have some access to camera control, though they wouldn't be in charge of the actual computer systems working them."

He nodded as he tumbled through the possibilities. Ryan trusted Mac Davenport, and Andy had no reason to think the longtime police officer wasn't innocent. But there were thirty-eight other police officers employed by the CBBT. While the pay was comparable to somebody working for a town or county law enforcement, none of them were rolling in money. He inwardly snorted, thinking how he'd had to save just to make a down payment on his small house.

It wouldn't take much for a massive drug gang to wave money in front of someone in law enforcement to turn a blind eye or, with a sleight of hand, make a camera go offline.

His chest moved as he inhaled deeply, and Ivy leaned back to hold his gaze. Her hand drifted up to cup his jaw, her fingers gently moving through his beard. Then her thumb glided softly over his lips.

"I wish I could make it better for you." She slid her arms down, then linked fingers with him and led him over to the sofa. Pushing him down, she knelt at his feet, and as she reached to untie his boots, he hastened to stop her.

"Babe, no. You don't need to do that," he rushed.

She held his gaze and slowly shook her head. "I want to. Let me take care of you. Please."

As she untied his boots and slid them from his feet, his breath caught in his throat. Such a simple act, yet one he couldn't remember anyone doing for him before.

She sat next to him and pulled his body into hers. The position felt strange to him, although not unwanted. Even with her smaller body, Ivy's arms wrapped around his shoulder, and she pressed the side of his head until his cheek rested against her breasts. He closed his eyes and breathed her in. And while his cock twitched at the feel of her soft breasts pillowing his head, he closed his eyes and reveled in the comfort she offered.

He blinked, feeling moisture in his eyes, and prayed he didn't show the turmoil of emotions that suddenly hit him. He couldn't remember ever being cradled. Held tightly against his mother's body as she offered maternal comfort. He craved her touch, realizing how much he'd missed hugs simply to receive the gentle, unselfish gesture that gave so much.

The women he'd been with in the past had been for a physical release, and hugs had never been part of a one-nighter. But this moment with Ivy filled his soul, and his heart ached as it beat in his chest. Swallowing deeply, he held her tighter and felt her arms tighten in response.

They lay on the sofa embracing while not speaking, just being there for each other. And he felt that if he was ever gifted with her in his life forever and they had children, his children would never know a day without hugs.

But he kept those thoughts to himself, at least for now.

Finally, she whispered, "Let's go to bed, sweetheart."

A part of him hated to move but knew that as soon

as they got in bed, they would hold each other again and give as much as they received. Lifting his head, he held her gaze as he stared into her beautiful face. "I love you, Ivy."

The worry lines were erased, replaced by the crinkles at the sides of her eyes as her smile widened. "I love you too."

28

Ivy looked around the room in awe of the women gathered for the American Legion Auxiliary meeting. The topic was now onto the next fundraiser, a five- and ten-mile run. She'd loved cross-country in high school and had continued running in college, although not competitively. Sighing, she wished she ran more now that she'd moved to the Eastern Shore, but thinking of the fundraiser gave her the motive to get back into training.

Many of the women there remembered her name from high school, even if they'd been older than she. Some of the women were her mother's age, and she also recognized their names as well. With Andy involved in law enforcement, she felt an instant camaraderie with others in the same profession or married to those serving.

Once she'd entered the large room in the basement of the Methodist Church in Baytown, she'd been engulfed by Colt's wife, Carrie, Ryan's wife, Judith, and

Joseph's fiancé, Shiloh. They introduced her to Billie, Jared's girlfriend. Callan's wife, Sophie, met them after the meeting, and they all agreed to work on the fundraising committee for the run.

"It won't be too much work with everyone helping," Carrie promised. "We can get volunteers from the various restaurants and vendors for food and drinks."

"Plus, we can have vendor sections for sales where a percentage of the profit goes to the fundraiser," Lizzie said. Ivy remembered Lizzy living on a farm when they were in high school, and she had taken it over when her grandfather passed away. Married now, she made and sold goat milk products.

"You've got to try Lizzie's lotions," Jillian said, sliding next to Ivy. "I've got some in the Coffee Shop and Galleria."

"I was in there the other day," she said with a smile. "The sea glass art is gorgeous."

"That's by Jade's husband. Jade is over there," Jillian said, pointing at a beautiful dark-haired woman standing nearby. "Her husband is Lance, a police officer for Baytown, and he's also a sea glass artist."

"Wow," Ivy responded, surprised and impressed all at the same time. "Is everyone here so talented?"

"Not me." A beautiful woman appeared at Ivy's side. "I'm an accountant. If it doesn't involve numbers, I'm hopeless," she continued, laughing. "Although it comes in handy when helping my daughter with her homework. By the way, I'm Amelia… most people call me Lia. I'm married to Aiden MacFarlane."

"Nice to meet you," Ivy said, realizing the common

sentiment was genuine. Andy had encouraged her to come to the meeting tonight, and she hadn't felt so welcome in... well, she wasn't sure she'd ever felt so welcome. "I'm an engineer, so I know what you mean."

"Oh, you're dating Andy!"

Ivy turned to see another woman walk toward them.

"I'm Sam. I'm a vet in the area and married to the man who runs the local shelter. Joseph. Anyway, Andy is so sweet. He's come into the shelter a couple of times looking at both kittens and dogs. I think because of his job, he was leaning toward kittens." Suddenly, the woman blushed. "I'm sorry, that was presumptuous. Now that you're together, you may have other plans. But come in anytime. We've got lots of animals to choose from."

A few minutes later, Ivy walked out of the church and straight to Andy's SUV. He'd dropped her off and then spent some time with friends at the pub. Now, he stared at her through the windshield with a wide grin. Her heart skipped a beat as she hurried over. He climbed down and met her with a hug before waving toward the other women offering "aws" and assisted Ivy into his vehicle.

"Looks like you had a good time," he said, pulling out onto the road.

"I did!" she gushed, reaching across the console to grab his thigh and give it a squeeze. "Everyone was so nice and so welcoming."

"I'm glad, babe. I knew they would be."

She sighed with pleasure and then cast her gaze out the window, her thoughts tumbling in her head as she watched the dark pass by outside. It didn't take long for them to get to his house, and by the time he pulled into his driveway, she sighed again, but with a heaviness pressing against her chest.

Andy must have heard the effort in her breath. He parked the SUV, then twisted to stare at her, his hand linked with hers still on his thigh. "What are you thinking? Is something wrong?"

"I can't remember having a group of women friends... Well, I was going to say since high school, but to be honest, it may have been longer. Maybe ever." She turned and opened her door, not waiting for him, the cab of the SUV now feeling too small for the emotions swirling around her.

He quickly caught up to her, and they entered the house together. They hung their coats in the hall closet, and she dropped her purse and keys on the kitchen counter. But if she thought he would let her walk away after what she said, she quickly discovered he wasn't.

"Okay, Ivy. Talk to me."

She looked up, recognizing the worry that had settled in his dark eyes. "I'm fine, Andy. Really. Tonight was lovely. And I'm excited to get to know and work with these women."

"But something took you into the past, and you didn't seem to like what you saw."

She shook her head slightly. "It's silly, really. It sounds like I'm making a mountain out of a molehill. You know as well as anyone that I had what seems like a charmed life. To complain would seem superfluous."

He reached over, placed his hand on top of hers

resting on the counter, and linked fingers. "Look at me." When she hesitated, he repeated, "Ivy, look at me."

She lifted her gaze and found his gaze warm upon her face.

"I don't care what kind of upbringing anybody had," he began. "Everybody has their own demons to face. Real or imagined. Big or small. Quickly slayed or devastating. But nonetheless, their demons. And I want to know yours." A grimace etched deep lines on his face. "Believe me, I know I was one of your demons. And I fucking hate that more than you can possibly know."

Not wanting him to think this was about him, she shook her head. "No, no. This isn't about you at all."

"Then tell me. What was it about tonight that made you think of the past?"

She pulled her fingers from his and reached out to grab a wineglass. Pouring one almost full, she grabbed a beer from the refrigerator and handed it to him. They walked in silence to the living room, both settling on the sofa, sitting close and twisted so that they faced each other.

"When I first started elementary school, my dad was the principal, and I was so excited to have him there. And for the most part, it was fabulous. But by the time I was in upper elementary, there were a few kids who got in trouble or parents who liked to complain, and suddenly having my dad be the one in charge made me feel different. Sort of like an outsider. I had friends, but I found that it was easier to have just a couple of good friends, knowing I'd never be popular.

"Then I felt freer in middle school until there started

being the natural preadolescent divide where on one side were the early maturing girls and the guys who were good in sports. Even when those girls and guys were smart, their popularity came from their bodies and athletic prowess. Being smart in middle school—especially being a smart girl in middle school who was a late bloomer, and her mom was a teacher there…"

He nodded slowly. "I see where you're going. While most people would be jealous of you because they thought you got special treatment because your mom worked there. You always had to fight a little harder, didn't you?"

"Our society praises those who play sports. Run fast, throw a ball, do gymnastics. Our society praises people who are beautiful, even when they're adolescents and still figuring out who they are. And I don't know about guys, but I can tell you that even the most confident teenage girl will spend time looking in the mirror, wondering what others see. And if the first thing they know about you is that you're a smart girl, it's as though everything else is secondary."

"And high school? I made that worse for you, didn't I?"

A rueful smile curved her lips as she shook her head. "I won't deny *Poison Ivy* became harder to take when it seemed like other people thought it was funny. But that was a very small part of high school. I had friends. I was at a school that my parents didn't work at. And finally, by about sophomore year, it was no longer such a bane to be a smart girl. And by the time I was a senior, I embraced what I was good at and was more accepting of what I wasn't. I still can't say that I had tons of friends, but the ones I had were good."

"What about college? I was in the Navy, so I didn't have that experience."

"Remember what you said about the camaraderie in the Navy? How much it meant to you?" At his nod, she smiled while shaking her head. "I didn't have that. As much as colleges recruit women to go in their math, science, and engineering programs, believe me when I tell you that it's very much a man's world. Females were greatly in the minority. Some engineering classes had fifty males and only two females. Can you believe that in this day and age, I had an asshole student in one of my classes tell me I should be at home cooking instead of taking up space in the engineering program."

Andy gasped, his eyes widening. "You're fucking kidding me?"

"I wish I was."

"I can't say what it was like for the women in the Navy, and I have no doubt that servicewomen have to fight so much harder for the same respect."

"I'm not crying, *poor me,* like I had it bad. I'm damn lucky with the parents I had, the education I had, and the job I have. And I'm not feeling sorry for myself. I suppose I thought, tonight it just all came to roost in my mind that for the first time in my life, I was surrounded by strong, smart, beautiful women, inside and out, working to make their community better. And they welcomed me with open arms. No one was trying to one-up anyone else. No one was trying to beat out anyone else for a better position. No jealousy. No stepping on toes. I'm not sure I've ever felt so supported by a group before."

"As sorry as I am for the memories it brought up, I'm still really glad you went, Ivy." He set his beer on the coffee table, then lifted her wineglass from her hand and placed it on the table as well. Then with his hands on her waist, he lifted and shifted until she straddled his lap. Holding her close, he held her gaze. "If I could, I'd go back in time and not only erase the shit that I tossed at you, but instead would have sung your praises so that you never had to doubt yourself."

She wasn't sure she'd ever heard anything more beautiful in her entire life. To think that this man wanted to take her pain away but also erase any from the past lightened the heavy burden that had settled on her heart. Her lips curved until her smile spread across her face. Now weightless in his arms, she kissed him, having no doubt this was the man she wanted in her life.

29

Andy stood just outside the wheelhouse and tried to hold on to his growing impatience. This time of year, they were not nearly as busy checking boating and fishing licenses as they were in the warmer weather, yet today, they'd already stopped and ticketed four boats. Two for not having the proper fishing license, another one for leaving the marina and not following the boating rules, and another one for coming into the harbor too quickly, causing a threat to the other boats that were docked.

"What the fuck is wrong with people today?" he asked.

Callan shook his head. "It's getting close to the holidays. I can't imagine what's going on."

Andy glanced over his shoulder as Jose steered them into the inlet. And he had requested they take a look since that was the last place they'd seen a possible camera sighting of the drug runners.

They each carefully perused the inlet but saw

nothing suspicious. "This is like looking for a fucking needle in a fucking haystack," he grumbled.

"Anything from Sam?"

"I've heard that the sheriff's department raided a house in the northern part of the county, arresting several gang members with drugs and drug paraphernalia around. According to Hunter, they had Blood gang tattoos, so with any luck, that'll cut down on some of the activity."

A call came in from Ryan, requesting that they come back to the station. Jose looked up and said, "I think the chief of police of the CBBT is with Ryan and I think they want you in the meeting, Andy."

It didn't take long for them to get back to the Baytown Harbor, where Callan waved Andy on while he and Jose took care of the vessel.

Hopping up onto the dock, he hustled inside and made his way to Ryan's office, where he found Mac sitting, as well. Greeting both of them, he took a seat at Ryan's invitation.

"Ivy came to me," Mac began, gaining Andy's immediate attention.

"Good. I wanted her to." Andy had begged Ivy to let the police handle the investigations, yet he was uncertain of all the CBBT employees, including the police working under Mac.

"What she brought to my attention is concerning, but I know it also came from a conversation you had with Officer Jeeves."

"Yes. He thought the camera anomaly was a problem, but he didn't know how to figure out what to do about it."

Mac sighed heavily, "I struggle thinking that any of the employees of the CBBT would have their hand in anything illegal or anything that would hurt us. But I haven't spent twenty-five years in law enforcement without learning to never underestimate the power of a payoff, blackmail, or sometimes just pure unadulterated greed."

Andy nodded, shooting a glance back and forth between Ryan and Mac, but remained quiet, wanting the two captains to lead the discussion.

"Ronald Jeeves came and talked to me, but I confess the way he spoke about what happened seemed to downplay the situation. I didn't follow through, and that's on me. Ivy asked me to meet her today, and she gave me the rundown of what had actually happened and her initial investigation of the systems. Well, she's not part of our department since she works directly with Ethan Courde, Deputy Executive Director of Infrastructure. Big title for a big job. But it allows her the ability to maneuver between departments because that's what the job requires. She's the perfect person to have on the inside if someone is fucking with the systems."

Unable to keep the sour expression from his face, Andy wasn't surprised when Mac asked, "You disagree?"

He grabbed the back of his neck and squeezed. "It's not that I disagree. I just wish she was more removed. We're in law enforcement, and while gangs are not a new entity, the VMP has had limited contact with them in the past. But we... and you have the training and the knowledge to deal with the threats, especially if someone is on the inside."

"It makes her vulnerable," Ryan agreed.

Nodding, Mac sighed again. "Yes. I feel like she's getting in the crosshairs as she tries to find out what's happening. Because from what she told me, there is no way what happened the other night happened by coincidence or accident. But I need her expertise to figure out who we're looking at."

"Can we keep her involvement to a minimum?" Ryan asked.

Mac rubbed his chin, his gaze down for a moment before lifting his head. "With over seventeen miles of bridge and two tunnels, there are a lot of places where the smaller boats go underneath the bridge. They usually stick closer to the shoreline, so their boats have less wind or deeper water to be concerned with. Either closer to the Eastern Shore or Virginia Beach. For someone to come at night isn't unusual, but for the cameras to crap out exactly where they possibly came through, it's too much for me to think that someone on the inside didn't help. And for that, I need Ivy's expertise."

"Any ideas?" Ryan asked.

Scrubbing his hand over his face, Mac said, "Ronald Jeeves is not the only officer who monitors cameras on a rotating duty shift. I know Ivy talked to Anne, but other people in the IT department could have manipulated the cameras, and Anne wouldn't know about it. She's a day worker, but a few others work shifts so they would be there at night. And, of course, there's the maintenance crew. They also work shifts and can physically manipulate the cameras underneath the bridges."

"What did the higher-ups say?" Ryan asked.

Mac scrubbed his hand over his face. "I talked to the executive director as well as Ethan, and at this time, we all agreed that caution needs to be of utmost importance. We'd prefer not to let too many people know about the investigation. None of the department heads will know. Ivy will work with me."

"What about Anne or the head of maintenance?" Andy asked.

"We can't assume anyone's innocence at this point. I've told Ivy not to talk to anyone else. Since I can't be sure of my own officers, even though that shits me to admit, then I can't be sure of even a department head. Ivy and I'll report only to Ethan. If asked by Anne, she'll just say that without any direction, she's not looking into it anymore."

"Can you trust Ethan?" Andy blurted.

Mac opened his mouth, then snapped it shut. "Right now, I'm not sure I'd trust my mother. But some people don't have the know-how or opportunity to alter camera images. I don't see how Ethan could be involved."

Ryan leaned back in his chair. "Unless he's directing someone underneath him."

"Fuck. Okay, fine, I'll have Ivy just report to me." Mac stood and, with a chin lift, walked out of the room.

For a moment, Andy and Ryan sat in silence, then finally, Ryan said, "Are you okay?"

With his top teeth pressed against his bottom lip, he sucked in a hissing breath, his nostrils flaring. "In truth? No. But somehow, this situation has become a runaway train. I thought we'd catch the boat and be able to nail down a few of the gang members. Maybe get the sheriff's department to shut down the local Bloods infiltration or at least slow it down some. But fuck... now it's close to home, and I hate that Ivy's right in the middle of it all."

"She just needs to be vigilant and cautious."

Andy nodded but didn't feel any better about the situation. Thanking Ryan, he walked back outside and headed to the vessels. It was past lunchtime, but he'd lost his appetite. He checked the flares, fire extinguishers, lights, and anchors. He made sure the equipment on board was still plentiful and in place. Stepping outside, he ran his practiced eye over the hull above the waterline and double-checked the ropes.

By the time the others returned from lunch, he was still antsy. Filling them in, he recognized the concern in their expressions, but none offered empty platitudes, for which he was grateful.

Ryan walked out onto the docks. "Got a call from Colt. He's got a proposition for you."

He was staring right at Andy, whose body locked tight and gave him his total focus.

"The sheriff's department has been watching one of the houses you, Hunter, and Sam visited. They're almost positive they've seen at least one suspected member of the local Bloods go in there."

"They want water surveillance?" he asked, a blade of excitement slicing through him.

"Yes. They figured you'd want to go."

"Need anyone else?" Jose asked. "I'm available."

Ryan hesitated, then nodded. "You can take the single engine. Jose, you pilot, and that'll leave Sam and Andy to watch."

Andy grinned, then turned and fist-bumped Jose.

"I'll tell Colt you're on board, and Sam will let you know when you'll leave."

As Ryan headed back inside the station, Andy sucked in a breath of cold, fresh air, glad to finally have something that might move them a step closer.

That night, the small boat glided through the water to the entrance of the inlet. Jose had cut the engine when they neared, then he and Andy used oars to bring them closer to where they could watch the back of the property. Once secure, Andy and Sam trained their binoculars onto the house. Roberta's house.

According to Sam, the sheriff's department had followed one of the known Blood members to the house, surprised when he didn't appear to hide his trail.

"Do you think he wanted the attention or just didn't care?" Andy had asked.

"I don't know. On a daily basis, they probably just have a recreational amount of coke or heroin in the house. It's when a shipment comes in by boat or land that it gets cut and then immediately shipped out."

"Are we looking for anyone specific or just seeing what's going on?"

"We have an informant from the Baltimore area who

has said that a shipment coming from the south will be arriving on its way to Baltimore. We'd like to see who's inside besides the woman who talked to us."

They ceased speaking, and Andy huddled in his thick jacket against the cold winter air, his binoculars trained on the wide glass windows at the back of the house. Several people were in the room, some seated and others milling around. The ones on the sofa would lean over the coffee table, and Andy watched as they snorted what he assumed was coke. Shifting his gaze to the kitchen, he spied Roberta talking with a tall man whose back was to them. Too far to define much about the scene, the man suddenly slapped her. Startled at the action, Andy watched as Roberta whirled and left the room. A few seconds later, a light came on in an upstairs bedroom. Several minutes later, he could see her standing at the window looking out, her phone clapped to her ear.

"Trouble in paradise?" Sam murmured.

"What do you figure her game is?"

"At best, a gang leader's main woman. At worst, a woman passed around, probably from one of their strip clubs or brothels. She cleans up well and speaks well, which gave her a chance to seem like a bored housewife whose husband is renting the house when we talked to her. It gives the place legitimacy on the surface."

"Wonder who she's talking to?" Andy continued to wonder aloud.

"Girlfriend, maybe. Bitching about the way she's being treated."

"No," Jose spoke up softly from the back. "She'd be

used to that behavior. I'd say she's more likely to be complaining to someone who she thinks can get her a better position. In the gang, she's seen as nothing more than property. But maybe she's got someone who's offering a better choice. Someone higher up."

Andy lowered his binoculars for a moment as he looked over his shoulder toward Jose. It sounded as though Jose understood something about the way Roberta was thinking.

Jose looked at him and offered a little snort. "Didn't come from middle-class." Inclining his head toward the house, he added, "I've seen the same scenario played out a lot of times growing up."

Andy nodded, then turned back to the investigation. He respected Jose too much to pry but hoped his friend would open up one day.

The party continued, and after a while, Sam said, "Okay, let's get back. I've taken photographs, and hopefully, we can identify some of the partygoers from them."

The three said their goodbyes on the dock, and as Jose secured the vessel, Andy walked to the parking lot with Sam. "What do you think?"

"I've got no doubt the Bloods are using that house as a temporary place to run drugs through. From what we saw, I think they get a shipment, cut it, and repackage it to be shipped out again. That increases their profit as a middleman between the cartels and the ones who receive the product."

"And the new shipment coming in?"

"I'll have Colt talk to Ryan and Mac about when to

check the cameras. It'll be in reverse this time. They'll have to pass the CBBT before triggering one of your cameras. But my guess is that this party tonight was just to gather those who'll be working the shipment."

With goodbyes said as soon as Jose joined them in the parking lot, the three men drove off, and Andy wished Ivy wasn't involved at all.

Roberta stood at the window looking out into the dark. Her cheek stung, and she blinked back the tears. "The fucking asshole hit me. I know, I know. I should have kept my mouth shut, but I was so angry."

Swallowing her pride, she whispered, "How much longer?"

She listened and then said, "Yeah... coming tomorrow night. I don't know when, but I'm sure Ty or Marcus will let me know and have me contact you. I just wanted to hear your voice tonight and know I'm not completely alone in this fucked-up house."

Disconnecting, she crossed her arms around her waist, pulling in.

30

When Andy's cameras alerted him to movement on the inlets again, Ivy looked up and groaned. They had just sat down to eat dinner, and it seemed as though every movement on the water had captured the camera's sensors.

"More deer?" she asked. Ivy had heard him grumble many times since putting up the cameras when the deer that wander the woods and beach at night made up for most of the sensors' alerts. He looked down, peering at the infrared image.

"Bingo," he breathed, and her gaze shot back to his. She leaned over to observe the motorboat cruising past the camera.

"Where is that?"

"The inlet closest to the house the sheriff's department suspects may have drug dealers staying in." He stood and moved from the table, bending to kiss the top of her head. "Sorry, babe, I need to make a call to the boss." He quickly dialed, and she shoved her food around her plate for a moment as she listened to him give Ryan the information. "Yeah, yeah. It came from the south. Okay, thanks."

Ivy waited until he disconnected and sat back down at the table before grumbling. "I wish the sheriff's department could just go in and arrest them. I'd think that catching them with the drugs coming in would be what they want."

He held her gaze with a lifted brow, and she sighed. "I know. It's much bigger than just one drug shipment. It's the whole gang activity." She grimaced, rubbing her forehead. "And, of course, the CBBT. Because if someone is making a change to the cameras or programs to allow undetected traffic, then that's a cybersecurity nightmare. I'll talk to Mac tomorrow—"

"No," he rushed.

Twitching slightly, she widened her eyes as she stared at him. "Wh—"

"Babe, I'm sorry, but my instructions were to only talk to Ryan, and he'd relay the information to Colt. They no longer want just anyone knowing what we find out."

Scoffing, she shook her head. "Mac's the head of the police force, Andy. You know that."

Andy said nothing, and slowly the meaning of both his words and his silence crept in. Gasping, she said, "You think Mac is... oh, my God—"

"Don't get ahead of yourself, Ivy," he warned. "No one is accusing Mac. It's just that anyone at the CBBT who has access to make a change in the security, either with the physical cameras or the programs, is now under suspicion."

Air rushed out as she slammed back against the hard wooden slats of the chair. "This is crazy. I love my job and the people I work with, but it's been nuts since I started there!"

He reached over and linked fingers with her. Inclining his head toward her splint, he asked, "How much longer?"

Recognizing his attempt to change the subject, she knew he was right, considering neither of them could solve the case themselves that evening, and focusing on it was becoming exhausting. "Physical therapy has gone well, and I only have a couple more weeks of it. When I finish, I'll go back to see the orthopedic surgeon, and maybe I'll finally be done with this."

He lifted her hand and kissed her fingers just above the splint. Her heart melted a little, just like it always did when he was sweet. As she stared into his chocolate eyes, a little sigh escaped. *He's always sweet.*

By the time they finished eating, his phone rang. "It's Ryan. He would have informed his contact at the CBBT," he said as he connected the call.

Unabashedly trying to listen, she learned little considering all Andy said was a few "yeahs" and "okays." Anticipation built, and when he disconnected, she pounced. "What did he say?"

He hesitated, and her breath caught in her throat. "Oh God. The cameras didn't catch anything, did they?"

His head slowly moved back and forth. "I'm sorry, babe. But this is much more now than just shutting down a local branch of a drug gang, which is bad enough. Now, there's an internal problem at the CBBT."

The oxygen seemed to leave the room, and she held on tightly, his fingers still linked with hers. "They've got to be stopped."

"I was told to tell you that you'll start your day across the Bay at the Virginia Beach offices. The executive director wants to meet with you. And you're to tell no one."

The next day at work, Ivy wondered how she would ever be able to concentrate. The drive across the bridge seemed interminable as her thoughts and stomach churned as much as the water below crashing against the pylons.

Walking inside, she hoped she didn't run into anyone she knew until she'd had a chance to be briefed. As soon as she stepped inside the executive director's office, she hadn't even taken off her coat before Owen Stuart moved behind her and closed his door. Waving her to a seat, she sat in the wooden chair in front of his desk and felt the weight of his heavy stare once he'd settled in his. Trying not to squirm, she waited to see what he would say.

"I received a call last night from Captain Ryan Coates of the Virginia Marine Police. It was followed by a call from Sheriff Colt Hudson, both giving me the information of what they suspected," Owen began. "It's my understanding that you already know about the situation."

She nodded, clasping her hands in her lap. "Yes, sir. I'm dating one of the Virginia Marine Police officers who is involved and had previously talked with both our Chief of Police, Mac Davenport, and the head of IT, Anne Baker."

"I don't have to tell you that this could be a public relations nightmare if we have somebody employed at the CBBT who's taking payoffs to alter either our cameras or our information systems."

She nodded but remained silent, considering there was nothing to add to his statement. She pressed her lips together as her gaze stayed on him.

"I'm giving you complete access to all systems," Owen continued. "As far as I'm concerned, you have carte blanche to check everything without notifying any department heads."

As much as she hated to agree, she replied, "I understand."

Owen inclined his head toward the chart on the wall behind his desk. She followed his inclination and observed a framed copy of the organizational flow chart of the CBBT leadership that was in every office. Each director, assistant director, and department head was listed next to their title.

She turned her gaze back to Owen as he instructed, "I need you to understand completely, Ms. Watkins. There is no one above looking at it. I need you to look at each system… and employee equally."

The names on the wall included Anne, Mac, Curt, Bradley, and Ethan. There were others, but it didn't pass her notice that her boss, friends, and other coworkers had their names prominently displayed on the chart Mr. Stuart was referencing. Sweat trickled down her back and under her arms, and she hoped she'd used enough deodorant that morning. Swallowing deeply, she nodded. "Mr. Stuart, I'm not trained in investigations per se, but I'll do everything I can to try to figure out how the anomalies are occurring."

"Excellent."

"But I think some people would question if they see what I'm doing."

"An email has already gone out this morning that says that in order for you to complete certain studies required by our mission, you will be looking at each department and have access to their data."

Unable to hide her sigh, she said, "I don't mind saying that I hope I don't find anything. I hate the idea that someone at CBBT is altering our security."

"I understand what you're saying, Ms. Watkins. And I hope for the same thing. But we have to be open to any possibility."

The heavy stare that he'd bestowed on her had now caused her stomach to flip flop. "So… I report my findings to…?"

"Me."

Trying to ignore the dig at Ethan, she nodded. "All right, sir, I understand." With that, she stood as he did and followed him to his door.

She'd barely made it down the hall when her name was called. Hiding her wince, she turned and plastered on a smile as Anne hurried forward.

"Girl, what on earth are you working on?" Anne grabbed her arm, her eyes wide as interest and curiosity practically vibrated from her. "Got the big chief's email first thing this morning."

"Hey, Anne. Oh, I'm just checking all systems to see if there are ways we can be more streamlined and efficient."

"Sounds like a huge project! Who else is working with you? I was surprised that my office wasn't involved."

"It's just me, but I suppose more may be added later," she lied, her plastic smile now feeling brittle.

"I thought maybe it had something to do with the camera video that we talked about."

"Well, I just have to do a lot of checking of various systems to see, um… how we can streamline things."

"Oh God, I hope that doesn't mean budget cuts!" Anne blurted, then looked around as though someone was going to jump from the walls and cut her position. "I love this job!"

"I'm sure… well, it's really just to see that we're all integrated, you know?" As soon as she spoke, she inwardly grimaced at how her lying skills sucked.

"Hmm, well, if you need help, just let me know."

"Sure," Ivy said with forced enthusiasm. Anne waved and hurried down the hall, leaving Ivy to walk slowly in the other direction, her stomach still in knots.

Walking into the parking lot, she heard her name again. Turning as Curt approached, she once more smiled as she greeted him.

"Hey, I got the email this morning about your

project. I figure this is as good a time as any since you're here to take a look at things under the bridge."

"What?" Her eyes bulged even though she tried to cover her surprise.

"Meet me at the first island. I'll show you what it's like under the bridge."

He climbed into his pickup truck and fired the engine before she had a chance to respond. Sighing, she followed and pulled off the bridge at the first man-made island that started the tunnel entrance from the south. Parking, she walked over to the side of the bridge rail, wrapping her coat tighter around her shoulders. There was an under-bridge inspector unit in place that looked very much like a cherry-picker bucket truck used to gain height, only this was one that was designed to hang over the side of a bridge.

By the time she made it there, Curt was already in the bucket. "Come on," he yelled.

Once more following, she wished she had dressed for the open-weather conditions as she lifted her arms and allowed him to fasten the safety belt around her waist. He gave a jerk and held her gaze.

"Want it secure. Don't want to lose you over the side of the bridge again."

She assumed his words were meant as a joke, but the memory was still too fresh for her to find any amusement in them. Grumbling, she grabbed the sidebar as they were lifted over the rail and then down underneath the bridge. Near the tunnel entrance, there were huge rocks below where the waves crashed.

"Modern miracle under here," Curt murmured, his gaze searching the area.

"Mmm," she agreed, clinging tighter to the bucket rail, wondering if she was as pale… or as green as she felt.

"See that?"

She forced her head to turn to look at where he was pointing and could easily spot the camera attached to the underside of the bridge. "Yes."

"I know you see the images that come from these, but I wanted you to see the actual cameras along every pylon. We not only use them to spot cracks, chips, and problems with the structure, but we also use them to look at the boats that come near the bridge. Got a lot of fishermen who come through, and some don't manage the water very well. They run into the pylons, and we have to come to check them out."

So far, everything he was telling her was information she already knew. Freezing even while bundled, she said, "Curt, this is really interesting, but why are you showing me this now?"

"Got the message this morning from the big chief. Figure you need to see things from all over to check."

Her chin jerked back. "I… I didn't…"

"I'll bet I was kept out of this latest info loop because you're looking at the camera problems. I just want to make sure you have all the facts. You've seen the results of the camera usage when we looked at the structure, and I thought it would be good for you to see them. We take the information from our cameras to identify where we might need to make repairs or for further study of the bridge and tunnels. And, of course, I've heard about the camera problems recently. I figure you're looking into that, too."

Pinching her lips tightly, she didn't confirm or deny but wished Owen had waited until she had her mind wrapped around her *new* assignment before sending out the email. She hadn't figured out how to play it yet. Blowing out a breath, she tried to force her thoughts into analytical mode as she focused on the cameras.

"They're too high for someone in a boat to manipulate, so for someone to alter the camera itself, they'd have to use an under-bridge inspector unit like this one," she stated.

He nodded slowly, his steely-eyed gaze staying on her face. "Yeah. And as you can see, you can't exactly just slip one of these out of maintenance storage and move it to a place on the bridge without people noticing. And then try to operate it by yourself? Don't think so."

More than one person altering cameras. Working in tandem. Night work. No one checking on them. Possibilities ran through her mind. "And who on your staff has access to the programs that can remotely move the camera angles?"

No response came and she turned from the concrete structure in front of her to Curt, whose jaw was now tight.

"Me. My second-in-command in maintenance, Rory Markum, and my assistant, Melanie Yanez."

Nodding, she continued to grip the metal side of the inspector unit but remained quiet as her gaze shifted over the area again. "Well, I think I've seen enough—" She was startled when she realized Curt's gaze was still pinned on her.

"I like you, Ivy. I think the chief has put you in a difficult position."

"What do you mean?"

"Has it occurred to you that someone might not want you discovering how things are being messed with?"

Her senses became hyper-alert. The sound of the waves below. The spray of water as it misted over them. The chill of the wind. The tenuous metal basket that held them with what she prayed was with security. Suddenly, he pressed a few buttons on the panel. Her heart leaped as they began to move, and her grip tightened. Slowly, they lifted back upward to the bridge. She tried to smile but between being afraid and cold, her face felt like cracking. Once her feet were firmly on the concrete, she offered a shaky thanks and goodbye, then headed to her vehicle. Starting the engine, she turned on the heat and held her hands in front of her until her fingers warmed. As she pulled out of the parking space, she spied Curt still standing outside talking to one of his workers. His head turned, and his gaze stayed on her until she was out of sight.

As she drove back across the Bay, she tried to force her thoughts on how to complete the project, but it was difficult with her shaking hands in her sight as they clutched the steering wheel. It didn't take long for her to notice a CBBT police car behind her. He was not too close, but he stayed right with her, and that had never happened before. "Jesus, is everyone intent on intimidating me?" she shouted. At the next tunnel, he turned off, and her shoulders slumped in relief. "It must have been my imagination." Looking at her reflection in the rearview mirror, she groaned, "Stop panicking." Unfortunately, her nerves outvoted her voice.

For the rest of the drive, she tamped down her nerves but was relieved when she pulled into the Eastern Shore CBBT parking lot. She sat in her car for a moment, feeling very alone. Finally, she climbed out and entered the building. Almost to her office, she spied Ethan coming out of his office and heading straight to her.

"Ivy! Owen sent out an email this morning about the new system analysis that you're doing. I have to say that I can't understand why I wasn't told about it."

"I'm not sure, Ethan. I just assumed it was all approved."

"It's fine," he said, waving his hand dismissively. "I was just surprised, that's all. Let me know if you need any assistance."

"Thank you," she said, hoping the smile she plastered on her face for the hundredth time that morning didn't appear as strained as she felt. Moving into her office, she quickly pulled up her emails and read the one everyone was referring to. *Yep. Owen had sent it to all directors and department heads before speaking to me.* Resting her head on her hand, she sighed.

31

Andy held Ivy as they lay naked in bed, her steady breathing indicating she was finally sleeping. He sighed heavily, and she shifted so that her cheek was on his chest as one of his arms curled around her shoulders. His free hand pinched the bridge of his nose as he thought back to their evening.

As soon as he'd gotten home from work, he'd walked into his house, but she wasn't there. Checking his phone, he'd missed a text saying that she was at her parents' house. Her message seemed odd, considering they'd spent every night for weeks at his house. She'd kept her things at her house, but he was ready to suggest she make the move official and live with him.

He'd immediately driven to her house and, when he walked into the living room, was surprised to find her sitting on the sofa with her knees cocked and her arms wrapped around her shins. A glass of wine and a multitude of wadded tissues were scattered haphazardly on top of the coffee table. She'd looked up at him, and his heart cracked as tears ran down her cheeks.

He'd rushed over, sat next to her, and pulled her onto his lap. There, safe in the comfort he was desperate to give, she'd talked about her day.

"I've been on this assignment for a few days, and I feel like everyone is looking at me differently. Suspiciously. Wondering what I'm working on and how it would affect them. And Mr. Stuart told me to check everything and that no one was above suspicion. Not even my boss!"

I didn't say anything but just let her get it all out.

"When I drove back from his office, I was followed by one of the cops." As though seeing I was about to jump in, she quickly continued, *"He only followed me for one of the sections, then turned around at the next tunnel. But still, it was unnerving. And that was after Curt had me go out on one of the under-bridge inspection units. It was cold and windy, and we were dangling in a metal basket over the side of the bridge so that he could point out the fucking cameras to me."*

At that, my anger built. "You've got to be fucking kidding me!" My words barely registered with her as she continued.

"That was after Anne grabbed me in the hall and wanted to know what was going on. And then, when I got back to my side, Ethan was wondering why he didn't know about my special project. I spent the rest of the day literally hiding in my office. And it's been the same for the past couple of days! I'm working to see if I can figure out what was going on, but it was me against the entire CBBT organization!"

My hands have been holding her hips, my fingers digging in with frustration. Seeing another tear slide down her cheek,

I reached up and covered her cheeks with my palms, wiping her tears with my thumb. "Babe, I'm so sorry. And I can't believe that you're out there on your own trying to deal with this for them."

She hiccuped. "And crying is so stupid, I know! It's just that I love my job. I love getting to know people and feeling like I'm part of the team. Feeling like people appreciate me for what I can bring to the game. And now, once again in my life, I've got a label slapped right on my forehead that makes people want to run away from me!"

Her last statement had gutted him as he thought back to how difficult he'd made her life when they were younger. All it took was a word. A moment of ugliness. A biting comment that made him feel better at the time but was so devastating to her. But she'd forgiven him, and somewhere along the line, he had to forgive himself. But now he felt the righteous anger that she was again put in the line of fire due to this situation.

She twitched in her sleep but pulled him closer with her arm wrapped around his waist. He smiled as the moonlight filtered through the window and caressed her face. She was beautiful, even with slightly puffy eyes. It still hit him how incredibly blessed he was to have her in his life. If he could erase her pain, he would. If he could carry her burdens, he would. If he could keep her happy every day for the rest of her life, he would.

"I love you, Ivy," he whispered into the night.

As though his words sifted through her dreams, she smiled as she slept.

Andy was in Ryan's office early the following morning, frustration filling every cell of his body. He sat with his boss and Callan, giving them the entire scoop on what Ivy had to do. "She's not an investigator. She's an analyzer, which gives her excellent skills, but they aren't the same thing!"

"No, they're not," Ryan agreed. He picked up his phone and made several calls. Once finished, he looked at Andy and said, "Get Ivy here at one o'clock. Have her tell her boss that she's got a doctor's appointment or something."

He pulled out his phone and called her. As soon as she answered, he instructed, "Babe, I need you at the station at one o'clock. Ryan has set up something with some of the deputies."

"What?"

"Ivy, please. Just come. I don't want any more evenings like you had last night. You aren't alone in this."

"Okay, but I can't just walk out of work."

"Tell anyone who asks that you've got a doctor's appointment."

"Oh, Andy. I'm a shit liar."

He chuckled and cast his gaze at the others in the room, seeing them listening to his one-sided conversation. "I know you're a shit liar, but give it your best. See you at the station at one."

Disconnecting, he nodded to the others. "Okay, done."

Ryan nodded. "Good. Both of you have morning patrol. Be in the workroom by one and bring Jose with you. Colt, Hunter, Aaron, and Sam will be here as well."

Andy offered a chin lift in thanks and walked out with Callan. Once outside, he turned to his friend. "What do you think is up? Don't get me wrong. I'm glad for the support. But I sort of feel like I've asked Ivy to walk into a lion's den."

Callan clapped him on the back. "It'll be fine. Ivy needs the support of local law enforcement, and that's what Ryan is giving her. I don't think the CBBT director meant to put a target on her back, but that's essentially what he's done. He should have known that people will talk, and that will make it more difficult for her to do what he's asked."

The morning patrol couldn't end fast enough, but finally, while Jose and Callan moved into the conference room, he stood at the front door, pacing until Ivy pulled into the parking lot. Hustling to her car, he assisted her out and wrapped her in his embrace. She immediately hugged him in return, her arms around his waist. They stood for a moment in the parking lot, silently gaining strength from each other.

Finally, she leaned back and held his gaze. "What's going on?"

"I'm not exactly sure, but after you were so upset last night, I became angry as hell you have to face the CBBT alone. Especially since what you're trying to get information on is tied into an ongoing investigation into gangs and drug trafficking. When I talked to Ryan this morning, he made some calls." Stepping back, he linked fingers with her and led her inside.

She came easily until they stepped into the workroom, and her feet stuttered slightly. Tightening his grip on her hand, he led her to two available chairs, waiting until she sat before he slid in next to her. With a nod toward Ryan, he reached over and rested his arm on the back of her chair.

Ryan smiled at her and began. "I'm not sure what Andy has told you, but we want to ensure that you aren't alone in your part of the investigation. While we have certain jurisdictions, I'm gonna turn this over to Colt. I know you've met, but I'll let him introduce his staff and take it from here."

Andy kept his gaze on her, wanting to make sure he understood her state of mind. Aaron offered a wink to Ivy, and her lips quirked upward.

"Okay," Ivy said, her chin lifted, her gaze clear as she nodded toward Colt.

"Ivy, I've brought Detectives Hunter Simms and Sam Shackley. I also have Deputy Aaron Bergstrom with us. They've been working specifically on the case of the gang members transporting drugs through the area. Because they are also using the water, the Virginia Marine Police are also involved. I know you're aware of this, but I just wanted to make sure the explanation was made."

She nodded, then replied softly, "I understand."

"It seems as though the Director of the CBBT has legitimate concerns about an employee possibly working with drug runners to keep visual evidence of their crossing in and out of the Bay from being investigated. I know you've spoken with Mac Davenport, but it's my understanding that what the Executive Director has requested of you is putting you out there by yourself. Is this correct?"

Ivy nodded. "Yes. Only a few departments have employees that could have either physically altered the cameras or altered the programs. One of those is the police force since they have access to the camera feeds, so that keeps me from working directly on this with Mac." Her brow furrowed, and Andy battled to keep from smoothing his hand over her forehead.

"Actually, Mr. Stuart didn't give me specific instructions other than he pointed at the organizational chart and emphasized that no one was to be spared my investigation."

Colt nodded. "Understood. The problem that we have with what he's asked you to do is that of investigating a possible crime when that's not your official training." He raised his hand and placated, "I'm not saying you don't have the knowledge or expertise to investigate something, because with your analytical background, that's essentially what an investigator does. They analyze. But when we investigate as trained law enforcement officers, we know the law as it applies to the situation."

The crease between her brows deepened as she nodded. "I could potentially mess up an investigation just by what I'm looking at. Is that right?"

"Possibly," Colt replied with a grimace. "The gangs don't want to be caught. They don't want their drug shipments halted or interfered with. If someone at the CBBT is assisting them, they don't want to be caught either. If they think you're working by yourself, then I think that could put you in danger. If it comes out that we're directing the investigation, then you're given a level of protection. You're no longer seen as acting alone."

Andy growled, the sound coming from deep in his lungs. Not surprising, considering every word Cole just said slammed into him. He also wasn't surprised when others around the table heard his growl. The other men barely sent a glance his way, and he knew if they'd been talking about any of their women, they would've done the same. Ivy's head snapped around, and she stared at him wide-eyed. His hand moved to her shoulder, and he leaned closer. "That's the reason we wanted to meet. We want to make sure you're being offered assistance and protection, as well as not circumventing the law."

She held his gaze, her lips pressed together, and the crinkle between her brows deepened. But she didn't deny wanting help. Turning back to Colt, she said, "As glad as I am to be able to work with you, I feel that it's only fair to let you know that this feels disingenuous to the director of the CBBT. I was told to report only to him. Discussing what I discover with law enforcement... well, I suppose it puts me in another awkward position."

"I knew that you'd feel caught in the middle," Colt acknowledge. "And I'd already taken the liberty of speaking with Owen Stuart before I came here today. I told him it was an ongoing criminal investigation and that we would like your cooperation without a subpoena, but if we needed one, we would do so." Colt finally smiled. "And I can assure you that Executive Director Owen Stuart pledged his support to law enforcement investigating the matter. He now realizes this cannot be handled in-house."

Andy heard a heavy sigh leave Ivy's lips, and the tension eased as her shoulders slumped in relief.

She nodded. "Thank you for that. I feel so much better."

"I know it's only been a couple of days, but is there anything you can tell us that might assist in our investigation?" Hunter asked.

Seeming to warm to the topic at hand, Ivy leaned forward and placed her hands on the tabletop, turning to offer a small smile toward Andy, which, in turn, warmed his heart and made him want to kiss her in the middle of this fucked-up situation. Clearing his throat, he simply offered her a smile and nodded.

"Curt Cellini, the head of maintenance, took me out, when I was quite unprepared, in an under-bridge inspection unit. It's like a cherry-picker for going over and under the side of the bridge. He and I have always gotten along fine since I started working, and I will say he's been a longtime employee of the CBBT. But I definitely got the feeling he was unhappy that his department was being looked into. But while we were under the bridge, he pointed out the cameras to me. I need to understand how they work, considering that they are used to monitor the structural integrity of the bridge. But as he pointed out, the physical cameras were inaccessible unless you were in one of the inspection units. And those aren't something you could just take out by yourself, maneuver by yourself, or lower yourself down. It would take more than one, and other people would notice."

Sam nodded, then asked, "So that takes out the maintenance department?"

"Not necessarily," she said. "The under-bridge cherry pickers are not used daily, but they are used at least three to four times a week. So someone could alter a camera and then let whoever is going to be using the boat know what sections to avoid."

"Fucking hell," Hunter said, scrubbing his hand over his face.

"But," Ivy continued, "I have checked the work orders and staffing for the days in question, and the same people were never out in the sections that had a problem. So that would indicate that someone on the maintenance crew is not the culprit. For that to happen, there would have to be at least six since two people are in a bucket at one time." She shrugged and added, "So, with that piece of information, I would tend to say that maintenance would not be the first choice. But then, I suppose, if someone gets enough money, they can share the wealth, and multiple people can be in on it."

Hunter nodded, then said, "Okay, so Curt Cellini's crewmembers are still possibilities."

"And there's more with the maintenance department. Curt and two in his department have the ability to move the camera angles from inside. Rory Markum, Curt's second-in-command, and Curt's assistant,

Melanie Yanez. They aren't involved in the programming but in the remote movement of the physical cameras."

"What else do you have?" Colt asked, looking up from the notes he was taking.

"The bridge police."

As the words left her lips, she lifted her chin slightly again as though expecting a backlash. Andy knew none would come. As she said… no one is above suspicion.

Continuing, she said, "Mac Davenport is known to you. He has an officer who is fairly new. Ronald Jeeves is from the Baltimore Police Department. He has the ability to monitor and work the camera feeds. I don't know who else because I've just started looking into them."

Colt continued to scribble as the other tapped into tablets. "Okay. What else?"

"The management information system is divided into two sections. They are both headed by people who I know. Anne is over toll equipment, advisory signs, and the computer network. Bradley controls the radio and telephone networks and the cybersecurity program." She sighed, looked down for a moment, then shook her head.

"I know this is hard," Andy said, reaching over to squeeze her hand as it rested on the table. "Everything you say feels like a betrayal."

Her gaze sought his, and relief streamed from her eyes. "Yes. Exactly." Looking back at the others, she cleared her throat. "Anyway, almost anyone from that division could have altered programs monitoring camera feeds. Well, as far as ability goes. But to make changes that aren't noticed by anyone else? Well, that's a different matter. Anne helped me discover the first time we checked on the camera intel. I don't know how closely she's looked at her department, but I can't imagine that she didn't check them out the first time we noticed a problem. There are also about fifteen people who work under her. Bradley? I don't know. He has about fifteen employees under him. I'm afraid I haven't had time to check his department."

Andy's gaze moved from her clenched hands to the faces around the table. He recognized tight jaws, glacial stares, and the occasional tic of fingers twitching, excessive tapping on a tablet, or, as Colt preferred, his pen scratching over a pad of paper.

"I feel that I need to dig deeper, because the department heads probably don't want a culprit to be in their department. Mac will feel that all the officers are above board. Curt would be horrified to think it was someone in maintenance. But I'm at the tip of the iceberg with checking on all the systems. Honestly, I'm out of my league here," Ivy said, her voice clear and her gaze now moving to the others in the meeting. "I need some direction, please."

Colt and Ryan shared a look before shifting their gazes first to Andy and then to Ivy. He waited, not surprised when Colt spoke first.

"Keep doing what the director wants you to do, Ms. Watkins. But you will not only report to him but to us as well."

She rolled her lips inward, pressing them between

her teeth, then nodded. She glanced to the side, uncertainty showing in her lifted brows as though to ask, *"What now?"* He scooted his chair back, and she followed his actions. They walked out of the meeting together, and when his arm went about her shoulders, the tension eased from her body.

Hearing footsteps approach, he turned and waited until Aaron caught up to them. His brother's eyes were warm as they focused on her.

"Ivy? Hang in there, okay?"

She smiled and reached out to squeeze his arm. "Thanks, Aaron."

He clapped his brother on the shoulder before he, Sam, Hunter, and Colt headed to their cruisers. Turning back to Ivy, he walked her to her car. Standing in the parking lot, he pressed her back against her car and leaned in, bracketing his hands on either side of her, cocooning her in his safety, wishing he could keep her there. No longer caring that he was technically still on duty, he kissed her, and as soon as her body melted into his, he devoured her lips until they finally separated, both panting.

"That's a taste of what you'll get tonight," he promised.

Her gaze held his before her lips curved into a wide, beautiful smile.

32

The following week moved by in both slow agony and the speed of a NASCAR race. Ivy felt energized as she delved through the various departments and systems to uncover layers of information, fascinated by the inner workings of the CBBT. And she felt exhausted when nothing, in particular, jumped out at her. Hating to think that someone at the CBBT would intentionally sabotage any system, she wondered if the gang members could remotely disable the cameras. And, in truth, she hoped that was what happened.

Ethan and the other department heads had been professional when she needed information from them, but she couldn't help but feel their lack of friendliness. *Alone while surrounded by others.* Leaning back in her chair, she snorted. *Jesus, it's like this damn assignment has made me... Poison Ivy.* Grimacing, she shoved that thought down, refusing to give it oxygen to flame any higher than it already had.

By the end of the day, she walked out of her building

and into the parking lot. *I just need to get through tomorrow, and then I can have a weekend break.* The idea of a weekend with Andy finally caused a smile to slide over her face. Approaching her car, she braced against the wind and thought of the impending holidays. With Thanksgiving next week, she'd have a shortened workweek and looked forward to a meal with Andy's family. Sybil had invited her, but the idea of being with Andy's family was exactly where she wanted to be. But to keep Sybil from pouting, she agreed they'd come by for dessert. *After all, who doesn't like extra desserts at Thanksgiving?*

Once inside her car, she hurried to start it to crank up the heat. Turning the key, she gasped when no sound was heard. Not even a grinding, clanking noise. Nothing. Continuing with no success, she finally banged her good hand on the steering wheel in frustration.

She dug in her purse for her phone but had no idea if Andy was off the water yet. Sending him a text, she let him know she was stuck at work because her car wouldn't start. Staring at the phone, hoping for the three dots of anticipation, she sighed. *Well, damn!*

Baytown now had an auto repair shop, so she looked up their information. *Jason... that's who runs it.* She remembered meeting him and his wife, Rose, at the fundraiser dinner. Rose ran the ice cream shop in town, and Ivy thought it would be the perfect place to kill time while someone looked at her car. Her call went to the after-hours voicemail, and she groaned once more.

Hoping Sybil was home, she started to call her when

a tap on her window startled her. Seeing a familiar face, she smiled and opened her door. "Hey."

"I heard you trying to start your car. Do you need a lift? I'm going into town and can take you if you'd like."

It was on the tip of her tongue to refuse, but waiting didn't seem to make any sense.

"Sure, that'd be great."

She climbed into their SUV and buckled in, wincing at the volume of country music on the radio. As they pulled onto the highway heading north, she glanced to the side as they tapped on the steering wheel to the rhythm. While the volume was loud, she relaxed in the seat, not having to worry about small talk.

"You can drop me off at the harbor, and I can get a ride home—" A sound behind her snagged her attention, and she shifted around to discover the cause. Suddenly, a cold hard object pressed against her temple.

"Stay still, bitch," a harsh male voice growled in her ear.

"Wh—"

"Shut the fuck up," he repeated, and the weapon barrel pressed firmer.

Her breath caught in her lungs, terrified of breathing too hard. The burn in her chest threatened to battle the stampede of her heartbeat. Shooting her eyes to the side, she stared at her coworker, who gave her nothing but eyes facing forward and a tight grip on the wheel. The SUV accelerated.

"Slow it down." The order came from the back seat. "You get pulled over, and we're all fucked."

They decelerated slightly. Ivy suddenly remembered

feeling terror while standing on the bridge. Terror managed to rob the voice while the mind continued to race with questions.

She wanted answers, but her body focused on breathing. They passed the turnoff for Baytown and continued for nearly ten more minutes before turning west. She tried to memorize the directions. Carlisle Street. Barton Road. Harvestdale. At the end of Harvestdale, the sedan slowed to turn into a driveway, and a large house filled her view.

The car had barely stopped when the pressure against the side of her head increased. "Out."

Aware that the driver's door had flung open, she did the same. Her arm was immediately grabbed and held tight by the man from the back seat. He forced her to walk toward the front. She stumbled, and he jerked her upright.

The driver was just in front of them and turned to mouth, *"I'm sorry."*

Air rushed out, and she nearly choked as she scoffed. *Sorry? Oh God. Sorry?*

The front door opened, and a bottle blonde with skintight pants and shirt met them in the foyer.

"I brought her, Roberta. I did what I was told to do."

The blonde offered a thin smile. "That's all any of us can do, Curt." She turned with a cursory glance at Ivy. "Come on in. I'll get the money Ty left for you."

Roberta led the way farther into the house with Ivy following, her feet automatically putting one in front of the other while the feel of the gun poking her back motivated her to keep walking and stay quiet. Now was not the time for heroics.

"Sit."

A hand grabbed her shoulder painfully and shoved her down into a chair.

"Jesus, Linc! You don't have to be so rough!" Roberta said, her hands landing on her thick hips, her long, red nails on display. She pursed her lips in disapproval, then looked down at Ivy. "Sorry, sweetie. It's not personal."

Ivy's face was frozen, her muscles unable to move into any expression that would make sense. Not fury. Not fear. Not incredulity. They were frozen in place other than the twitch next to her left eye, where she swore she could still feel the gun pressed even though it now dangled from the fingertips of the man called Linc.

Activity seemed to move all around as several people walked in and out of the room with bags and a few suitcases. She bit on the inside of her bottom lip, allowing the pain to force her brain to work. *Think... think... memorize.*

"I need to leave. I don't want to be here any longer than I have to," Curt said, lifting his hand, palm out.

"Sure thing, sugar," Roberta said. She walked over to a kitchen drawer. Pulling out a large envelope, she turned and handed it to him. "It's all in there."

Curt started to walk out of the room, his gaze not having landed on Ivy at all since they'd entered the house.

"Why?" The word came out barely more than a whisper, but Ivy's desire to know why Curt participated in her kidnapping overcame her fear of speaking.

He stopped with his back to Ivy, then dropped his chin and sighed. Twisting around to look over his shoulder, he contorted his face. "I'm sorry. Really… this is so fucked up. I'm so sorry."

She glanced nervously toward the man who held the gun. He stood in the next room, directing a few others as they carried boxes to the door. Roberta faced her but remained quiet. Ivy pressed her lips together, her chest heaving. "That's not a reason."

Curt shook his head. "I had no choice." Shooting a glance toward Roberta, he hurried to the front door and slipped out.

Blinking, wondering if that would help her wake up from the nightmare, Ivy watched Roberta offer a little shrug.

"I told you, honey. It's not personal."

"This doesn't make any sense. I don't understand what's happening," she whispered, desperate for Roberta to look at her with sympathy. Maybe even to promise it would end soon and they'd let her go. She tried to steady her breathing but felt the swell of panic rising like the tide.

Roberta leaned over and whispered, "It's best if you don't know." Then she stood and offered a small smile as though she'd just imparted the most wonderful news. She turned and walked up the stairs, leaving Ivy in the chair, unbound but guarded. And considering the guard had a gun, her ass stayed right where it had been placed.

Andy stood in the wheelhouse as the VMP vessel pulled into the dock at the end of the day. They'd spent the afternoon helping a stranded fisherman whose boat engine had died. He'd attempted a cursory diagnostic to see if the fix might be easy and they could get the fisherman up and running enough to return to the harbor.

The fishing boat was old, and it had not proven to be a simple task. Eventually, Andy worked his mechanical magic so the boat could head back to the Baytown Harbor under its own power. They'd just watched the fishing boat dock and were ready to head to the station dock when Ryan rushed from the building.

Jared and Joseph were in the boat with Andy, and right behind them was another VMP vessel with Jose, Bryce, and Callan.

The look on Ryan's face sent Andy on instant alert, and as he stood waiting to see what had happened, he realized Ryan stared straight at him.

His stomach plummeted as three people ran through his mind—his dad, Aaron, or Ivy. Something happening to any of those three would have been devastating news, but nothing prepared him for Ryan's words.

"Colt has deputies watching the house on Harvestdale because, with the activity there, it looked like they may be feeling the heat and are pulling out. Half an hour ago, they spotted a black SUV arrive and recognized Ivy as being led inside the house by a man identified as Lincoln Hargrove. Goes by Linc. Big name for local Bloods. He had a gun on her."

For a few seconds, Andy simply stared, mouth open, his brain a step behind what his ears heard, and his body a step behind his brain. "Oh God!" he finally blurted. He darted to the edge of the deck to jump over onto the dock.

Ryan called out, "No! The sheriff's department and DEA are getting ready to invade the house—"

"And put Ivy in the fucking crossfire?" he roared.

Ryan threw his hand up, his forefinger raised as his cell phone clapped once again to his ear. "Parker Inlet? Got it. ETA, six minutes."

Looking up, he said, "The deputy reporting said it appears they are getting ready to leave the house. They've loaded a silver boat docked outside the house with boxes, probably filled with drugs. Two men are on the dock, but they just brought out Ivy and are moving her toward the boat."

Andy stood on the deck, his feet rooted to the floor, his body wired tightly, and his heart threatening to pound out of his chest.

Joseph's hand landed on his shoulder. "Easy, man. Let Ryan get the intel needed, so we don't waste any time."

Ryan radioed, "All vessels. All crewmembers. VMP three. VMP five. VMP one. North to Parker Inlet."

While Andy's body moved like molasses, he was grateful the other officers didn't waste a second. Jose backed away from the dock as Jared did the same. Joseph grabbed Andy by the shoulders and pulled him back into the wheelhouse.

"Fucking focus, man."

With the VMP radio tuned to the sheriff's radio station, they listened to instructions as the dispatcher sent out codes for police, fire and rescue, hazmat, and the Coast Guard. Ryan radioed that DEA reported having speedboats in the Bay near the CBBT ready to stop the drugs from passing from the Bay.

Ryan coordinated from the station, his voice relaying the information coming specifically from Colt.

"I don't understand how they got her," Andy muttered, unable to process Ivy being in the hands of a deadly drug gang. "She should have been home by now. She got off work almost an hour ago." He pulled his phone from his pocket and spied a missed message from Ivy. Guilt slammed into him as he read it. "Her car didn't start."

Joseph looked over his shoulder and surmised, "It was probably tampered with."

"But she wouldn't have just taken a ride with anybody," he insisted.

"Then it was someone she knew. Someone she trusted." Joseph's face was as hard as his words.

As Jared sped their vessel toward the inlet, Andy radioed Ryan. "Do they know who took her?"

"Just got an update. The sheriff's department has identified the SUV that brought Lincoln and Ivy to the house. The car belongs to Curt Celini. He drove off about ten minutes after they arrived at the house. Colt has deputies following, but it looks like he just went home. They've got him under surveillance."

Andy felt his gut jerk back as though he had been physically punched. Ivy had been certain that the department heads wouldn't be the ones in with the gangs.

They slowed as they neared the inlet. The Coast Guard moved in close to the VMP boats, and Andy looked over at the 41-Interceptor vessel they were driving. It was a fast, sleek vessel designed for speed and controllability, as the CG had the ability for high-speed chases. On any other day, he would be envious of the watercraft, but now, his only thought was gratitude for so much support for the mission. And the fear of needing something so powerful in order to save Ivy.

With his heart now lodged in his throat, he heard Ryan's voice over the radio.

"Be advised, sheriff department and DEA ten twenty-three. Ten nineteen in progress. Ten seventy-four. Ivy spotted at the dock."

Sucking in a deep breath as his heart was firmly lodged in his stomach, he tried to clear his mind. His brother would be there with the other deputies and DEA as they closed in on the house or gave chase to anyone who'd left. Ivy was being held hostage, but at least she was alive. Looking toward the other VMP officers and friends nearby, he drew strength from the resolve in their gazes.

33

Ivy walked on wooden legs, her hands still unbound, a testament that the kidnappers didn't see her as a threat. And she knew it was the truth. Too many of them were around for her to do anything to help her situation. One of the men was in front and the other behind. And she'd seen guns in the hands of both. *There's nowhere to run that they couldn't shoot me in the back first. No way to kick or punch my way out of this, even if I had the strength or knowledge of how to fight.*

And as much as it galled her, she couldn't plead, argue, or convince them to let her go. She'd seen at least five men inside the house as they busied themselves with packing and had never once tried to disguise or cover their faces. Every TV crime show she'd ever watched gave evidence that these men were not afraid of her. *Because they'll kill me.*

Her chest ached with the way her heart had pounded ever since the gun had been placed against her head and with the effort it took to breathe just to keep from passing out.

When Roberta walked upstairs after leaving her parting wisdom of *"It's not personal"* still ringing in her ears, Ivy had tried to analyze what was happening. Small plastic-wrapped bricks were boxed up and taken outside. It didn't take a genius to know she was at a suspected gang house, and they were preparing to leave. Roberta had walked back downstairs minutes later, a suitcase bouncing down each step until she arrived at the bottom and managed to get it to roll along the foyer to the front door.

Roberta had barked out an order to one of the men who headed her way with a grimace on his face, but he rolled her suitcase outside. The others had continued to work, including the man called Linc, who had laid the gun down as he carried boxes outside.

Their conversations had remained low, but no one seemed to care that she overheard. And now, when someone finally walked over to her again, it was to point a gun at her and tell her to follow them.

So, here she was, walking to what was her certain death. Shot. Drowned. Beaten. She stumbled, and the man behind her grabbed her upper arm with a bruising grip. The air was colder, and without her hat or gloves, she was chilled to the bone in spite of her coat. Perhaps, the chill came out of terror, and her blood had halted its path through her body.

At the end of the path, they came to a private wooden dock with a silver boat moored. She'd never paid much attention to boats even though she grew up near the Bay. She knew the difference between one with a flat bottom that the crabbers and oyster fishermen would use and the larger, multi-engine ones that were taken much farther in the Bay for line or net fishing. She knew there were even larger ones, including sleeper cabins and a kitchen for pleasure cruising, or yachts moored in the marina.

But this vessel looked like something from a fancy boat show. Solid silver. Long and deep. Sleek. It could almost disappear on the water. With four huge motors mounted on the back, she was sure it could speed along with the idea of outrunning anyone chasing them.

She stood at the end of the dock while the two men climbed aboard, giving her a chance to see that another man had already been in the hull when his head popped up before the rest of his large body came onto the deck. He looked over at her, then his gaze slid up and down before he turned away.

Her thoughts warred. *If I get on board, they'll kill me. If I stay here, they'll kill me.* Clarity broke through the cacophony in her mind like the sun breaking through the clouds over the Bay. *Today is the day I'm going to die.*

Regret streamed through her—regret that she would not see her parents again, and they would have to live knowing how she died. Regret that she did not get to have the life with Andy that she'd already come to crave. Her chest quivered as she looked to the side, wondering if she could make it to the trees before being shot in the back.

Suddenly, the sound of shouting from the house rang out, and Linc jumped from the boat and grabbed her arm, dragging her toward the vessel. "No!" She tried to dig her heels in, but the slick dock gave her feet no purchase to halt their progress.

Linc picked her up and tossed her into the bottom of the boat. Her body slammed into the hard surfaces of the deck, and her head cracked against the steering wheel. She cried out in alarm and pain, and the stars that swam through her vision rivaled the ones from the clearest night sky. She tried to scramble to her feet, but the man standing at the wheel placed his booted foot on her sternum and pressed down. Jerking her gaze up as she instinctively grabbed at his leg, she spied his narrow eyes threatening to crush her with no remorse if she tried to move. Her resolve to escape wavered as terror gripped her soul.

Shouting and gunshots seemed closer but were soon drowned out by the roar of the motors firing to life. The entire boat vibrated, and as she lay on the deck, the quakes rolled through her. With one man down in the hull, Linc and the pilot, whose foot she was still under, fired their weapons as they ducked. The boat pulled away from the dock, and she felt the forces pulling on her as it made a sharp U-turn.

The speed increased, and the front of the boat lifted. The pilot raised his boot off her chest, and she sucked in air. He focused on steering, and Linc was turned away from her, firing toward the dock. Ivy scrambled to her knees with her hands still on the floor of the boat. Keeping her head down so she wouldn't be caught in the gunfire, she could tell the boat was leaving the inlet.

The pilot cursed and shouted out, causing Linc to

whirl around now that they were out of range of gunfire from the dock. Her body tensed, expecting him to look down and see she was no longer lying flat, but he was looking out into the distance. His curses now joined the pilot's, and he turned to face away from her once again, ducking as he continued to shout.

Wanting to jump over the side of the boat before they got too far into the Bay, she lifted just enough to peek over the edge, seeing a multitude of other vessels around.

The engines' roars kept most other sounds from hitting her ears, although she thought she could hear someone on a loudspeaker, giving her hope that the police occupied the other vessels. But she knew these men would not give up or give in easily.

Linc stood as they accelerated again, but he rocked back and forth on his feet, unsteady in the fast-moving boat. He held the side with one hand, then leaned against the edge when he lifted both hands to fire his gun again.

Seeing him waver against the side of the boat, she shot upward. Without thinking of the consequences, she slammed into Linc's back as hard as she could, not wanting him to fire at the police. As luck finally went her way, the pilot turned, and the boat swerved at that moment. Linc's body tilted forward, and when he lost his balance, he flipped over the side and into the water. She gasped in shock as she squatted down again. She'd only meant to make him drop his weapon, but he was now in the water. Pressing her lips together to keep from crying out, she stared at the pilot who'd looked over his shoulder, his brows lowered at not seeing Linc.

He shouted more curses as he cut the steering wheel sharply again, causing the boat to swerve in the opposite direction. She dropped her hands to the deck to avoid having the same fate as Linc. Cold water sprayed on her face as the boat cut through the Bay, turning in circles, and she gasped, her chest heaving. Blinking, she stared at the third man who raced up from the hull, ducking as he approached her.

He lifted his gun, and her heart stumbled in its beating. She instinctively threw her hands in front of her as though she could stop a bullet. A sneer slashed across his face, but suddenly, it was gone in a pink spray. More water splattered her face. She blinked and swiped at the moisture in her eyes. Blinking again, she stared at her palm as the Bay water spraying over the edge of the boat caused rivulets of red to run down her arm. The man lay next to her, blood pooling all around him, and his face obliterated.

She opened her mouth to scream, but no sound came out. Turning from the gory sight, she scrambled a few feet away, then stopped to press against the side of the boat. Keeping her eye on the pilot, she was terrified to move out of fear of getting too close to him. He was the only gang member left on the boat, and when he turned around and looked at her, his face was a picture of rage. His eyes bulged as he bared his teeth.

He reached down toward his weapon but had to turn away to grab the wheel as he steered the speeding boat. He grimaced as he looked forward, unable to take his eyes off where the boat was going. The boat slowed as he turned again, and his curses rang out.

With the sound of the motors lowered slightly, she could hear the amplified voices calling for him to halt. The gunfire had stopped. Not willing to wait for him to have another opportunity to shoot her, she peeked over the side. She observed gray and blue boats surrounding them but had no idea if Andy was among them. The edge of the boat dug into her palms as she clung to the metal. Glancing behind her, she spied the shoreline but wasn't sure how far away they were. Once again, clarity in the midst of chaos hit. *He'll use me as bait to get away, then kill me.* Looking at the shoreline again, she blew out a deep breath. *I can make that. No matter what, I have to make that!*

Waiting for him to face forward again, she unbuttoned her coat and let the arms slide to the deck. Then without looking at him again for fear she would chicken out, she launched over the side, arms and legs swinging in a world-class belly flop, not caring how she landed until the slap of cold water hit her. *Shit, shit, shit!* Terrified he would turn around and run over her with the motors, she surfaced to take a deep breath, dove down as far as she could go, and kicked in the direction of the shore.

But the cold water made her movements sluggish, and fear kept her breathing erratic. Rising to the surface again, she swiped at her eyes as she jerked her head from side to side. Her ears were met with shouting and motors revving, but she couldn't see over the waves, with her head barely bobbing above the surface. Unable to discern if a gray boat in the distance was friend or foe, she looked back toward the trees. Moving her arms and legs in a sloppy attempt to swim, she moved slowly, now terrified she would freeze or drown before being shot.

Suddenly, her body was ensnared by something, and she fought, trying to dislodge her trap. Arms encircled her torso, but instead of pulling her down, her head was lifted, her face above the water.

"Ivy! It's me! I've got you, babe!"

Shivers darted through every muscle as she clutched the arm securely wrapped around her. Twisting her head around, she stared into dark eyes. And smiled.

34

From the moment they'd arrived at the mouth of the inlet, Andy's nerves of steel had turned into twigs and kindling, ready to snap and ignite at any moment. He was grateful that the other VMP officers were in touch with Ryan and Colt, and having the Coast Guard flank them gave him a chance to swallow down his anxiety.

The property was on the other side of the tree line, and knowing Ivy was being held there ate at his thoughts. He wanted to storm the castle, draw his weapon, annihilate every gang member who'd dared to even lay eyes on her, and lay waste to their whole empire.

Hearing shots being fired and a female's scream of "No!" were like a bullet to his heart, and he jerked his focus back to the shoreline. Next, the revving of motors filled the area, and his gut clenched. A silver AMG Nighthawk, at least forty feet long with four motors, roared out of the inlet toward the multitude of law enforcement boats surrounding the area.

The VMP vessels would have no chance of giving chase if the Nighthawk made it to the Bay's open waters but felt certain the Coast Guard's Interceptor and now circling helicopters would be able to. Others could care about the drugs and the gang members, but he only had one concern. *Ivy? Where the fuck is Ivy?*

As the Nighthawk approached, he trained his binoculars on the vessel but only observed two men, one driving and one with a weapon he was discharging randomly toward them. Staying low, he focused on them when another person wearing a green coat suddenly rose from the bottom of the boat and pushed the man with the gun. He toppled forward, and Andy watched, stunned, as he flipped over the side. The third person ducked out of sight, but he knew that green coat. It was the same one Ivy had been wearing this morning when he kissed her goodbye before they'd left for work.

"Holy shit!" The exclamation came from around and through the radio as others witnessed the scene before them. Ivy was still out of sight, but without taking his eyes off the Nighthawk, he knew Callan's vessel was moving in to pick up the gang member in the water.

"We've got to get closer," he growled, now knowing Ivy was in the boat. "We can't let them get out into the open Bay."

"On it," Jose said from the wheelhouse.

The VMP vessels formed a semi-circle, hoping to provide enough of a deterrent for the Nighthawk's pilot, but Andy also knew desperate men would easily decide to ram into one of them, especially if the

Nighthawk's hull was fortified. "Come on, Ivy," he whispered. "Let me see you again."

Another head came into view. A third man must have been in the hull of the boat, and his focus was down as he lifted his gun. Andy's heart stopped beating, but before he could blink, a shot was fired from the CG helicopter, and the gang member's head was gone. His body dropped down, and the pilot twisted around but was unable to do anything while keeping the Nighthawk under control.

All semblance of professional control left Andy as adrenaline spiked, and his heart started beating again. Then another movement caught his attention, and before he had a chance to gasp at the sight, Ivy stood and vaulted over the side of the boat, her arms and legs windmilling as she hit the water.

"Get to her!" he shouted at Jose, no longer caring what the Nighthawk was doing. If it slipped past them, then the CG could stay with them.

Her head disappeared from sight, then popped up above the surface. She looked around as though to get her bearings, then went back under the water. Jared grabbed the life preserver, and Andy shucked out of his outer coat, double-checking his life jacket. As soon as they were close, Andy jumped into the Bay.

Diving down, he swam with powerful strokes until his hands came into contact with her body. Grabbing her, he propelled them to the surface with his legs, then worked to keep her face above the water. She fought, her feet pedaling and her hands clawing at his arms.

"Ivy! Ivy! It's me. Calm down, baby. I've got you.

You're safe!" he shouted, his mouth close to her ear. She jerked and twisted around, her gaze landing on him.

Her pupils were dilated, so he continued more softly, "It's me, baby. I've got you. I've got you."

Her chest expanded, then deflated quickly as realization dawned in her eyes. He wanted to hold on to this memory forever... the fear melting as she relaxed and her gaze not leaving his. Her fingers tightened their grip on him, no longer trying to dislodge his hold.

"Andy!" Jared shouted.

Andy hated to look away, but at Jared's interruption, he knew he needed to get her out of the cold water. Looking to the side, he reached out with one hand and grabbed the flotation device, and allowed Jared to pull him and Ivy to the side of the VMP vessel. He shifted Ivy in his grasp and supported her as Jared pulled her out of the water. Not waiting, Andy hauled himself up and onto the deck.

Andy picked her up and carried her into the wheelhouse, where warming blankets were ready. Ivy's lips were blue, and her body was wracked with shivers. Her mouth quirked weirdly, and for a few seconds, he wondered if she was having a stroke. Then it hit him. She was trying to smile.

His fingers went to her blouse, and he ripped the front, buttons scattering. "Get a dry shirt," he ordered Jared, who quickly produced an extra VMP long-sleeved T-shirt. Divesting her of her sopping wet shirt, he pulled the dry shirt over her head and weaved her arms through the sleeves. Leaving her pants for now, he gently forced her to the floor, where he and Jared swaddled her tightly in blankets. Then while Jose guided them to the harbor, he stripped his shirt and replaced it with a dry one as well. Sliding to the floor, he pulled her still-shivering body close to his and enveloped her in his embrace. With his lips near her ear, he whispered, "Jesus, babe, I've got you. I love you."

She twisted in his arms, and this time, her smile was less wonky as she blinked away the tears. "I love you, too."

With her tucked safely in his arms, he could finally breathe without pain and slow his racing heart. Pulling her in tighter, he smiled. He wanted this feeling to last forever and prayed she did, also.

"Andy, we are so glad you're there with her."

"Thank you, Mrs. Watkins. That means a lot to me."

"Well, tell her we'll be back next weekend for at least a week. And we'll be home for a while before having to come back to check on her grandmother."

"I promise I'm taking care of her, but I know she can't wait to see you."

Andy kept his voice low as he talked on the phone with Ivy's parents. Saying goodbye, he disconnected and tossed his phone onto the table. Standing in his kitchen, he sighed, feeling as though he could crawl into bed with Ivy and sleep for a year.

By the time they'd made it to the VMP station, they were met by Zac and the Baytown rescue squad. Zac had wanted Ivy checked out, but she'd insisted she didn't need to go to the hospital. Ryan called his wife, Judith, who wanted to see Ivy at the clinic. While Sybil brought clean clothes, Andy drove Ivy to the doctor's office, where Judith x-rayed her wrist and examined her.

Judith gave her a new splint but was pleased to announce that she had not damaged her wrist further, so Ivy was still on track with her surgeon's plans. She would forgo a week of physical therapy and then be able to start it up again. When thrown into the boat, the hit on Ivy's head created a lump but no concussion. Other than the bruises on her arm where she'd been grabbed, she'd made it through the ordeal with minor physical injuries.

Ivy had been pleased, but Andy's blood pressure and anger rose every time he thought of what-if. She'd finally clutched his face and drew him close.

"Baby, I'm here. Once again, you were the first thing I saw when I came out of the water. Safe in your arms which is where I want to be."

She'd kissed him lightly, and the tight band around his chest eased.

When they left the clinic, Andy drove them back to the station, where they found it to be a hub of activity. Colt and Sam were there to take Ivy's statement. As she relayed everything that had happened, once again, her grasp on Andy's hand kept him from punching the wall.

After her statement, they gave an update on the events that had transpired. The local Bloods had set up a temporary place to stay in the house at the end of Harvestdale. It was large enough to hold a number of people, had enough acreage to keep neighbors from seeing what was going on, and the dock provided the perfect place for late-night deliveries or pickups.

The gang had started to move from the location after a late land delivery had come in from Baltimore and were going to take it south by boat. It seemed that one of the members noticed a sheriff's vehicle nearby and figured their days were numbered in that location. In the sweep, Colt's deputies managed to arrest Tyrone Johnson, one of the Bloods from Baltimore, and Linc Hargrove after he was scooped out of the Bay by the Coast Guard. Roberta, Ty's girlfriend, was the "face of the house" if anyone came by. She was stopped as she attempted to evade police in her vehicle driving north back toward Baltimore.

The DEA had taken possession of the Nighthawk boat, and early reports noted an estimated two million dollars' worth of cocaine in the hull.

Ivy had listened quietly to what Colt was explaining but finally shook her head. "No one has mentioned Curt. How was he involved with a drug gang? And me? Why me?"

Sam had looked at her for a moment with sympathy in his eyes. His gaze shifted to Andy, then back to Ivy. "There's a lot we don't know yet, Ivy. He's been arrested on charges of kidnapping, but there will be more charges to follow. He hasn't said a lot, but it's our belief now that he was the one making program changes to the security cameras on the CBBT that allowed the drug-running boats to pass undetected."

"But why? He was a longtime employee with the CBBT. He only had a few more years until retirement."

Her gaze searched the group before landing on Andy's face. Her expression was pained, and he knew she felt the betrayal from someone she'd known. His hand squeezed hers, but without more information, he'd wait to see what Sam could share.

Sam had offered a heavy sigh. "Why did he end up working for them? We've only known of his involvement for a few hours. The investigation will take time, but I can tell you that he said he was being blackmailed. He admitted his college-age daughter living in Baltimore got involved with drugs. Not only using but also selling. And the gangs don't play when it comes to using anyone they can to move their product." He'd shrugged before sighing again. "I'm sure more will come out with the ongoing investigation, but I know that doesn't help you deal with his involvement in your kidnapping."

"He knew I'd find out about the bridge cameras," Ivy had said softly. Her shoulders were stiff, and her chin lifted. "And I would have. He might have been able to hide it from others, but I would have found out. I was close to determining that it wasn't Bradley or his group from cybersecurity. And it didn't seem like a computer change was occurring, which would clear Anne and her group. Bradley was anxious for me to discover what was happening so that his cybersecurity team could tighten their procedures."

Sam nodded. "Again, we have a lot of investigating to complete, but I'd say you're on the right track with that assumption. Now, how he became involved with them other than his daughter? We don't know yet."

With that, it appeared that Ivy's body leaned a little heavier against Andy, and he'd wanted nothing more than to get her home. They left soon after, but she'd insisted on hugs for everyone first, thanking them profusely.

By the time they drove to his house, she was almost asleep. While she'd taken a hot bath, he'd fielded numerous phone calls from friends who wanted to check on them. Finally, by the time he'd gotten her into bed, he was ready to turn the phone off. His conversation with her parents was the last one he planned on answering until the next day.

Showering, he crawled into bed and curled his body around Ivy's. He closed his eyes, but all he could see was her jumping over the side of a speedboat into the water. She shifted around and blinked her eyes open.

"Stop thinking," she whispered, her lips curving slightly.

"How can you smile after all that happened today?" he asked just as softly.

"Look where I am. I'm right where I'm supposed to be. Twice, Andy, I've needed a hero, and twice, you've been there for me."

"I'll always be there for you," he vowed.

"Counting on it, sweetheart."

She smiled, and he kissed her. He'd meant for the kiss to be a touch. A soft reminder they were together. A gentle whisper between them. But she moved her hand to clutch his jaw, angled her head, and took the kiss deeper.

Grinning, he was happy to oblige. It was much later before they fell asleep, once again curled around each other.

35

Andy stood at the head of his kitchen table, which he'd expanded with the addition of a card table on one end. The golden-brown Thanksgiving turkey was in front of him, just waiting for him to begin carving.

As he looked around the room, his chest squeezed at the realization of what was happening. The kitchen counter was filled with food ready for the hungry guests. Ivy's parents, Joanne and Edward, had just made it back to town in time for Thanksgiving and offered to host the meal, but Ivy insisted that it would be too much trouble and wanted to host it herself. At his... their house. His and Ivy's.

She'd fully moved in a few days after the second watery rescue. Now her clothes hung side by side with his. Her toiletries were sharing space with his. Her car was parked next to his. And she slept in *their* bed.

Ivy had spent the morning in their kitchen cooking with Joanne and Sally, filling the house with the scent of delicious food and the sound of laughter. On the counter was Joanne's cornbread dressing from a recipe handed down in her family. Ivy handled the mashed potatoes, green beans, turkey, and gravy. Sally delivered the corn pudding and an assortment of pies.

Andy looked down at his hands holding the carving knife and noticed they were shaking. How could something so simple mean so much to him?

Pop walked over and clapped him on the shoulder. "Feels strange, doesn't it?"

He sucked in a quick breath as he nodded, swallowing over the lump in his throat.

"Your house, your family at your table, and you at the head of the table. Looks good on you, Son."

He blinked rapidly and grinned. "Couldn't have done it without you, Pop. You're the reason I am who I am."

Now it was his dad who blinked rapidly before offering a nod and walking to where the others were gathered. Pop pulled Sally to his side and kissed her forehead. Edward and Joanne were standing near Ivy with smiles on their faces. Aaron was with his new girlfriend, Belinda. She was pretty and seemed sweet, but Andy felt sorry for her if she didn't realize she was just the girl who fit the holiday family meal date. But at least Aaron was attentive with his arm around her as he also nodded toward Andy to start the proceedings.

Andy offered Edward to say the blessing, and when the "amen" was said, Andy grinned widely toward Ivy and carved the turkey. Soon the sounds of more laughter and chatter filled the room, along with the groans of delight as everyone ate.

By the time coffee and dessert were served, he

leaned back in his seat with his arm resting along the back of Ivy's chair and looked around the filled table.

Family. He'd spent a lot of time in his younger years angry that his mom wasn't there. He'd focused on her leaving. But family wasn't about who left. Family was about who stayed. Who didn't mind getting their hands dirty when needed. Who didn't mind the hard work it took to take care of each other. Who stepped up, stepped in, and stayed. Family was the heroes who earned their place at the table by being there when needed.

Ivy shifted and leaned against him, twisting to hold his gaze with a soft smile curving her lips. "You okay?"

"Couldn't be better," he replied and bent to kiss her lightly. And he knew the words were true.

Get ready for the next Baytown Hero... Jose's story!
A Hero's Surprise

ALSO BY MARYANN JORDAN

Don't miss other Maryann Jordan books!

Baytown Boys (small town, military, protector romantic suspense)

Coming Home

Just One More Chance

Clues of the Heart

Finding Peace

Picking Up the Pieces

Sunset Flames

Waiting for Sunrise

Hear My Heart

Guarding Your Heart

Sweet Rose

Our Time

Count On Me

Shielding You

To Love Someone

Sea Glass Hearts

Protecting Her Heart

Sunset Kiss

Baytown Heroes - A Baytown Boys subseries

A Hero's Chance

Finding a Hero

A Hero for Her

Needing A Hero

A Hero's Surprise

For all of Miss Ethel's boys:

Heroes at Heart (Protector Romance)

Zander

Rafe

Cael

Jaxon

Jayden

Asher

Zeke

Cas

Lighthouse Security Investigations

Mace

Rank

Walker

Drew

Blake

Tate

Levi

Clay

Cobb

Bray

Josh

Knox

Lighthouse Security Investigations West Coast

Carson

Leo

Rick

Hop

Dolby

Bennett

Hope City (romantic suspense series co-developed with Kris Michaels

Brock book 1

Sean book 2

Carter book 3

Brody book 4

Kyle book 5

Ryker book 6

Rory book 7

Killian book 8

Torin book 9

Blayze book 10

Griffin book 11

Saints Protection & Investigations

(an elite group, assigned to the cases no one else wants…or

can solve)

Serial Love

Healing Love

Revealing Love

Seeing Love

Honor Love

Sacrifice Love

Protecting Love

Remember Love

Discover Love

Surviving Love

Celebrating Love

Searching Love

Follow the exciting spin-off series:

Alvarez Security (military romantic suspense)

Gabe

Tony

Vinny

Jobe

SEALs

Thin Ice (Sleeper SEAL)

SEAL Together (Silver SEAL)

Undercover Groom (Hot SEAL)

Also for a Hope City Crossover Novel / Hot SEAL…

A Forever Dad

Long Road Home

Military Romantic Suspense

Home to Stay (a Lighthouse Security Investigation crossover novel)

Home Port (an LSI West Coast crossover novel)

Letters From Home (military romance)

Class of Love

Freedom of Love

Bond of Love

The Love's Series (detectives)

Love's Taming

Love's Tempting

Love's Trusting

The Fairfield Series (small town detectives)

Emma's Home

Laurie's Time

Carol's Image

Fireworks Over Fairfield

Please take the time to leave a review of this book. Feel free to contact me, especially if you enjoyed my book. I love to hear from readers!

Facebook

Email

Website

ABOUT THE AUTHOR

I am an avid reader of romance novels, often joking that I cut my teeth on the historical romances. I have been reading and reviewing for years. In 2013, I finally gave into the characters in my head, screaming for their story to be told. From these musings, my first novel, Emma's Home, The Fairfield Series was born.

I was a high school counselor having worked in education for thirty years. I live in Virginia, having also lived in four states and two foreign countries. I have been married to a wonderfully patient man for forty-one years. When writing, my dog or one of my four cats can generally be found in the same room if not on my lap.

Please take the time to leave a review of this book. Feel free to contact me, especially if you enjoyed my book. I love to hear from readers!

Facebook
Email
Website

Made in the USA
Columbia, SC
05 June 2023